THE FAIRLEY BROTHERS IN JAPAN

"David Starkey's *The Fairley Brothers in Japan* is a raucous, episodic novel provoking outright laughter, penetrating sadness, and wonder, often at the same time. It is sort of Don Quixote meets The Blues Brothers. But that description is both an exaggeration and an understatement. Thirty plus years after an early success as a folk/rock band in 80's America, the two brothers attempt a comeback in Japan. The story vividly explores the outrageous complexity of Japanese culture, the confluences of the international music scene, the irrationality of a collaborative creative process, but most importantly—the betrayals, conflicts, and undying love between two talented brothers. If you like a novel that's turn-the-page fun to read, yet complex psychologically and emotionally, then you're going to love *The Fairley Brothers in Japan*. Beautifully written, this is a must read."

—**JIM PETERSON**, author of *The Sadness of Whirlwinds*

"If you love the spirit of live music, the comeback, and family finding their way, you will love this book. David Starkey is a gifted, natural storyteller with a poet's attention to detail and hope. This book is captivating and thoroughly delightful."

—**LEE HERRICK**, California Poet Laureate and author of *In Praise of Late Wonder: New and Selected Poems*

"I love a good road trip novel and *The Fairley Brothers in Japan* is just that: an endearing story of two brothers' journey to reignite their youth, with an evocative musical backdrop. It's a gentle, compelling ride which drew me into their relationship and the Japanese culture. The sort of novel which stays with you for days after you finish it."

—**IVAN WAINEWRIGHT**, author of *The Other Times of Caroline Tangent*

"Very early in David Starkey's *The Fairley Brothers in Japan*, one of those brothers, Chris, 'had the warm feeling that nothing very bad could happen to him in Japan.' This, despite the fact that it's 2022, and he's there to meet his brother Andy for the reunion tour of their folk-rock duo, more than thirty years after their (humiliating) last performance. Chris's warm feeling proves, um, misleading, but if you are holding this book in your hands, you should savor the warm feeling that something very smart and funny, full of insight and earned wisdom, is about to happen to you."

—**H. L. HIX**, author of *Constellation*

"David Starkey's *The Fairley Brothers in Japan* is the emotional and compelling journey of musician brothers Chris and Andy. The writing—sentence by sentence, scene by scene, page by page—is down-to-earth, graceful, and lyrical. In uniquely reimagining the road novel, Starkey powerfully forms *The Fairley Brothers in Japan* through song titles, song lyrics, and interviews with the folk-rock duo. Starkey's vivid and detailed images illuminate the brother's emotions while capturing the texture of Japan's landscape and culture. And the images and details are as economical, elegant, and evocative as a haiku.... As the Fairley Brothers journey through their shared and conflicted memories and grief, their bonds of brotherly love, family, and music, the reader experiences their yearning for meaning and song so the circle will be unbroken."

—**FRED ARROYO**, author of *Sown in Earth: Essays of Memory and Belonging*

"David Starkey has given us a masterclass in novel writing, and he has managed this with a cast of characters that hasn't a whiff of charisma... I loved both brothers because they're rendered with compassion, dark humor, and the essential knowledge that a real writer holds about the human condition: We really don't understand each other at all and the three most important words in any language are 'in spite of.'"

—**LOU MATHEWS**, award-winning author of *L.A. Breakdown, Shaky Town*, and *Hollywoodski*

THE FAIRLEY BROTHERS IN JAPAN

THE
FAIRLEY
BROTHERS
IN JAPAN

DAVID STARKEY

KEYLIGHT
BOOKS
AN IMPRINT
OF TURNER
PUBLISHING

KEYLIGHT BOOKS

AN IMPRINT OF TURNER PUBLISHING COMPANY

Nashville, Tennessee

www.turnerpublishing.com

The Fairley Brothers in Japan

Cover and book design by William Ruoto

Library of Congress Cataloging-in-Publication Data
Names: Starkey, David, 1962- author
Title: The Fairley Brothers in Japan: a novel / by David Starkey.
Description: Nashville, Tennessee: Turner Publishing Company, 2025.
Identifiers: LCCN 2024046680 (print) | LCCN 2024046681 (ebook) | ISBN 9798887980652 hardcover | ISBN 9798887980669 paperback | ISBN 9798887980676 epub
Subjects: LCGFT: Road fiction | Novels
Classification: LCC PS3569.T335815 F35 2025 (print) | LCC PS3569.T335815 (ebook) | DDC 813/.54—dc23/eng/20250228
LC record available at https://lccn.loc.gov/2024046680
LC ebook record available at https://lccn.loc.gov/2024046681

Printed in the United States of America

FOR STEPHEN, SAYA & SANDY

The hat remains
but where now
is the body it once sheltered?
Ah sad and transient world
beneath the sky
—Saigyō

THE
FAIRLEY
BROTHERS
IN JAPAN

PROLOGUE

TELLURIDE BLUEGRASS FESTIVAL

Telluride, Colorado
Saturday, June 18, 1988

The Fairley Brothers, Chris and Andy, were happy to have the gig, even if it was on Telluride's secondary stage and at three p.m. on the sort of hot summer day when festivalgoers were likely to retreat to their lodgings for a joint, a glass of beer or wine, a nap, a quick roll in the hay, or all of the above.

Although they had had success with their second album, which featured two Top Forty hits, their latest record—their fourth—had been a critical and commercial dud, and it was only the fact that the affable Andy Fairley was friends with Norman and Nancy Blake, and Peter Rowan of the Free Mexican Air Force—two acts that had considerable clout at that year's festival—that they were there at all.

The crowd was thin and unenthusiastic as the brothers took the stage. They could no longer afford to pay a backup band, so it was just the two of them and their acoustic guitars.

At Chris's suggestion, they began with their biggest hit, "Whenever I Hit the Road," and for the duration of the song, the audience was with them, some people singing along with the chorus: "Whenever I hit the road—the road! / Whenever I hit the road." Most listeners clapped at the end.

Andy was sure that if people just *listened* to their new record, they would love it, so at his insistence, their second number was "On Your Own," which he felt was a can't-miss hit. On the album, the track was a piano ballad, and their two guitars didn't quite capture the song's melancholy. The response was tepid, and when Andy said into his microphone, "This is another one from our new album," audible groans arose from the crowd. As the brothers harmonized and strummed their six strings on "Don't Give It Away," people began to leave.

The stage manager had told them that they had thirty to forty-five minutes, depending on the audience's response, so before Andy could say anything, Chris called out, "Here's another one you may remember hearing. It's called 'Turpentine.'" A smattering of applause greeted his announcement of a song from their third album, and audience departures slowed while they sang the bluesy number, but as soon as it was over, most of the crowd, as if by telepathy, got up and began to leave.

Chris glanced over at the stage manager, who was making a sawing motion across his neck, but Andy said, "Here's a new one, written by my big brother, of course, that I think you're really going to dig." He began playing "If You Want to Rock (You Must Learn to Roll)," which was, in fact, one of the songs Chris was proudest of having written. "If You Want to Rock" contained a meaty solo, to which Chris added flourish after flourish—although the riffs didn't sound nearly as full on his Martin as they had on his Les Paul, with the effects box in high gear.

The exodus continued. A rangy shirtless bearded man wearing a cowboy hat positively glowered at the brothers as he left his seat. When the song came to an end, before either of them could say anything, their mics went dead, and over the PA the stage manager said, "Give it up for the Fairley Brothers, Jim and Randy." There was a tiny smattering of applause punctuated by several *boos*. "Thanks very much, boys. And everybody out there, hang on. We'll be right back with Chris Daniels and the Kings."

"Jim and Randy?" Andy mouthed to Chris as they unplugged their guitars and placed them in their cases.

As they walked off the stage, no one greeted them or commented on their performance. They walked down the stairs and out into a roped-off area full of trailers for the other acts. None of the trailers were for them, so they made their way silently back to the Econoline van they'd rented in LA, which Andy had insisted would be necessary for all the touring they would be doing after their comeback performance.

Chris glanced at himself in the rearview mirror, then looked over at his brother. They were two good-looking blonde guys from Southern California. He was twenty-eight and Andy was twenty-four. Their entire lives should have been ahead of them, but it didn't seem that way to Chris. It felt like everything good had already come and gone.

As he started up the van, Chris said, "That was our last concert, wasn't it?"

Andy looked at Chris. He tried to smile but couldn't.

ARRIVAL

Tokyo
Saturday, August 6, 2022

The flight attendants on the All Nippon Airways Boeing 787 announced that passengers deplaning at Narita Airport would need to wait until all international transfers were off the plane. There weren't many people disembarking for Tokyo, and a quick look over his shoulder convinced Chris that he was the only person still seated who wasn't Japanese or of Japanese descent.

He took his phone from his pants pocket and looked, for approximately the tenth time since the plane had left LAX, at his brother's email message:

> Chris dude this is going to be so epic!! That Honda commercial is playing all the time on TV and online. Fumiko got us at least one gig a day people cannot get enuf of Fairley Bros!!! I'll meet you by the Shinkansen tix office in Tokyo station at 9:15 on Sunday morning and we ride up to Hokkaido. I've never been!! Super psyched big Bro!!!!!

A lack of logical punctuation and an excess of exclamation marks had been a hallmark of Andy's writing since he was a boy. He had always been the eager one.

Twenty minutes after the final international transfer passenger had left the plane, everyone else was invited to deboard. Chris took his duffel bag from the overhead bin and returned the bows of the flight attendants as he headed up the jet bridge into the airport.

Once inside, the line snaked up and back, past a series of stanchions and queue barriers. At the end of the line were ten young women making sure that passengers had been tested for COVID within the previous seventy-two hours. Chris showed his paperwork and was waved into a long hall that ended with a visa and passport check. He showed the border agent the paperwork indicating that he was a close relative of a permanent resident of Japan, then bent down to have his face photographed. The unsmiling agent, a middle-aged man, gestured in the direction of baggage claim, and Chris went downstairs to collect his luggage. Miraculously, not only his rolling suitcase but also his guitar case were waiting for him by a carousel that had already stopped turning. He collected his things and was stopped once again at the exit, where he handed the inspector two pieces of paper declaring that he was carrying nothing illegal.

Finally, officially, in Japan, he looked around the airport for an ATM, or at least an information booth, but none of the signs in English gave a hint as to their whereabouts. Chris headed right, found nothing useful, then turned back in the opposite direction and stumbled upon an ATM and a sign pointing to the Narita Express.

He withdrew ¥50,000—about $330—and took an escalator down to the tracks, where he fumbled with the automated ticket machine. With the help of a very courteous but non-English-speaking Japan Railways assistant, he made his way onto his assigned train car.

Google Maps told him that Narita was an hour from Tokyo Station. He was sweating and tired, with a sore neck and a crick in his back, but he tried to enjoy the quiet ride into the world's largest city.

Out his window, rice paddies, telephone lines, and endless suburbs rolled past. As he leaned back in his chair in the mostly empty car, Chris had the warm feeling that nothing very bad could happen to him in Japan.

His room in the Courtyard by Marriott Tokyo Station was just large enough for him to place his suitcase on the desk. He leaned his guitar case against the wall and dropped his duffel, which was serving as his gig bag, on the bed. He unzipped the duffel, which contained extra guitar strings, instrument cables, three tuners with replacement batteries, a collapsible iPad stand, and a Bose two-input S1 Pro multi-position speaker, finding, to his relief, that everything was there and undamaged.

Andy had said bringing the Bose speaker, which would hold a charge for six hours, would be a good back-up in case they had any PA problems. Chris wondered what sort of gig would require a speaker that small; then he remembered their last dates before Telluride, in 1988, which had been rife with audio fuck-ups, and their disastrous turn through Ireland in 2017, and he realized that his brother was probably just using common sense.

Chris checked his phone: It was nearly nine p.m. If he managed to stay up another hour, he could take a Benadryl and probably sleep through most of the night and more or less beat jet lag. He took the elevator down to the lobby. The Good Table Dining & Bar was open. Bonnie Raitt's version of "Runaway" drifted out the front door. Chris was shown to a seat where he ordered a margarita with salt on the rim, and a steak, medium rare, that came with a garnish of something pickled and strange. He ate and drank, then took the elevator back up to his room, where he slept fitfully, dreaming of home.

SHIN-SAPPORO WEDDING
CHAPEL & BUSINESS HOTEL

Sapporo
Sunday, August 7

Andy Fairley sat on the Tokaido Shinkansen as it sped north past Odawara toward Tokyo Station, mentally listing what he hoped to accomplish in the next two weeks. He wanted to reconnect with his older brother, who was recently retired and would now have time to regularly visit him and his wife, Fumiko, in Kyoto. He dreamed of a Fairley Brothers comeback, ignited by the Honda commercial, yes, but one that developed naturally once Japanese listeners had the chance to listen to the Fairley Brothers' four album catalog. Ideally, that growing popularity would lead to the recording of a new album. Andy had written a few new songs he liked, and he knew that his brother had continued to compose material long after the band had broken up.

Mostly, though, Andy hoped Chris was not going to be an asshole if everything didn't go exactly to plan, as had happened daily in Ireland, five years earlier, the last time they'd tried to tour together.

As the Shinkansen approached Shin-Yokohama, Andy nestled his AirPods in his ears and pulled up the Honda commercial on YouTube.

It was a thirty-second spot, which began with a focus on the Honda logo. The camera pulled back to show a dark blue CR-V barreling down an urban highway. A remastered and heavily sweetened version of the Brothers' "Whenever I Hit the Road" chugged along in the background. The CR-V faded into the word "Hybrid," and the camera pulled back once again to show the compact SUV, this time zooming up a dusty mountain road. The song's chorus, "Whenever I hit the road—the road! / Whenever I hit the road," played as the image faded to the car parked by a lake, facing a sunset. The image crossfaded to an interior of the CR-V's heavily automated dashboard, and then the car was sailing through a city at night, with one more iteration of "Whenever I hit the road!" The final note was sustained an extra moment as a title came up announcing, "The All-New CR-V."

And that was it. The brothers had each received twenty-five thousand dollars for a one-year use of the song in Japan. There was a discussion of featuring the song in the more lucrative American market, but the advertising agency there had decided to go with something by Cardi B instead.

Still, it was a sign that the Fairley Brothers weren't entirely relegated to folk-rock history, and as the train got closer to Tokyo Station, and the other passengers began gathering their luggage from the racks and moving toward the doors, Andy preferred to dwell on the positives: Good things were happening, and he was about to see his big brother for the first time in five years.

Andy rubbed the base of his neck as he stepped off the train—a minor stress headache or two was to be expected at the beginning of a tour. He made his way through the bustle of face-masked commuters, taking the escalator from the tracks down to the station below. He saw Chris standing alone, surrounded by a wheeled suitcase, a duffel bag, and his guitar case. At six foot two, Chris had always been tallish in America, but he looked positively gargantuan among the people hurrying through the station. He was older, of course, his blonde hair cut shorter and mostly faded to gray. He stooped a bit, too, but he was still good-looking. They both were, Andy thought, without undue pride, which had surely played a role in their modest success.

Chris caught sight of Andy on the escalator, though he pretended not to. He could see his brother studying him, and, from his peripheral vision, Chris did the same. Andy was smiling that crooked grin that had always made him the favorite of their female fans.

Then Chris waved at his brother, and Andy stepped off the escalator with his duffel bag and his guitar case, put them down, and embraced Chris.

"You still look the same," Andy said, stepping back from Chris.

"Ah no, that's a lie, I know. But you do. Or younger maybe."

"Another lie." Andy looked up at a digital clock on the wall. "We can talk on the train. You bought a Japan Rail Pass, right?"

"Just as you advised."

"Great, so let me pop into the ticket office. I need to buy my ticket and reserve seats for us."

Chris stood outside the glassed-in office as Andy moved through the ticketing process with dispatch. Soon, they were feeding their tickets through the turnstiles and following electronic signs upstairs toward their track. Chris had tried not to overpack, but it was still a strain going up the steep stairs while shouldering his bulging duffel bag and toting the suitcase and guitar case.

It was humid, and both brothers were sweating when they arrived at the sign for their coach number. Chris let out a long breath and looked around. "So far," he said in a quiet voice, "since I arrived at the airport, walked from this extremely busy train station to my hotel and back, I've seen only three people who haven't appeared to be Japanese."

"Considering the visa process and COVID restrictions, I'm not surprised," Andy said. "All that paperwork I had to give you to show I live here and that I'm your brother—it's a lot."

"Sorry about that."

"No, no—no worries. It was worth it to get you over here so we can play together again."

Chris nodded.

"Don't you feel it, big brother?" Andy asked. "That excitement at the beginning of a tour? The feeling that anything can happen in the next two weeks?"

"I do feel that way, though I'm not sure I'd call it excitement. More like trepidation."

"'Do what you fear, and your fear disappears.'"

"Is that your idea?"

"Something I read on the Internet. I'm not sure if it's copyrighted, but it could make a good tagline for a chorus."

There was no time for more talk because the arrival of the train was being announced, in Japanese and English, and then the Shinkansen, long and sleek, rolled into the station. Those in line with the brothers went on high alert, as though the train might take off without them if they weren't paying attention.

The trip from Tokyo to Sapporo was a long one, almost seven hundred miles. They spent four and a half hours on the bullet train, watching through the tiny passenger windows as rice paddies blurred into small towns of hip-roofed houses, which became, in a blink, sprawling suburbs and cities with soaring apartment blocks, and then rice fields again. Construction cranes and billboards, telephone poles and laundry drying on apartment balconies, bamboo groves and hilltop copses—it all sped by in a high velocity scroll.

The train was quiet, as were the passengers, but the brothers bought Sapporo beers from a young woman wheeling a cart up and down the aisle and talked about Chris's recent retirement from human resources at the Los Angeles Department of Water and Power. "You took that job right after the band broke up," Andy said. "I mean, no offense, but that's always seemed like a kind of perverse decision. From being a rock star to doing desk work all day."

"The salary was good, and it was steady work. I've told you this. Good retirement benefits, too. No offense, but don't you kind of feel...vulnerable, still having to teach English as a foreign language on an hourly basis? No job security. No retirement fund."

"Japan and U.S. Social Security have a reciprocal retirement agreement. I'm not without means, you know. And Fumiko will have a good pension. I've had a good run."

"I don't remember. How many jobs is it since we called it quits in '88?"

Andy gazed up to the ceiling of the train, then shut his eyes. "Let me think. Right afterwards, I didn't do much. Just spent the last of the royalty checks. Then I worked as a personal assistant for Shifty LaRue—"

"That shitty movie producer."

"Right. Then I did a summer as a fire lookout in Oregon, then I was a bartender at the Viper Room for, what, eight years? After I got fired, I played for spare change on Hollywood Boulevard for a week, which was a low."

"I'm trying to remember when that was."

"Not sure. Late nineties? And then I stayed with you for six months, but that wasn't a job."

Chris nodded pensively. "Sounds right."

"But I got back on my feet after that, thanks to you, big brother. That's when I took that course on teaching English as a foreign language, and then it was, wow, the world: Cambodia, Vietnam, Malaysia, South Korea, Russia, Kazakhstan, Côte d'Ivoire, Uruguay, and where? Oh, Argentina. I think that's all of them."

"And tending bar in Ireland."

"I was kind of burned out. Same thing over and over in my conversation classes: 'What is your favorite color and why?' 'Which do you prefer, cats or dogs?'"

"I get that."

"I actually started out bartending in the Faroe Islands, and then I sort of slipped through the mesh of employment regulations into Ireland with the help of a friend."

"Which was how you got us those gigs five years ago."

Andy nodded. It was a subject he wasn't ready to address, so he said, "And then Japan, of course. Where I met Fumiko. I feel like I'm finally settled."

"That's good," Chris said, draining his beer, placing it in the netting attached to the back of the seat in front of him. He stood up and retrieved his Bose noise-canceling headphones from his duffel bag. "All this personal history makes me tired," he said as he sat back down. "Maybe we could take a rest now?" His brother gave him a thumbs-up.

The Shinkansen passed under the Tsugaru Strait via the world's longest undersea tunnel, but both brothers were sleeping and didn't wake until the train was pulling into the Shin-Hakodate-Hokuto Station.

They carried their bags to the only train going north, a local express that ran along the bleak coast of Uchiura Bay. The foliage by the tracks was often lush and green, but between the trees and bushes, they caught glimpses of closed hotels, rusting factories, and little weedy towns with boarded-up storefronts.

It was a four-hour journey and seemed to take twice that long. Andy had two warm beers in his duffel bag, and they sipped them slowly, as though this might be their last nourishment of the day. After an hour, they had exhausted their fund of small talk, both wary of diving deeper into anything that might derail their tour at its outset.

Andy shut his eyes and thought of his wife, and what she might be doing at that moment. Probably Fumiko would be getting home from work. She'd make herself a cup of green tea and turn on the television, maybe sleep for a while on their comfortable couch. Then he imagined her making soba from scratch—mixing and kneading the dough, rolling and folding and cutting it into noodles, then boiling them and taking them out just in time. But of course, she would probably be too tired to make soba noodles after a long day at the bank. Maybe she'd just stop for Lawson fried chicken on the way home.

Chris shut his eyes and thought of what his ex-wife might be doing at that moment. Larissa was remarried to a money manager at J.P. Morgan named Stuart. It was probably the middle of the night in Brentwood. They would be snuggled up with each other, sleeping, maybe even making love. They certainly wouldn't be thinking about Chris Fairley hunched over in some uncomfortable train seat on a faraway island.

As the train approached Shin-Sapporo Station on the outskirts of the city, the brothers roused themselves. Andy said, "Let's just leave our bags at the main station and walk around Sapporo a bit."

"But isn't Shin-Sapporo where our gig is?"

"Yeah, but this is just a suburban station, and the gig's not till nine." He held up his phone. "It's not even six."

"Have you been practicing?"

"Of course," Andy said. "I've been playing along with every one of our albums for months. What about you?"

"Same."

"So, we're rehearsed. We'll get some dinner and head back in plenty of time."

"Are you sure? What about a sound check? I don't want to be late."

"Come on, Chris, this is like half the point of the trip, right? We play music but we also see Japan."

Chris had promised himself that he would have fun, no matter what, so he nodded in agreement. As the train eased out of the station, Andy went to the bathroom, and Chris took a Clonazepam from the pill case in his pocket, washing it down with the last of his warm beer.

After a few minutes of following the signs in the central station, they found the coin lockers and squeezed their guitar cases and luggage into three of the largest compartments.

Outside, Sapporo was warm and humid, though not as steamy as Tokyo. The brothers walked past the taxi stand and down a wide boulevard with restaurants and hotels, clothing and electronics shops, convenience stores, and a Starbucks. Whenever they reached a red light, the pedestrians, nearly all of them masked, would wait until the light turned green, even when no cars were to be seen. "They kind of go overboard, don't you think?" Chris asked.

'What are you talking about?"

"I mean, following the rules. Even when you don't have to."

Andy shook his head and sighed. "There's nothing wrong with following the rules."

At what seemed like every corner, giggly young Japanese women were passing out free cardboard masks of Pikachu—pointed brown ears, yellow face, and bright red circles on his cheeks. "The most beloved Pokémon," Andy said. "Should we take one?"

Chris shook his head. "Definitely not."

Andy looked down at his phone.

"By the way, where are we going?" Chris asked.

"Spicy ramen. How does that sound?"

"Okay. But where is it?"

Andy gestured vaguely ahead of them. "Up here somewhere."

They kept walking, passing a number of restaurants that clearly served spicy ramen. A pink and purple bus with an anime girl and the word "Vanilla" painted on the side stopped beside them. A jingle blared from the speakers, then a woman trying to sound like a little girl shouted something joyfully.

"What's she saying?" Chris asked.

"I wouldn't swear to it, but I'm pretty sure she's a character in a TV show and she's inviting us to follow her on Instagram." Andy motioned for his brother to get in the frame for a selfie with the bus in the background. The brothers smiled, unconvincingly, but Andy looked at the photo and said, "Good enough. Fumiko can post it on our own account."

"We have an Instagram account?" Chris asked.

"We do now."

They turned into a covered pedestrian shopping arcade and walked past pachinko parlors and bars and restaurants and convenience stores. It was crowded with shoppers, every single one of them wearing a mask. "Spending money seems to be the main pastime in Sapporo," Chris said.

"You're saying it's not like that in America?"

"No. Just all the lights and music and recorded voices. It's kind of an overwhelming come-on."

"I guess so. Honestly, you don't even notice it after a while."

They passed a vending machine with a stencil of a rugged mustached Anglo man with a pipe stuck between his lips. "Suntory Coffee Boss" the lettering below the man read. "Why is Ernest Hemingway selling coffee in Japan?" Chris asked, pointing at the machine.

"That's not Ernest Hemingway. That's Coffee Boss. He's the boss of coffee."

Andy's phone finally directed them to a small restaurant with kanji-covered curtains instead of a door, and a photograph of a bowl of ramen covering the lone window.

Inside was a single counter with eight chairs. Tacked to one wall was a photo of Anthony Bourdain. Above his picture, written in Sharpie, it said: "Magnificent! Many, many thanks." Below, was a drawing of a knife, a florid, indecipherable signature, presumably Bourdain's, followed by "and the No Reservations Crew." Next to the handwritten thank-you note was another photo of the chef. Bold Arial font proclaimed: "Anthony Bourdain came to the here."

The brothers sat down and ordered two large Sapporo Classics and two large bowls of spicy ramen. The lone chef behind the counter immediately went to work, stirring noodles into boiling water and mixing in spices and oil, doing everything so deftly that the bowl was set down in front of them in just a few minutes.

"How is it?" Andy asked.

"Not bad. Bouquet of wet rags and a note of mop water in the finish."

"Seriously?"

"No, it's actually pretty good."

As they ate, Chris kept looking at his watch. "We should probably get going, huh?"

"Yeah, sure, but we have plenty of time."

Chris nodded and ate his soup; this was something annoying he remembered about his brother, how he always cut it close getting to the gig. Even after sound check, Chris would have preferred an hour just to warm up, go over a few songs, meditate and breathe.

As he dipped into the vegetables and shrimp in his ramen, Andy recalled how irritating he found Chris's need to always be at the gig *hours* early. And for no good reason, really. Chris was just too anxious, always had been. But what was the use in arguing this early in the tour, before they'd even played their first gig?

Andy paid for the dinner and typed a different route back to the station on his phone. It was growing dark, and when they were a few blocks away, an explosion of lights and disco music came from a makeshift stage in the middle of the street.

It was a Pikachu parade. Six life-sized Pikachus waddled down a runway, waving and blowing kisses at an adoring audience, many of whom were wearing the cardboard Pikachu masks. The Pikachus were accompanied by three young men wearing white pants and fluorescent orange shirts and three young women in pink ballet costumes. They danced and waved and generally urged the crowd to show their love for the cuddly Pokémon.

"Maybe we should grab a couple of masks and wear them when we play the wedding?"

"Are you serious?" Chris said.

"Kind of. Japanese love to nerd out. I think they'd like it."

"Sorry, man. No fucking way."

"Suit yourself," Andy said, picking a discarded mask off the asphalt. "I'm taking one anyway. In case of emergency."

The lobby of the Shin-Sapporo Wedding Chapel & Business Hotel was dominated by a three-story Disneylandesque façade of a Christian church, with stained glass windows that appeared to be plastic and twin steeples that were surely made of Plexiglas. To the left was a little stage, where the brothers would presumably set up and play. To the right was a fifteen-foot-tall plastic Christmas tree, undecorated in August.

The seats facing the faux church were half-filled, and a few guests wandered through the aisles, looking puzzled. Everyone wore light blue medical-grade face masks. There was no sign of the bride and groom.

"It's kind of late in the evening for a wedding, isn't it?" Chris asked.

Andy shrugged. "All I know is they want us to start playing at nine."

They checked in and took the elevator up to a small bare room with twin beds on the fifteenth floor. "I've got a bad feeling about this one," Chris said as he opened his suitcase and plugged in the mini steam iron he'd packed.

"Wait, big brother, do not do this to me yet. Just give it a chance."

Chris let out a long breath. "I'm just saying." He took out a dark blue polo shirt and black slacks, and began ironing them on the desk, while Andy pulled an apparently wrinkle-resistant shirt and pants from his duffel bag.

In fifteen minutes, they were both dressed, coiffed, and ready. "Got your tuner and capo?" Chris asked. Andy gave him a thumbs-up, and they picked up their guitar cases and headed for the elevator.

Downstairs, the ceremony had miraculously come together. Mendelssohn's "Wedding March" played over the lobby's loudspeakers, and a minister stood in front of the fake church's closed doorways. Andy and Chris waited near the front desk as the bride and groom, in Western dress, moved slowly down the center aisle. When they reached the minister, the music ceased, suddenly, and the ceremony proceeded in Japanese.

"So, like the wedding and the reception are in the same place?" Chris whispered to Andy.

Andy made a *Beats me* face, and in a few minutes the couple was married. The "Wedding March" picked up where it had paused, and the bride and groom turned back down the aisle, the guests applauding and waving at them with both hands.

A fiftyish woman in a dark purple dress sidled over to the brothers. "You the musicians?" she asked, gesturing toward their guitar cases.

"Sure are," Andy smiled.

The woman shook her head. "Should have been set up an hour ago."

"We were told to be here at nine," Andy said, smiling somewhat less brightly.

"Well, go over to stage now. That man there, he show you what to do."

"You got it," Andy said, as Chris glared at him, and the brothers headed toward the stage opposite the plastic tree.

Two microphones had been set up, and a hotel employee showed them where to plug in their guitars. A light, tinkling jazz had been playing over the PA while the guests mingled, but as Chris took out his phone to check the time and saw "8:59" turn to "9:00," the music ceased and the woman in the purple dress stepped onstage and spoke into one of the microphones. She said something in Japanese that ended with an approximation of "The Fairley Brothers" and "Whenever I Hit the Road."

As she left the stage, there was a polite round of applause as the guests took their seats. "We haven't played this in five years," Chris said, "but I understand it's pretty popular in a car commercial here right now. So, thank you, Accord, or Civic, or whatever."

Silence. Andy nodded, *Go on*, and Chris counted out four, then hit a G chord and the Fairley Brothers were touring again.

When the song ended, the audience applauded, and the bride and groom, who had been standing to the side, bowed at the brothers. Andy bowed back, and Chris followed, a beat behind.

Immediately, Chris launched into their second biggest hit, "Take Me Till Tuesday," which had been helped up the charts, entirely by accident, by the fact that the band 'Til Tuesday had a hit at the same time, "Voices Carry." Chris assumed that this song, too, would be familiar to at least some at the wedding, but the faces were uniformly blank, and the applause this time was anemic.

"Let's do 'The Psychics Are Crying,'" Andy said, and they began the long, moody song, which opened with a solo in E minor that Andy knew Chris loved to play.

However, a minute into the song, before they'd even reached the first verse, the woman in the purple dress stood up and walked to the lip of the stage, shaking her head and making an "X" with her index fingers.

"Is something wrong?" Chris asked

"Only 'Hit the Road,'" she replied.

"Excuse me?" Andy said.

"We only pay you to play that one song."

Chris gave her an exaggerated shrug, with his arms outstretched. "But we've already played it."

"Play it again." She bowed, then forced a smile. "Please."

"I think we'd better do it," Andy muttered.

"I mean, okay, but, wow," Chris said. "Not what I was expecting."

"That's life," Andy said, and hit the opening G chord himself.

Back in their tiny hotel room on the fifteenth floor, the brothers sat drinking cans of Sapporo that Andy had filched from an ice bucket near the undecorated Christmas tree. He had pulled back the curtains, and the window, which didn't open, looked out on Shin-Sapporo Station and a scattering of office parks. The nonsmoking room smelled of cigarette smoke.

Andy had turned the TV on without the sound, and a commercial was playing for elastic knee supports. A beauty stylist bent over a customer, a busy mom picked up toys, a businessman hurried through a train station. They all smiled before the camera zoomed in on their knees.

Andy said, "Well, we made almost a thousand dollars. That's not bad."

Chris shook his head. "I don't know. We played 'Whenever I Hit the Road' *five* times. Do you think all our gigs are going to be like this one?"

Andy shook his head vehemently. "Uh-uh. No way. This was just opening night jitters."

"We weren't jittery: That lady was."

"I guess so." They sipped their beers, and Andy said, "I should have put on the Pikachu mask."

"Save it for tomorrow," Chris said. He stood up and walked to the window. "Hopefully it won't be as shitty as today."

Andy silently counted to ten, while below them the lights on the outskirts of Sapporo twinkled. Gradually some of them went out, like the extinguished glow of dying stars.

HOKKAIDO ART FOREST
LUNCHTIME CONCERT SERIES

Sapporo
Monday, August 8

The next morning, Andy was up before Chris. He dressed and went downstairs to the lobby, where he sat down beneath the enormous plastic Christmas tree. He called his wife, and Fumiko wished her husband good morning, then said: "I'm sorry. Sounds like from your text messages that it was bad last night."

"I want to think it was a one-off thing," Andy replied.

"You told me your brother was difficult."

"Yeah. But it was difficult for me too. Embarrassing. Playing the same song over and over. But I smiled and I did it, and we got paid. I don't know. It's like when we were kids—he's such a pessimist."

"I'm sure today will be better," she said, then began talking about a romantic drama at work involving two married people. Andy half-listened as he watched four salarymen, all wearing black suits with dark gray ties, each attempting to bow lower than the others. The man making the final bow seemed as though he would tip over for a moment, but he recovered, and they all made another round of bows. Their business concluded, they departed the lobby just as four young men Andy recognized from the wedding spilled out of the elevator. They stumbled toward the restaurant, all looking as though they had spent the night praying to the porcelain goddess.

When Fumiko finished her story, Andy said, "I'd better get going. I love you, Fumi."

"Love you too."

Chris woke to find Andy watching soundless TV. It took Chris a moment to realize what he was seeing: A man dressed as a praying mantis caught dragonflies with a butterfly net, then kissed each one before letting it go.

Back in the television studio, three other adults, also dressed as insects, apparently traded quips while bright yellow kanji flashed across the screen.

"Is this a favorite show of yours?" Chris asked.

"Totally." Andy looked over at his brother. "Kidding, of course. It's just that the Japanese watch a lot of TV, and you start doing it yourself. But I didn't want to wake you up."

Chris yawned, stretched his arms, and sat up in bed. "So, where to to-day? Hopefully not another wedding?"

"Not to worry. We've got two gigs. One at noon, a lunch concert series, and another at a kind of community center, at sixish—they were flexible about the time."

"What time is our train?"

"Actually, the train service in Hokkaido isn't very good. Remember I told you to bring your international driver's license?"

For a moment, Chris panicked; then he remembered that a month or two earlier he had, indeed, paid a visit to the AAA office in Woodland Hills.

"In fact," Andy continued, "we probably ought to get going pretty soon. I'd like to stop on the way and see the giant Buddha. Are you okay with that?"

"I never say no to a giant Buddha."

Just then loud music blared from outside the window. The brothers pulled back the curtains to see a squad of men in gray uniforms, arrayed in neat rows, doing calisthenics in front of a building site.

"What's that?" Chris asked. "Some kind of army thing?"

"Construction workers," Andy said. "That's how they warm up. I think it's also supposed to be a sort of team-building exercise. We do something like that at my work every couple of weeks."

The brothers watched the workers do jumping jacks and deep knee bends and lunges and squats, and then the music stopped, the workers ap-plauded, turned, and began heading toward the scaffolds and girders and cranes.

"Hard to imagine union guys going for that in the States," Chris said.

Andy nodded. "Their loss."

The brothers showered, shaved, and packed, and were checked out by nine. The car rental office was next door to the hotel, and while Andy went to get the car, Chris waited out front with their bags and guitars, thumbing through the American news on his phone: inflation, outrageous gas prices, the threat of civil war. Meanwhile, on a gray day on the outskirts of Sapporo, businessmen and businesswomen and schoolchildren in their uniforms walked toward the train station. Each person passing by gave Chris a quick, appraising—if not surprised—glance, then looked away, as though they had no idea he was standing there.

Twenty minutes later, Andy pulled up in a midsize silver Toyota. Andy popped the hatch, and Chris loaded the car.

"What model is this?" Chris asked, settling into the passenger seat.

"An Aqua, I think. They don't sell it in America." Andy was bent over the touch screen. "I had them change this to English, but it's still making me use kanji to enter our destination."

"Is that a problem?"

"It's just...I can speak Japanese okay, and sort of read it, but writing it is something else."

"Take your time."

"Don't worry, I will."

For five minutes, Andy looked back and forth from his phone to the touch screen. "I think that's it," he said, finally. "The Hill of the Buddha."

Andy started the GPS, and soon they were headed south—driving on the left-hand side of the road—down a four-lane commercial boulevard, onto an expressway, and then off again, winding through a huge cemetery crowded with polished granite pillars with gold lettering. Beyond the cemetery, Andy turned onto a winding country highway that paralleled a river.

"This gig seems pretty far out of town," Chris said.

"Maybe. All I know is that Fumiko says it's a popular lunchtime concert series, and that it's at one of the most beautiful outdoor sculpture gardens in Japan."

"So, we're playing *outside*?"

"I don't *know*, Chris," Andy snapped. "Jesus. Give me a break. I'm doing the best I can."

"Okay, okay, sorry. Just trying to picture it ahead of time."

"Why don't you Google it and see?"

Chris did, and the photographs showed a variety of intriguing sculptures in a parklike setting. "There's probably a pavilion, or something," he said. "For bands."

The road narrowed, with trees pressing in close on both sides. Chris opened his mouth to comment again on the rural nature of the location, then thought better of it and said nothing.

A little after ten, they reached what looked like the gates of a movie mansion. Two men in bright green safety jackets waved red flags to usher in cars.

On the left of the entrance drive was a long, perfectly straight line of replicas of the Rapa Nui statues. Each Moai was fifteen feet high, with a flat, frowning face and long arms that reached almost to the ground. The last two statues wore enormous face masks over their mouths. It had begun to drizzle, and the figures, which appeared to be made from concrete rather than stone, dripped with rain. The general effect was of a diminishment of the original, as though the iconic statues had always been nothing more than a tourist draw.

That impression was deepened when they reached the end of the row of megaliths and found a version of Stonehenge, considerably smaller and less stonelike than the original.

"Egad," Chris said when they had parked the car.

"I know," Andy said, "but that's not the highlight. Have you ever heard of Tadao Ando?"

Chris shook his head.

"He's a world-famous Japanese architect, and he designed what we came to see."

"The giant Buddha?"

Andy pointed through the rain-splattered windshield at a large mound planted with lavender bushes. "Actually, it's that hill surrounding the Buddha."

"I don't see any Buddha. Unless you mean that stone thing sticking up from the middle."

"I think that's the top of his head. Let's get out and take a look."

Chris struggled into the North Face rain jacket he'd brought, and Andy pulled a clear plastic umbrella from his duffel bag. As they walked toward the entrance, Chris asked, "And how far is the gig from here?"

"According to Google, like ten minutes?"

"And we'll surely be playing inside."

"Surely," Andy replied.

They entered a rectangular concrete space, with a shallow reflecting pool in the center. Down a low vaulted tunnel, they could see the base of the Buddha. They walked along the edge of the pool, then through the tunnel and down to a series of low steps leading up to the enclosed space.

It was, the brothers agreed, spectacular. A circle of gray sky framed the top of the polished stone statue. Rain slid down the Buddha's face so that he appeared to be weeping, despite his enigmatic smile.

They took pictures with their phones, including a couple of selfies. "I'll send these to Fumiko to post on Instagram and TikTok," Andy said. "She's also made us a web page and is keeping a kind of tour blog."

"Is there really that much interest in the Fairley Brothers' tour?"

"Some. But we also have to generate the interest ourselves. At least that's what Fumiko says."

"I'm looking forward to meeting her," Chris said.

"My wife is an extraordinary individual."

Hokkaido Art Park turned out to be only five minutes away. Andy pulled up to the gate at eleven and spoke with a guard in Japanese. The guard took a map from the rack, circled a building with a Sharpie, and handed it to Andy. "They're expecting us," Andy told Chris, as he drove up a winding road to a parking lot in front of a two-story concrete and steel modernist structure built into a woody hillside.

The brothers walked into the building, but it appeared to be empty. Tinted floor-to-ceiling windows let in some overcast light on the mostly bare space: orange carpets and unmanned reception desks.

"Wrong place maybe?" Chris said, hopefully.

Andy looked down at the map in his hand. "Pretty sure this is the building the guy circled." He called out, "*Konnichiwa*?" but no one answered.

At one end of the room, a staircase led down to a lower floor, and the brothers followed it to discover a large room with rows of empty chairs in front of a stage set up with two comfortable-looking stools, two microphones, and two guitar stands. "That would be us," Andy said.

"The only thing missing," Chris replied, "is an audience."

Andy looked at his phone. "It's still forty minutes to showtime. Why don't you go out and get the guitars, and I'll text Fumiko for details and see if I can find the person in charge."

By the time Chris returned, Andy had located the organizer, a flustered young woman in a dark-blue business outfit. They were conversing in Japanese, with Andy several times asking her to repeat herself.

When they finished speaking, the woman bowed deeply to Andy then backed away to the wall, looking thoroughly miserable.

"Problem?" Chris asked, already knowing the answer.

"Well, yes. Sort of."

"What's a 'sort of' problem?"

"So, the reason we were able to get on their schedule, which is normally set a year in advance, is because the act that was supposed to play today, a Nu jazz combo called Outré, had to cancel. If I understand correctly, the venue sent out an eblast to the concert series subscribers saying there was no concert today, and then, after Fumiko booked the gig for us, Miss Tawada here was supposed to send out another eblast saying we were playing, but she got busy and forgot until about an hour ago when Fumiko texted her to see if we were here yet. So, she got everything set up, but we may not have much of an audience."

"Ah," Chris said, sitting down in one of the chairs set aside for the audience. This is what you get, he thought, for believing things will go right.

"It's an honest mistake," Andy said. "And she feels 'deeply ashamed.' Those were her words: 'deeply ashamed.'" He looked at his phone. "It's eleven thirty. In ten minutes, Miss Tawada is going to announce our performance over the loudspeaker system that goes out all over the park. So, we should get an audience."

Chris smiled tightly. "Then I guess we ought to set up and do a sound check."

The brothers discussed their set list, plugged in their guitars, and played half of the bluesy "Turpentine" to an enthusiastic young man at the sound-board who gave them two thumbs-up.

At eleven forty, the announcement went out over the loudspeaker, and about ten minutes later, three families with young children wandered in and tentatively took seats in the back rows. One couple had a baby in a stroller, the second had two toddlers, and the third had mischievous-look-ing twin boys who appeared to be about six. Miss Tawada sat in the front seat, and a lone elderly man with a cane sat somewhere in the middle.

Promptly at noon, Miss Tawada came up to the stage and, in Japanese, read very softly for nearly five minutes from a printed introduction. Chris recognized only the names of their albums and hit songs and "Honda." Andy nodded knowingly, although he understood only a fraction of what she said in her whispery voice.

When Miss Tawada sat down, the brothers walked in from the wings and began playing.

In the middle of their third song, "The Psychics Are Crying," a group of bo-hemian-looking and possibly drunk young men entered through the back doors and began to talk rather loudly throughout the song. When it was over, one of the young men called out something in Japanese that ended with "Outré."

Andy said something back to them in Japanese.

One of the young men took out his phone and waved it at Andy. "Outré!" he shouted.

"*Iie* Outré," Andy said.

Miss Tawada, blushing deeply, hastened back to the men and, after much discussion, ushered them out.

The family with the baby used the commotion as an opportunity to escape, but the other two families remained grimly in their chairs.

When Miss Tawada retook her seat, Chris said, "We had a little trouble with our third song last night, too. Must be jinxed, but now we want to play something we think you're going to like."

The brothers launched into "Whenever I Hit the Road," and the sparse audience did, indeed, perk up. The old man with the cane tapped it against the floor in time to the song and even sang along with the chorus.

"Glad you liked that one," Andy said. "And thank you to Honda for giving the Fairley Brothers a chance to reintroduce ourselves to Japan."

Assuming the program was over, Miss Tawada stood up, but Chris began playing "Pickled and Juiced," mumbling into the microphone: "We've got a few more, if you don't mind." She sat back down. "This song features my brother Andy on the blues harp, and I think you're going to really like his solo."

Indeed, Andy took a harmonica from his pocket, and his solo caused the children in the back to break into applause. He waved at them and called out, "*Domo arigato!*"

Just when Chris thought the misery was nearly over, Andy unexpectedly began an old Carter Family standard the brothers had played back in their earliest days. Chris followed along, unsure how ironic the chorus was meant to be: "Keep on the sunny side, / Always on the sunny side, / Keep on the sunny side of life!" The crowd enjoyed that one, and the duo played three more songs, though they were met with ever decreasing attention from the twin boys and waning enthusiasm from the remaining sets of parents, until Chris noticed a clock off to the side indicating it was ten to one.

"This is our last song," he said, and the brothers launched into their traditional closer, "Dark as Dark Can Get," the final song on their most popular album. Despite its title and rather grim lyrics, the song itself was upbeat, ending in a fever pitch of guitar strumming.

"Thank you, Hokkaido Art Forest!" Chris said, standing and bowing. Andy stood up and bowed, too, whispering, "You don't have to be sarcastic."

"I'm not," Chris said, his smile tighter than ever.

The families quickly vanished, but the elderly man came over and insisted on shaking both the brothers' hands. He spoke to Andy in Japanese. When he finished, Andy translated: "He says he used to listen to us on the radio the year he spent in Ohio working for Honda. He didn't learn much English, but he knows the words to our songs."

Chris bowed and said, with frank sincerity, "Thank you, sir. That means a lot."

The old man patted Chris on the arm, then turned and left.

As they were packing up their guitars, Miss Tawada approached them with an envelope thick with bills. "Thank you very much," she said in English.

"No, thank *you*," said Andy. "We really enjoyed it."

She spoke to Andy in Japanese, then bowed. He returned her bow and said to Chris, "She says she apologizes again, a thousand times, for her email error, and that we are free to enjoy their buffet and to stroll around the gardens, if we'd like."

"How much time do we have?"

Andy opened Google Maps on his phone, typed in a city, and said, "Looks like the drive is about two and a half hours. If we leave here before three, we should be fine. Like I said, the next place seemed pretty flexible about our starting time."

"The community center?"

Andy cleared his throat. "That's right."

"What kind of a community center is it?"

Andy shrugged. "Not sure. I'd have to ask Fumiko."

"Maybe you could do that? Before we get there?"

"No problem at all."

The Fairley Brothers took advantage of the lunch buffet, located in another building, filling their plates with yakitori, vegetable and shrimp tempura, okonomiyaki pancakes, and bowls of soba.

Afterwards, they walked out into the sculpture forest, which was something of a wonder. The rain had stopped, but the ground was wet, and the air was thick with humidity. Cicadas screeched from what seemed like every tree. Little concrete fountains led to a concrete teepee. Inside, they sang an a cappella version of "Whenever I Hit the Road" that was deep and echoing.

Chris suggested leaving for the next gig, but Andy said they had plenty of time, so they strolled past slabs of polished stone and pillars of rough concrete. Dotted among the landscape were statues of human beings in various stages of joy and distress.

As they sat on a bench overlooking a rotund figure who seemed to have been welded together from the spare parts in someone's toolbox, Chris said, "Molly would have liked this place."

Andy didn't answer immediately. Finally, he said, "Really? You're going to go there? On the second day?"

"It was just a random thought. She liked quirky, odd places." Chris rubbed his face. "Do you think about her much?"

"If I'm honest, Chris, not really, no. Why? Do you?"

"More than I should, probably."

"My God, that was over thirty-five years ago. Move on, right?"

"I have, mostly. It's just...now that I'm retired. And Larissa's long gone."

"Yeah, well, we can talk about it another time, okay? Right now, we need to get going if we're going to make our evening gig."

"Sure thing, little brother. We'll talk about it another time."

FURANO VALLEY FLOWER FOREVER
FLOWER FARM GIFT SHOP

Furano Valley
Monday, August 8

In December of 1985, the Fairley Brothers were playing the final shows in support of their only gold album, *Dark as Dark Can Get*. The last two shows were back-to-back nights at home in Los Angeles at the newly renovated Wiltern theater, but at the time the brothers and their band were headlining at The Warfield in San Francisco.

After almost two years on the road, they were confident and poised and had even developed something of a schtick, with Andy ribbing Chris about the solemnity of his songwriting, before the two of them would launch into a number that took full advantage of their well-rehearsed harmonies.

They were discussing one of those harmonies—Andy felt he hadn't been hitting the high E's on Chris's A's—as they walked up Columbus Boulevard toward a garlic-heavy Italian restaurant they both loved.

They paused on the corner of Columbus and Broadway to watch a young man spinning around on his back on a sheet of cardboard, a boom box cranking out Kool & the Gang's "Get Down on It." A cold, salty wind was coming in off the Bay.

Chris felt someone tap his shoulder. He turned to see a young woman about his age with black hair and bright blue eyes. "Do you like breakdancing?" she asked.

He shrugged. "Who doesn't?"

She looked over at Andy. "And your brother?"

"I'm very athletic," Andy said, extending his hand to the woman. "Andy Fairley. How are you?"

"I know who you are," she said. "Both of you. I have your records, and I'm going to your show tonight at The Warfield."

"A fan," Andy said, smiling his big, winning smile. The groupies gravitated toward him, and he felt bad for his brother—but not that bad.

"Actually," she said, pointing her thumb at Chris, "mostly of his. I love the songs he writes."

Andy took a step back, and gestured toward his brother, as if to say: *She's all yours.*

Before the brothers knew it, the woman, Molly Moore, had invited herself to lunch with them, and they were soon splitting a bottle of Chianti, and then another, over a meal of gnocchi alla Romana and fettuccine Bolognese.

"I'm kind of over the hardcore scene here," she told them. "I mean, like, the Dead Kennedys, or whatever. They have one idea, then they beat it to a pulp. But you guys, on the other hand, especially Chris, you know how to make a song, to create a little world you can go inside of and feel safe."

"And depressed," Andy added with a laugh.

"Safe and depressed are not antonyms," Molly Moore said.

After a couple of hours of eating, drinking, and talking, they left her outside the restaurant, smiling and waving. "That's that," Chris said to Andy in the taxi back to their hotel. "They want my mind, not my body."

"That's not exactly true," Andy said. "You've had your share of...female companionship."

"I guess. But it's not very satisfying, not in the long run. One moment they're here. The next—poof! They're gone."

However, when the lights went up that night, Molly was in the front row, smiling and waving again.

After they'd finished their second encore, Chris sent a stagehand out to bring her back to their dressing room.

There, in the cramped space plastered with peeling posters from previous shows, seated between the two sweaty brothers, she became larger than life, whipping her long black hair around as she told wild tales about her dysfunctional family in Daly City and her alcoholic grandparents in Cork.

They ended up at a jazz bar back in North Beach, the cigarette smoke so thick they finally walked outside into the night air for a reprieve. Molly reached up to kiss Chris, then took him by the hand, waving goodbye to Andy. "Don't worry," she said. "I'll have him back to you by morning."

Both brothers were recalling flashes of that first day and night with Molly, as the GPS on the Toyota Aqua guided Andy back north, past the giant

Buddha, up along the river highway, through the labyrinthine cemetery, into Sapporo and onto the E5 toll road.

After Andy had taken the ticket from the automated tollbooth, he said, "How about we break this weird silence with a little music?"

"What did you have in mind?"

"I was thinking our first album. I wouldn't mind playing a few more songs off it."

"Okay." Chris synched his phone's Bluetooth with the multimodal interface, and soon Apple Music was playing "Sunday Afternoons," the opening track on their 1984 album, *Meet the Fairley Brothers*.

Chris turned down the volume. "I'm still kind of amazed that we got a contract for that record. 1984 was *not* a good time to be a folk-rock duo. I mean, what were the big hits that year?"

"I don't know," Andy said, "like, 'What's Love Got to Do with It?' 'Hello' by Lionel Richie. 'Jump' by Van Halen."

"Exactly. Lots of synthesizers. 'Ghostbusters.' 'When Doves Cry.' Even the Boss was all synthed out. Remember 'Dancing in the Dark'?"

"Of course. And 'Girls Just Want to Have Fun.' It was not a really introspective era."

"All the more amazing," Chris said, "that we were able to put out *Meet the Fairley Brothers*."

"'Good things happen to good people,' as Mom always said."

"She also told us there was a Santa Claus."

Andy shook his head. "Right you are, Debbie Downer."

For a while, they listened to themselves from thirty-eight years ago, as the mostly razor-straight highway stretched out in front of them. They left Sapporo's suburbs, the E5 slicing through corn and wheat fields and endless squares and rectangles of rice paddies. In the distance, a mountain range was growing closer as they headed northeast. Occasionally, the brothers sang along with the album, harmonizing with their twenty-something selves.

The songs, Chris thought, were well crafted and clear, like photographs that included just the right amount of detail.

"Do you remember those early demos we sent out?" Andy asked. "That punk rock thing we had going on?"

"It's amazing how different the exact same song sounds when you slow it down and swap out buzzsaw electric guitars for acoustics."

"We could have been a great punk band."

"I doubt it," Chris said. "I don't think we ever had enough attitude to really pull it off."

Andy shrugged. As he remembered it, they had always had plenty of attitude. The track shifted and they both began singing along with "I'll Love You Longer Than a Bob Dylan Song," the college radio mainstay that had enabled them to record their next album, *Dark as Dark Can Get.*

Just past Iwamizawa, Andy turned off onto Highway 116 and headed northeast into a narrow valley. It was early afternoon, but the area looked abandoned. No one was in the fields. No cars passed in either direction. The gas stations were boarded up. Even the houses with cars parked out front had their windows shuttered, as though the owners planned to be gone for a long time. "Kind of creepy," Andy said, and Chris nodded in agreement.

They continued listening to *Meet the Fairley Brothers* as the road began gaining altitude and wending into the mountains. The trees seemed to press in toward the asphalt. They passed a reservoir on their right, its water level a good twenty feet below the high-water line.

The lake made Andy think of a trip he and Chris had taken with their grandfather in the now distant past. Andy would have been in grammar school, Chris just starting junior high. Their mother's father, a transplanted Texan, was widowed and lived eight hours north, in Sacramento. They didn't see him much, but when they did, he was always friendly and encouraging. One summer he had taken them to Lake Amador in the Sierra foothills for a weeklong fishing trip. Initially, Chris had griped about sleeping in a tent, but by the time they were ready to leave, both boys had become capable bass fishermen and decent amateur astronomers, and their grandfather had imparted self-help nuggets like "That's no hill for a stepper" and weather assessments such as "Boys, it's hotter than the hinges on a depot stove."

Reminiscing, Andy took a turn too wide and Chris poked him in the arm: "Pay attention, dude." Andy considered for a moment sharing his reminiscences. Then he thought, Why spoil my memories?

As the road climbed, red-and-white-striped poles began appearing, presumably to mark the shoulder when Hokkaido was deep in snow.

The album ended. "You want to skip ahead to *Never Believed You Anyway*?" Andy asked.

"Sure, why not."

Chris scrolled to their third album and hit the play arrow. The car filled with the familiar sound of the title track, Andy taking the lead and Chris joining in on the chorus: "I don't care what you say / I never believed you anyway."

They listened to the album as the highway changed names, dipped below the summit of the mountain range, then began to meander downhill, following the course of a narrow river. While "Blue All Week Long" wove its dirgelike way from verse to chorus to verse to extended guitar solo, Chris stared out the window and made a vague comparison and contrast between the two great loves in his life. Larissa, his ex-wife, was smart, funny, financially savvy, pretty though not gorgeous, and seemed utterly devoted until the day she left him. Molly Moore was also smart and funny, but she was absolutely gorgeous and a spendthrift who he always knew would end up leaving him. Larissa was certainly the better catch, but what did it matter in the end, now that he was all alone? He reached into his pocket for the Clonazepam he'd stashed there earlier in the morning and swallowed the pill dry.

As they entered the outskirts of Furano, the GPS sent them around the town, to the north and into the wide Furano Valley, where the clouds were low and heavy.

"Where, exactly, is this community center?" Chris asked. "Wouldn't it be in the middle of town?"

Andy let out a deep breath. "The thing is, it isn't a community center, per se."

"Oh, for God's sake. What the hell does that mean?"

"Just that it's a...de facto community center. The Furano Valley is famous for its flower farms, and the gig is at the biggest one. It's a huge tourist draw for people from all over Japan."

"So, what is it? Like a barn or something?"

"Obviously, I've never actually seen it. Fumiko assures me that it's a good gig. The pay sure is: one hundred thousand yen and they cover our hotel in town."

"How much is that, like a thousand dollars?"

"Almost. More if you count the cost of the room."

"And we just play our set?"

"I'm sure they'll want to hear 'Whenever I Hit the Road' at least once, maybe more, but otherwise, I'm guessing we have a decent amount of leeway to play whatever we want."

"Really?" Chris began chuckling. "What if we did a cover of 'Where Have All the Flowers Gone?'"

"Yeah, I mean, do you know it?"

"That's why we've got these iPads with Bluetooth. They scroll, we sing."

"All right," Andy said. "Anything else?"

"How about the Stones' 'Dead Flowers'? That's an easy one."

"It's a little ironic for a flower farm."

"It's post-ironic," Chris said, "like the Fairley Brothers themselves."

"In that vein, why not 'Every Rose Has Its Thorn' by Poison, or 'Sugar Magnolia' by the Dead?"

"Okay, and maybe the song about going to San Francisco?"

The two of them harmonized: "'Be sure to wear some flowers in your hair.'"

The GPS sent the Aqua deeper into the Valley and told them their destination was five miles away.

"Whatever kind of space it is," Andy said, "we'll make it our own."

The road cut through a grid of small fields dotted with barns and greenhouses, then past larger fields of barley shimmering in the light breeze, and finally uphill to an enormous gravel parking lot that was mostly full of cars, with several tour buses parked to the side. Andy took a ticket from the parking machine. "Remind me to get this validated."

The brothers dug their guitar cases and gig bags from the back of the Aqua and walked over a rise that revealed a panorama of flower fields crisscrossed by dirt roads. Great swatches of yellow, purple, pink, red, white, and orange flowers undulated across the hills, beneath the louring sky.

"Pretty," Andy said.

"No doubt. But I don't really see a place to play, do you?"

Before Andy could respond, someone cleared their throat behind the brothers. They turned to find a dapper elderly man wearing a blue and violet ascot. "Welcome," he said, in unaccented English. "You must be the Fairley Brothers."

"We are," Andy said, looking down at his phone, "and you must be Mr. Saito?"

"Indeed, I am." He bowed, and the brothers bowed in turn. "I'm a big fan of your music. I listened to your records quite a bit when I was studying botany at UC Davis."

"It's always good to meet a fan," Andy said.

"As you might imagine," the elderly man continued, "we're very proud of the Furano Valley Flower Forever Flower Farm." He gestured down the hill. "As you can see, we have tractor rides, and guests can rent ATVs. And our flowers, of course, are world-famous. We grow marigolds, pansies, irises, columbine, geraniums, petunias, and lavender, among others. We also have an alpaca farm as well as a knitting center. You might want to have a look at the alpaca wool sweaters before you depart."

"It's quite a place," Chris said, trying to politely cover his nose against the unequivocal smell of manure. "We were just wondering where the community center is where you want us to set up."

Mr. Saito pointed up the hill to a mint green barn with a bright pink roof. "Normally, we'd have you in there, but we're in the middle of renovations right now, so we're going to have to improvise somewhat."

"We're getting used to improvising," Andy said.

Mr. Saito cracked a modest smile. "A necessary quality for a musician, I would imagine."

"So," Chris asked, sounding gruffer than he meant to, "where's the gig?"

"Follow me," Mr. Saito said, and moved at a fast clip toward a two-story yellow building.

Inside was a souvenir store. People browsed rows of flower-themed knickknacks, stuffed anime characters, bobble-headed kittens, wooden dolls, Japanese fans, boxes of candy, and bundles of incense. Mr. Saito pointed to a slightly raised platform in the back of the store behind a flower-themed card rack. Three small tables, each with three tiny chairs, were already filled with middle-aged men and women drinking beer. Several of them waved when they saw the Fairley Brothers.

"You've got to be kidding," Chris said.

"No," said Mr. Saito, "I'm afraid I kid you not. If you want to get paid, here is where you will play."

Andy smiled at their employer. "A quick conference with my brother," he said before pulling Chris by the shirtsleeve into an aisle filled with flower-scented soaps. The mixed bouquet of rose, lavender, peony, and lilac was overpowering. "Big bro, I think we have to do this."

"We don't have to do anything, Andy. It's humiliating."

"What about those people waiting to hear us?"

"All nine of them? Come on."

"Well, I'm going to play. And I will suck if you don't join me."

Sighing, Chris followed his brother back to the minuscule stage.

The brothers squeezed themselves and their equipment onto the platform. Chris insisted on getting the gift shop's Wi-Fi password from Mr. Saito, then when their iPads were mounted on their stands, he took a Sharpie from his bag and wrote out a set list on the back of a flyer for the llama farm and taped it to the floor.

The Fairley Brothers' first number was "Where Have All the Flowers Gone?" followed by "Wildflowers" and "Build Me Up Buttercup," which received uproarious applause from the three tables and attracted a dozen curious souvenir browsers. By this time, most of the members of the audience were holding their phones up to record the show.

"It's great to be here in Furano," Chris said. "Over the years, my brother and I have frequently discussed the possibility of playing at the Furano Flower Farm Gift Shop, but we always thought it was an impossible dream. And now we're actually here." Silence. "Rock on, Furano!"

Andy raised an eyebrow. The audience clapped excitedly.

"Would you like to hear a new one?" Chris called out. His question met with only a smattering of uncertain applause.

"What 'new one'?" Andy said. "You didn't tell me anything about this."

"Something I wrote. It's a kind of country number with a darkly comic edge."

Andy lowered his voice. "Sounds intriguing. But shouldn't we have rehearsed it at least once before we played it to a live audience?"

Chris shrugged. "I mean, yes, it's kind of spur of the moment, but just follow along. Other than the little walkdown at the end of the chorus, there are only four chords. Starts in F, ends in C."

Chris strummed an F chord and began singing:

Things have been bad since you left me
Old J.D. is my new best friend
And sometimes I'll make a poor choice
Like when I parked the car...in the kitchen...again

Andy rolled his eyes, as Chris continued:

I parked the car in the kitchen
Kind of run into the kitchen sink
But the refrigerator's still working
So I think I'll get me another drink

As the song continued, detailing the speaker's propensity for parking his car in his kitchen, Andy gradually figured out the chords and haltingly joined in on guitar. Some of the audience members' phones went down into their laps, but others kept on recording.

When the song was over, and the listeners had politely applauded, Andy whispered to Chris, "I think we owe them what they came out to hear."

Chris shrugged and they played what one listener loudly called "the Honda song." By the first chorus, "Whenever I hit the road—the road! / Whenever I hit the road," most of the patrons had migrated to the back of the store to video the Fairley Brothers.

At the close of the song, Mr. Saito stepped onto the stage, waving both his hands, and spoke in Japanese, which evoked another round of applause.

"What did he say?" Chris asked Andy.

"He just thanked us for coming, and I guess the show is over."

"I think we ought to do an encore," Chris said to his brother. And then, in his microphone, "Do you want to hear one more?"

The audience erupted.

Chris typed into his iPad, then said, "This is a little number by a band called Spinal Tap. It's called 'Listen to the Flower People.'"

"I don't know it," Andy said.

"Just look at my iPad and follow along."

Andy wasn't the only one who apparently didn't know the song. The audience listened tentatively, clapped with restraint, then immediately began leaving.

Mr. Saito nodded at the departing guests and handed an envelope of cash to Andy.

"What'd you think?" Chris asked him.

"Unconventional, and unnecessarily sarcastic," Mr. Saito replied. "I would have preferred to have heard more originals, especially from your third album, which is my favorite."

"You like *Never Believed You Anyway*?" Chris asked dubiously.

"'Turpentine' rocks. And the record has a kind of thematic coherence that your other records lack." He coughed into his fist. "I've always wondered: Is it about a real person?"

The brothers looked at one another. "Not really," Andy finally said. "It's more of an amalgam."

"Ah." Mr. Saito cleared his throat. "Well, your assistant—Fumiko, I believe?—should have the address of your hotel in Furano. And you're welcome to look around at the flowers if you'd like."

"Thank you," Andy said. "You've been very kind."

"It was...an experience." Mr. Saito bowed slightly, turned, and disappeared down a hall past the cash registers.

As the brothers began packing up, a pretty woman in her late fifties appeared. "I am Mrs. Watanabe."

"Nice to meet you," Andy said, turning to her.

"I have all your records."

"That's great," Andy said.

"I mean, I have them here, in my bag." She pulled out four LPs protected by plastic sleeve covers. "I am hoping you will sign them all. Both of you." She pointed to the Sharpie lying on top of their set list.

The brothers paused their packing as she carefully took each album from its sleeve and handed it to them for their signatures. When an album was signed, she waved it in the air until the ink was dry, slipped it back into its case, and nestled it in her bag.

"And now I say goodbye," she said, bowing.

As she turned to go, Andy said, "Wait." The woman looked back. "Do you want to have dinner with us?" She hesitated, and Andy added, "Dinner with the world-famous Fairley Brothers? Who could resist such an offer?"

The woman dipped her head slightly and said, "I could." She hugged the bag containing the albums to her chest and disappeared into the crowd of shoppers that were once again milling in the aisles of souvenirs, ignoring the Fairley Brothers as though they did not exist at all.

"What was that all about?" Chris asked. "I thought you were happily married?"

"I am. That was for you."

"*Really?*" Chris asked, narrowing his eyes.

"Really," Andy replied, feeling largely certain that he was telling the truth.

It was raining and nearly dark by the time the brothers pulled into the parking lot of a business hotel across from the Furano train station. Andy insisted there was no possibility of their musical equipment being stolen if they left it in the car overnight, and they hustled their suitcases inside as the rain pelted down on their parkas. After checking in, they took the elevator to a fifth-floor double-room that was slightly larger than the one in Sapporo, but with the same white walls with similar brown accents, the same white bedspreads with brown throw rugs. Andy sat down on his bed and searched for "best restaurants near me." In a few minutes he held up his phone. "There's a place a hundred yards from here that specializes in local wild game."

"Lead on, Macduff," Chris said.

The restaurant was two inclement blocks away, and when, dripping wet, they entered the anteroom, the proprietress tried to shoo them back outside.

"She says it's full right now," Andy translated. "We can't come in."

"Tell her we can't go outside—we're the Fairley Brothers."

"Seriously?"

"You can at least try."

Andy said something in Japanese that only made the owner grumpier. She had her hand on Andy's chest and was pushing him out the door, when Chris began to sing, "Whenever I hit the road—the road! / Whenever I hit the road." He took a deep breath and sang the lines again, this time with Andy harmonizing.

The restaurant went silent. Then the diners began to cheer. "Honda CR-V!" someone called out, then let out a big, booming laugh.

The woman who had been so determined to keep them out now practically dragged them inside, down a narrow hall to a private back room with the walls painted dark red. They took off their shoes and sat cross-legged at a low table on a tatami mat.

They requested two large beers and drank them down before the waitress returned to take their orders. Andy asked for sake and the "Oh So Giant" bowl of miso soup with venison, duck, and vegetables, and Chris ordered the roasted bear in ginger soy sauce.

When the waitress had gone, Andy said, "It seems kind of wrong to eat a bear."

"I hear you. Nevertheless, there it is on the menu."

"If they had roasted humans on the menu, would you eat them?"

"I mean, are they tasty? How much do they cost?"

Andy took a sip of his beer. "LOL."

"Did you just say, 'LOL'?"

"Yeah. It's how you indicate something isn't funny."

When the food arrived, the brothers ate their meal in a silence punctuated only by the occasional appearance of the waitress or the proprietress checking to see if they needed anything. Andy almost asked his brother how his meal was, but Chris was bent over his plate, stabbing at the bear with his chopsticks as though it were still alive.

They paid and began walking back to the hotel, the rain still falling, the street glistening with puddles.

As they reached the train station, Andy detoured beneath the station overhang and stopped. Chris stepped out of the rain, and Andy said, "Look, I don't know if I should be concerned about you, or just annoyed, but I thought this was going to be easier."

"I'm sorry, man. Sometimes I don't know why I feel or act the way I do. I'm sixty-two years old—you'd think I would have figured it out by now. It's just this thing inside me, like it doesn't want me to be happy."

"So we're not having a fight?"

"I'm not," Chris said.

"Then why did we not say a word to each other during dinner?"

"Maybe we're just tired," Chris said. "It's my fault. I'm used to being alone, so this is a lot of 'together time' for me."

"I get that, I do. We can always get separate rooms. We'll just have to pay for the second one."

"Is that expensive?"

"It's not cheap."

"Let's just keep doing what we're doing. It's not bad. In fact, it's kind of fun."

"I agree," Andy said, clapping his brother on the shoulder and leading them back into the rain.

Upstairs in their room, Chris flopped down on the bed, and Andy turned on the television. Five analysts were watching a TikTok video of a woman falling down a flight of stairs. They laughed as she twisted her ankle and hit the landing. There seemed to be some discussion of the mechanics of the fall, as it was replayed, again and again, in slow motion.

Andy looked over at his brother who lay there with his eyes closed. "When I'm down," Andy said, "one thing that always makes me feel better is the onsen. Do you want to try it?"

"The what?"

"It's like a hot springs spa, but it's in the hotel."

"I mean, sure. What does it involve?"

"It's kind of complicated, but if you just do what I do, you'll be fine."

"Okay, why not?"

Andy pointed to two robes that were hanging near the door and two pairs of slippers. "Strip down to your shorts, then get in those," Andy said. "Also, take the towel and the washcloth."

"Is this going to be weird?" Chris asked.

"Only if you make it that way."

Both the robes and slippers turned out to be too small, but the brothers squeezed into them, picked up the towels and washcloths, then took the elevator down to the basement.

A sign pointed them to a changing room. Two sides of the room contained mirrors and sinks. On the third were shelves with baskets, where they stowed their robes, slippers, and underwear.

Naked, holding their towels and washcloths, they passed through a door into a larger room with a steaming shallow pool in which lay two men, silent and still, their eyes shut. One wall was lined with showerheads at navel height. Chris dutifully copied his brother, who sat on a low wooden stool and washed his hair, then soaped himself down. After rinsing off with their washcloths, they walked over to the pool, where Andy folded his towel and placed it away from the water, folded his washcloth and put it on top of his head, then eased himself in.

"I'm lost now," Chris said.

"Why? Just do what I did."

Chris gingerly stepped into the water. "Shit, it's boiling!" he yipped, withdrawing his foot.

"It's supposed to be. Just get in."

Chris took several steps into the pool, then eased himself into the hot water. "Just for the record, I'm feeling extremely uncomfortable right now."

"Duly noted."

"What now?" Chris said when he had finally settled into a semi-comfortable position.

"Just relax."

"How can you relax when there are so many rules?"

"How can you relax when there aren't any rules?" Andy replied.

It was a short soak, less than five minutes, then they were out, toweling themselves off and returning to the changing room. "I can't remember the last time I saw your naked butt," Chris said.

"Ditto."

When they were dressed in their robes and slippers, and headed for the elevator, Andy asked, "How was it?"

"An experience, for sure. But next time I think I'll pass."

LAKE AKAN FOLK FESTIVAL

Lake Akan
Tuesday, August 9

Andy woke up, his head throbbing—possibly from the sake he'd drunk with his meal the night before, possibly from spending two full days with his brother—and shook out three ibuprofen pills from the bottle by his bedside. Watching Chris sleep, Andy remembered how, on weekend mornings during their childhood, he would sit near his brother's bed, willing him to wake up. It never worked. Christmas, too, Chris would snore and squirm and snore some more, while Andy felt as though he would jump out of his skin if he couldn't get to the tree and begin opening presents. This morning, though, as Andy rubbed his temples with his fingers, he was more than happy to let his brother rest.

Chris, unaware of Andy's eyes on him, was dreaming of Molly Moore, but his dream didn't make sense. In it, he and Molly were a long-married couple, gray-haired and content, welcoming Andy to their home for Thanksgiving dinner. Andy's wife was a blur—part angel, part pitchwoman for a laundry commercial. When they sat down to eat and Chris reached over to carve the turkey, it melted into a sea of maggots.

Chris woke with a start and rubbed his eyes. Andy was watching the muted television again—an infomercial for a hair replacement creme. A dumpy man in a gray sweatsuit appeared to be testifying to the product's virtues. Bright-colored kanji plastered the screen.

"It's almost seven," Andy said, turning at the sound of his brother waking. "I was going to get you up in a few minutes. We've got another double bill today. We have the two o'clock slot at the Lake Akan Folk Festival, and then we have a ten p.m. gig at a jazz club in Kushiro."

Chris scratched the back of his head. "I'm sorry, I haven't really been following the schedule. Are those good gigs? Are they close?"

"Yes, and sort of. I think it's about a four-hour drive to Lake Akan, and then Kushiro is a couple of hours from there."

"But we get paid, right?"

"Of course. Lake Akan is, like, a thousand dollars each, and the jazz club guarantees half that, plus half the gate."

"We're not really a jazz act, are we?"

"The woman Fumiko talked to said that there's not a lot of live music in Kushiro, so she's hopeful the place is going to be packed. Also, a guy with a blog that apparently has a pretty big following wants to interview us. This would be right after the folk festival thing. Fumiko says it could really help our brand."

"Our 'brand'?"

"You know: our identity. What makes us, us."

"Ah," Chris said in a tone of deep skepticism.

"The more people are aware of us, the bigger our audiences are going to be. If we can go viral, we're going to see some serious spectators out there."

Chris reached over and drained the cup of water on his nightstand. "Okay, well, I signed on for this. Whatever you have going on, I'll go along with it."

"That's what I like to hear my big brother say. So maybe take a shower, and let's get on the road as soon as we can."

After checking out of their hotel, the brothers filled up with gas at a Showa Shell station and bought coffees and plastic-wrapped mango bread from a 7-Eleven. With Andy driving, they headed south down the Furano Valley, then along the Sorachi River to where it branched into the Nishitatsupu River, with its narrow valley of farms and villages.

The morning sun made both brothers feel hopeful, and several times they turned and smiled at one another. "You know," Andy said, "I realize these first three gigs have been pretty shitty, but I really enjoy just, like, the *process* of performing. The satisfying *click* sound your guitar case makes when you unlatch it, or thinking up the set list for the gig. I like the feel of my fingertips on the strings, even just tuning up, watching the digital lines get in sync on the tuner: E, A, D, G, B, E. It all makes me feel like I'm doing something important."

"Well, we are doing something important. Sort of. I mean, making music is important, whether or not anyone gets it, or even listens to it."

"That's kind of a positive statement, coming from you," Andy said.

"It is. Maybe I'm sick or something."

In Minamifurano, when Andy pulled over at a Seicomart to use the toilet, Chris typed the title of their fourth and final album into Apple Music, and, when Andy began driving again, he hit play without comment.

Despite its sardonic title, *What the Folk?* was a mournful record, with perhaps a little too much fuzz guitar accenting the choruses. The lush green margins of the two-lane highway seemed to comment on the music, though the brothers interpreted that commentary differently. If the verdure north of Ochiai made Andy feel briefly downcast, Chris was suddenly charged with a ray of optimism. And while the towering pines on the twisting mountain road further south seemed gloomy and foreboding to Andy, the trees struck Chris as regal and aspirational.

In Tomamu, they entered the Hokkaido Crossing Expressway, a road that burrowed through long tunnels as frequently as it was above ground. When *What the Folk?* ended, Chris played The Replacements' "Bastards of Young" and then the Weavers' "Kisses Sweeter Than Wine."

"Paul Westerberg and Pete Seeger," Andy said. "Interesting combination."

"Kind of sums up our aesthetic, wouldn't you say?"

"Maybe." Andy drummed his fingers on the steering wheel as an endless forest flashed past their windows before they entered another tunnel. "So, tell me what's been going on? I feel pretty out of touch, even after spending three days with you."

"What do you want to know?"

"I mean, we haven't talked much since Ireland. That was five years ago. How'd you spend the pandemic?"

"Alone, mostly."

"Yeah, sorry. You still miss Larissa?"

"Way more than I should," Chris sighed. "She just got tired of our marriage, and I don't really blame her. Twenty years with me would be enough for anyone."

"Oh, you're not that bad," Andy said, coughing out a laugh.

"It got so that I didn't want to do anything after work. I'd write a new song every now and then, and Larissa always encouraged that, but I didn't have any interest in playing them to people, or even recording them. The older I get, the more distant our success feels, you know? These three little 'gigs' we've done so far, mostly what I feel when I'm up there is embarrassed, like, do I really want to make these people suffer just to placate my ego?"

"I get that," Andy said, "but it's not really accurate, is it? Even at the wedding, a couple of people were digging us. And the other two places we had real fans out there. That old guy with the cane in Sapporo. That lady with our albums at the flower farm. Even grumpy Mr. Saito. Not to mention the fact that we're getting *paid* to do this. We've got at least one gig a day for almost two weeks. If you'd been here longer, I'm sure Fumiko could have booked us all over the country."

"Yeah, okay, but this is all based on a fluke. Honda just happened to pick what they no doubt thought was a piece of quirky nostalgia, and, weirdly, people liked it. In one country only, I might add. And who knows for how long? A month from now, it'll be some other ditty on some other commercial, and we'll be forgotten again."

"Chris, dude, you can be a serious bummer."

"I know, I know, I know. I try to stay upbeat, but this—this *feeling* comes out of nowhere and brings me down."

"Like depression?"

"Depression, anxiety—whatever. It's not debilitating, but it certainly doesn't make things any easier."

Andy wasn't sure what to say, so he said nothing. The Weavers continued playing on Apple Music. Now they were singing "On Top of Old Smokey," one of the first songs the brothers had learned together, and suddenly Andy, and then Chris, were singing along.

When the song finished, Andy said, "Do you remember the alternate version?"

"I do," Chris replied, pausing the music so that they could sing a cappella:

On top of Old Smokey
All covered with sand
I shot my poor lover
With a red rubber band

I went to her funeral
I went to her grave
Instead of throwing flowers
I threw a grenade

After a pause, Chris said, "You couldn't sing that one anymore. You'd get canceled."

Andy nodded in agreement. "Maybe that's not such a bad thing. But back to your life. No offense at all, dude, but do you have anything *upbeat* to report?"

"I don't think I have cancer."

"You what? *Did* you think you had cancer?"

"For a while, maybe. And I'm still not one hundred percent sure. I have to get a CT scan when I get back. Kidneys, spleen, pancreas. That sort of thing."

Andy, his brows furrowed, glanced over at his brother. "What happened?"

"I had blood in my urine. My doctor sent me to a urologist, and he gave me a cystoscopy to check for bladder cancer."

"What's that? A cyst...whatever?"

"Do you really want to know?"

"Sure."

"I hope you never have to have one. It's one of the great indignities of the aging male."

"Go ahead: I can take it."

"So, it's an outpatient procedure. You go into this room, and take off your pants, and lie back on a table."

"Doesn't sound that bad so far."

"Then a nurse comes in, and she takes a syringe and shoots this numbing gel straight into your urethra."

Andy took his right hand off the steering wheel and covered his crotch. "Jesus, God. Ouch."

"Don't worry: It only gets worse. They wait a few minutes for it to numb things, but, let me tell you, it's a pretty iffy anesthesia. Then the doctor comes in and sticks this thing called a cystoscope up your penis. It's like a long wire with a tiny camera at the end, and they've got it wired up live, so you can watch if you want to."

"Did you watch?" Andy asked, his right hand now clutching his jeans.

"The doctor kept telling me to, and I kept telling him I didn't want to see anything. Anyway, he's about halfway there, then he goes, 'Okay, hang on, this is the bad part.'"

Through clenched teeth, Andy said, "The *bad* part?"

"Yeah. They have to push the camera thing through your internal sphincter to get to the bladder."

"Oh my God, I feel like I'm going to have to pull over. This is really making me queasy."

"Imagine how I felt," Chris said. "But basically, when he gets the camera where he wants it to go, he looks around for less than a minute, then he pulls the thing out, and you're done. He thought my stuff looked okay."

Andy took in a long breath, then let it out. "Remind me to die before I get to that stage because *wow*."

The E38 went east past Obihiro, then headed north, where the brothers exited at Hombetsu after paying an exorbitant toll. The E61 was narrower, and narrower still at Ashoro when it became Highway 241, which wound northeast through the mountains toward Lake Akan. Andy asked for some driving jazz from the fifties or sixties and Chris chose Hank Mobley's *Soul Station* and Grant Green's *Idle Moments*.

Chris shut his eyes, and the music had him replaying Larissa's goodbye speech. She had made a nice dinner—soft jazz in the background, candles, wine, filet mignon—but while Chris had been at work, she'd spent the day gathering her things and moving them to the home of Stuart, the money manager. Halfway through the meal, she gently told Chris all the reasons she no longer wanted to live with him: his refusal to pursue a career in music, his inability to have fun or take risks, the monotony of their evenings and weekends together, the fact that neither of them were getting any younger, and when happiness presented itself, well, you had to grab it. As she spoke, she cried more than he did, although when she shut the front door behind her, Chris collapsed on the floor weeping.

Meanwhile, Andy could think of nothing but the cystoscopy.

The miles seemed to move sluggishly, as though the landscape resented whoever refused to pause and admire its dense, verdant beauty.

It was noon when they arrived in Lake Akan, a tiny resort town perched on the southern shore of a large, pleasant lake punctuated by tree-covered Mount Oakan on its northeast side. Souvenir shops alternated with small restaurants and tourist hotels.

Exhausted, the brothers found a parking lot near one of the boat docks and walked several blocks to the festival stage, hidden in the pines along the lake, from which could be heard American folk music sung in Japanese. As they got closer, Andy recognized "Puff the Magic Dragon" and began singing along in broken Japanese.

"Impressive," Chris said, as they stood at the edge of the crowd, looking for someone in charge.

"I'm making up a lot of the words, but I'm in the ballpark," Andy said. He pointed to a man with a ponytail and a leather cowboy hat, standing near the soundboard. He seemed to be criticizing an underling. "I'm betting that's our guy."

They walked over to him, and Chris tapped his shoulder.

The man turned around. He was deeply tanned with a handlebar mustache. "Busy right now," he said.

"We're the Fairley Brothers," Chris replied.

"Hmm. You cut it close. We didn't know if you can show."

Andy said, "My wife told you we'd be driving from Furano."

"Furano is a long way."

"Tell me about it," Chris said.

"Well, you here now. You go on at two."

"We'll be ready," Andy told him.

The brothers fetched their guitars from the Aqua, found an empty picnic table, and wrote out a set list. They would have fifty minutes onstage and decided to do two songs from each of their four albums, closing with Chris's "Car in the Kitchen." Chris sent Andy the song's lyrics and chords from his phone, and they rehearsed it twice. As they strummed their guitars quietly by the banks of the lake, a kingfisher skimmed along the surface. With its long gray bill, pronounced black and white tuft, and orange breast, it looked like a speckled explosion of feathers.

Sitting in the wings, waiting to go on, Chris counted eighty people in the audience. Everyone was masked. A few people were focused on their phones, but it was mostly a respectful audience. It took a long time to get to Lake Akan; you really had to like your folk music to make the trip.

When the time came for them to play, Chris nearly tripped on the steps leading up to the stage, and the crowed *Ooohed* sympathetically, then clapped when he righted himself. That little miscue seemed to endear them to the audience, and each song was warmly received. Not surprisingly, "Whenever I Hit the Road" and "Take Me Till Tuesday" garnered the most applause, but each song, even "Ray Guns in the White House," the nine-minute opus off *What the Folk?*, received patient attention.

"Do you think they understand us?" Chris whispered to Andy before they began "Car in the Kitchen."

"Does it matter? They seem to be enjoying themselves."

They began playing, and the audience's phones, which had been held high for video recording during "Whenever I Hit the Road," but had mostly been in their laps since then, were suddenly up and recording again:

I don't deny I've been drinking
Sometimes you just can't win
And last night is one good example
I parked the car in the kitchen again

I parked the car in the kitchen
Put the keys in the fresh fruit bowl
But there ain't been no fresh fruit there for a long time
I think I'm in need of damage control

When they finished, they received their largest round of applause.

After they left the stage and were packing up their guitars, a man in his forties in a blue suit coat and a thin blue tie with a neat salt-and-pepper goatee approached and said, "Hello."

"Hello there," Andy said.

"I'm Daisuke Hayashi. Fumiko Yoshida said I could interview you for my website, folkrockjapan.com?"

"Right, right," said Andy. "Of course. Do you want to go talk over a meal somewhere?"

"There is the little Ainu village nearby. I'm curious about it."

"Let's go then," Andy said, and the three of them, the brothers carrying their guitar cases, strolled up the street.

"Is there really a folk-rock scene in Japan?" Chris asked.

"Not as much as there used to be, of course, but one of the first big bands to sing only in Japanese was a folk-rock group called Happy End. They sound kind of like the Grateful Dead, but, in a way, they're like our Beatles. Have you ever seen the movie *Lost in Translation*?"

The brothers nodded.

"One of the songs you hear, 'Kaze Wo Atsumete,' is by Happy End. From their album *Kazemachi Roman*."

Andy translated for his brother: "'Gather the Wind' from *Wind City Romance*."

"You speak Japanese," Daisuke said, impressed.

"Badly, but I try."

They turned a corner and stopped at an archway presided over by three enormous Plexiglas owls. Totem poles were planted in the median, and at the far end of the one-block street was what looked like a ceremonial house. On either side were tourist shops, their folksy facades barely covering the peeling paint and rusted ironwork of the homes to which they were attached.

"Kind of a down-market Disneyland," Chris said, "though the same basic idea, I suppose."

"There's actually a *real* Ainu museum I'd like to see," Andy said. "On our way back to Honshu."

Chris looked puzzled. "I mean...okay. But I have to admit: I don't even really know what you're talking about. What's an Ainu?"

"They're the native people of Hokkaido," Daisuke said. "Mostly we, the Japanese, left them alone, but in the nineteenth century, Japan started getting land hungry, and so we came up here and basically wiped them all out."

"Jesus," Chris said. "Though it makes sense, in a way. This place does have a kind of cheesy Native American vibe going on. Like the conquerors making money off the conquered."

"Maybe," said Andy, guiding his brother toward the entrance of a restaurant, "we can just leave the Ainu in peace for a while? I'm looking forward to telling Daisuke our story."

The restaurant, which was decorated with wooden carvings and faded posters of northern landscapes, was empty, but a waitress rushed out from behind a curtain to seat them. Andy said something to her in Japanese, and she replied, nodding vigorously.

"What did you say?" Chris asked.

"I just asked if it was okay if we were here for a while, and she said that was fine, to stay as long as we liked."

Chris and Andy propped their guitar cases against a bookcase. Daisuke ordered for them, listing the dishes that would be served: kaisen don, hot rice topped with crab, roe, and salmon; Ishikari nabe, salmon and tofu in a miso broth; and Hokkaido ramen in a chicken broth with scallops and corn. With a large Sapporo beer in front of each of them, Daisuke turned on his iPhone's voice memo app and the interview began.

Two hours later, when Daisuke pressed Stop on the app, all three were exhausted.

"Wow," Andy said, "I feel like I've just relived the first twenty-two years of my life."

Chris nodded. "And it wasn't any better this time around, unfortunately."

"I thought it was fascinating," Daisuke said. "Epic, really. And now the first part of your story, as told by yourselves, will live forever on the Internet. Hopefully we can continue at another time?"

Chris groaned. "The whole thing feels so...transient. Like, big deal: we did something and now it's gone."

"Ah, but do you know Kenkō's *Essays in Idleness*?" Daisuke asked.

Both brothers shook their heads no.

"He writes in one essay, and I'm quoting from memory here, so it won't be perfect: 'If people were never to fade away like the dews of Adashino or the smoke over Toribeyama, but stayed on forever, how things would lose their power to move us. The most precious aspect of life is its perishability.'"

"I get that," Andy said.

"I get it, too," Chris said, "though I'm not necessarily convinced."

Daisuke smiled.

"Anyway," Andy said, "I appreciate your taking the time to listen to us. Unfortunately, as much as I want to believe otherwise, I tend to think my brother is right. For most people, we're just the creators of a jingle for Honda." Turning to Chris, he said, "Nevertheless, the Fairley Brothers is a real thing, a real band. I think we deserve to have our story memorialized."

"Yes, you do," Daisuke said. "Most certainly. And now, may I pay for the bill?"

"We've got it," Andy said. "And we do need to get going. We've got that gig down in Kushiro tonight."

Andy called for the check, and the waitress, clearly ready for them to leave, appeared immediately. Andy paid, and they all stood up and shook hands.

"Until we meet again," Daisuke said.

Chris raised his eyebrows. "Which may be a long time."

Daisuke grinned. "You never know." Then, waving both his hands, he turned and left.

"Dude," Chris said, "we've got to scoot. We're really cutting it close again, and that stresses me out."

"No worries, big brother. We'll make it. And I have a feeling that this interview is going to be worth its weight in gold."

DIZZY COLTRANES JAZZ
NITE SOCIAL CLUB

Kushiro
Tuesday, August 9

The drive south from Lake Akan was on a mostly two-lane highway through thick forest that led to a mountain pass shadowing the shallow, rocky Akan River. It was, indeed, only two hours to Kushiro, but despite its beauty, the monotony of the landscape made the trip feel longer. The brothers listened to Neil Young albums—*Tonight's the Night, Time Fades Away, Comes a Time*—and having said so much to Daisuke Hayashi, did not speak to one another.

Still, memories from those days drifted in and out of their minds. Andy recalled a young woman he met after a concert with a dragon tattoo on her chest and abdomen, its open mouth engulfing her nether regions. Chris kept returning to a gig at a San Francisco bar when, for the span of several songs, he completely blanked on where to put his fingers on the fretboard. He could remember the feeling—as though someone had taken an apple corer and removed a piece of his brain.

With evening coming on, they left the mountains and drove into a broad valley of rice paddies and small farms. Andy received a text from a former teaching colleague who lived in Kushiro. "Dinner before the concert?" the text read. With his left hand on the wheel, Andy typed with his right thumb: "Yes. Say where."

The GPS took them to the Kushiro docks, and then east along Shinfuji dori. Warehouses and cranes and clusters of storage tanks lined the road, with tractor trailers pulling out of factory gates. "If I remember my Wikipedia correctly," Andy said, "Kushiro has the northernmost port in Japan that is free of ice year-round."

"A surefire guarantee of a great local music scene," Chris replied.

It was after eight and dark by the time they pulled into a pay lot across from the business hotel where they were scheduled to spend the night. Andy looked at his phone. "My friend is waiting for us at that restaurant right next door, and the bar is just a few blocks away. I'll check in really quick, then we can deal with everything else later on."

"Not to belabor a point, but I feel like we're cutting it close again."

"Don't worry, big bro. Why don't you head over to the restaurant and meet up with Jamie Ed?"

"*Who?*"

"Jamie Ed Gainey. He's from South Carolina."

"Of course he is."

"A really great guy," Andy said defensively.

"It goes without saying."

Andy walked to the hotel lobby, and Chris swallowed a Clonazepam with the last of his energy drink before crossing the narrow street to the restaurant, a dimly lit place with photographs of meat dishes in glass cases on the walls outside.

He stepped inside the tiny entrance area and was face-to-face with a large man in his early thirties with a big red beard. "You must be Chris?" the man said.

"I am. Jamie Ed, I presume?"

Jamie Ed reached out a knuckle for a fist bump. "I would shake hands, but COVID and everything. Plus, touching is not really a big Japanese thing." He took a step back and looked Chris over. "I can see the resemblance." Chris shrugged, and Jamie Ed asked, "How's your trip going?"

"Today was pretty good. The previous two days..." Chris sighed.

"We don't always know what's important until long after the event is over."

"Ah," Chris said. "Sounds very Japanese."

"Well, I grew up in Florence, South Carolina. But I've been here three years, teaching. First, I was down in Kyoto with Andy for a year. A *great* guy, by the way, your brother, and then the last two years up here in Kushiro. It's kind of off the beaten track, but the pay is better because it's so isolated, and the cost of living is lower. Plus, my girlfriend is from here."

The door opened and Andy rushed inside, giving Jamie Ed a big bear hug.

"No touching in Japan," Chris said.

"You can't stop this one," Jamie Ed laughed, clapping Andy on the back.

A hostess came out and led them down a dark corridor and up a flight of stairs. The restaurant smelled of grilled meat, spilled beer, and cigarette smoke, with an afternote of stinky shoes.

When they had taken off their own shoes and were seated at a low table in a small room behind a pair of red curtains, Chris said, "Can you remind her we don't have much time? I don't want to be late."

Andy said something to the woman standing at the table and she replied at length, then bowed quickly several times and left. "You just order on this iPad," Andy said. "She says it'll be out quick. And I ordered three beers."

"Well done," Jamie Ed said. He let out a long breath. "Man, I can't believe I am having dinner with *the* Fairley Brothers."

"You're a fan?" Chris asked.

"I mean, more so *now*. Since I met Andy. But it was mostly my dad, back in Florence. When I was growing up, he couldn't get enough of you guys. He'd be playing your CDs and singing along while he tinkered in his workshop behind the house. If one of you gets sick and has to miss a gig, just let me know 'cause I probably know all the words to your songs."

"In other words, you had a little too much Fairley Brothers growing up?" Chris asked.

"Is there such a thing as *too much* Fairley Brothers?"

Andy and Chris spoke at the same time: "Yes."

The three men made their dinner selections, entering them into the iPad. A few minutes later, there were three frosty Sapporos on the table, and ten minutes later, their meals arrived. Andy and Jamie Ed mostly talked about their teaching successes and failures—the latter, especially—while Chris smiled politely and nodded and picked at his Japanese pancake. The okonomiyaki had looked good on the menu, and it had tasted okay the day before at the Hokkaido Art Forest café, but this one was soaked in ginger and Worcestershire sauce and was, therefore, in his opinion, not good.

After a half hour, Chris took out his phone and showed Andy the time. It was 9:15. "Forty-five minutes. Shouldn't we get going?"

"Maybe we'd better."

They paid—no tip, Chris still couldn't get used to that—then retraced their way down the stairs, passing a red-curtained room where the diners were laughing riotously.

Andy and Chris took their guitars from the Aqua, and with Jamie Ed, they walked the four blocks to Dizzy Coltranes Jazz Nite Social Club. The entrance was through a sliding door in an alley. The sign was in kanji, but it was decorated with a silhouette of Dizzy Gillespie blowing a trumpet on the left side and John Coltrane playing his saxophone on the right.

"No apostrophe in the bar's name," Chris said.

"Apostrophes are for losers," Andy replied.

"They do know we're not a jazz act, right?" Chris said.

"Fumiko made that really clear."

Jamie Ed pulled back the sliding door for the brothers to enter. It was a small place, dark, with fairy lights strung along the bar and behind a stage that looked barely big enough to accommodate a drum kit, much less any other instruments. At the moment, there were only two barstools and two microphones in microphone stands.

Behind the bar was an oldish white-haired man and a middle-aged woman. Two middle-aged men were sitting at the bar, sharing a loud story.

Andy walked over to the white-haired man. "Akiran-san?" he asked.

The man bowed impressively low, and they spoke in Japanese for a while. Andy turned to Chris. "He says he is deeply honored to have the Fairley Brothers playing at his establishment this evening."

Chris looked around the club. "That's really great, but did we get the date wrong? Or the time?"

"Nope. Ten o'clock. His daughter, Eiko, will help us with the sound check."

"Can you ask him if he's expecting more people?"

Andy spoke with the owner. "He says in a perfect world, the entire city of Kushiro would be here. However, Kushiro—let me see if I can remember this—'is a shitty town full of shitty idiots who don't appreciate it when someone is...'" He trailed off and looked at Jamie Ed.

Jamie Ed said, "'When someone is giving a pearl to a pig.' Like, people here don't appreciate your music."

Chris looked around again. "I can see that."

"Don't worry," Andy said. "We still get paid even if people don't show up."

Just then, a boisterous group of men and women in their twenties burst into the club. "Your fan base," said Jamie Ed.

The young people looked around, apparently surprised by the lack of patrons, and said something to the owner. Chris made out the word "karaoke." The owner shook his head, and the group retreated back into the street. When they were gone, the owner spoke to Andy again.

Andy translated: "Typical shitty idiots of Kushiro."

A lone Japanese woman in her early thirties walked into Dizzy Coltranes Jazz Nite Social Club, and Jamie Ed walked over and gave her a bear hug. "My girlfriend!" he said to everyone. "Shiori."

Shiori looked both embarrassed and pleased, as she waved with both hands at the brothers and the people at the bar.

"She's a big fan," Jamie Ed said. "A *really* big fan."

"Maybe we should get set up," Chris said to Andy. "Since we're getting paid, one way or the other."

His brother nodded, and Eiko came from around the bar and went over to a small mixing panel in a dark corner of the club. The Fairley Brothers took their guitars from their cases, tuned up, and played the first verse and chorus of "Wake Up Little Susie." Eiko gave them a thumbs-up from the shadows, and Andy asked, "Shall we start?"

"Unless you want to wait for an audience," Chris said.

"People will show up. Surely not everyone in Kushiro is as shitty as Akiran-san says."

In the end, though, Kushiro proved almost as indifferent as the owner of the club had predicted.

One couple came in two songs late. They listened politely but left after the fourth song.

A lone drunk man tottered in, sat down, folded his arms across the table, put his head down, and promptly fell asleep.

The two men at the bar continued their drunken, desultory conversation, raising their voices so they could hear one another above the music and lowering their volume between songs.

Halfway through the first set, an elegantly dressed woman in her late forties or early fifties sat down at the table closest to the stage. She smiled at the brothers and mouthed the words to a few of their songs, though she didn't seem to be deeply familiar with the material.

At the break, Andy took Chris by the shirtsleeve and walked over to introduce himself and his brother.

"I know who you are," she said. She wore a wide black hat and a black silk scarf and a pearl necklace, which she fingered as she spoke.

"And do you live in Kushiro?" Andy asked.

"Nearby. A small town: Shiranuka." She turned to Chris. "Perhaps you will come to visit?"

Andy said, "I'm sure he'd love to. Right, big bro?"

Chris smiled politely, attempted a bow, and pulled Andy to the far side of the club. "That's not my scene, man."

"What? A beautiful lady wants to get to know you, a long-divorced and lonely man, and you're just, 'Nah, I'll pass.'"

"Something like that."

"There's something wrong with you, Chris Fairley."

"I know that."

While Andy went to hang out with Jamie Ed and Shiori at the bar, Chris sat at a far table and nursed the beer Eiko brought over. He knew what was wrong with him. At sixty-two, his libido was starting to fail him; instead, he wanted companionship and intimacy, the sort he'd had with Larissa for years, and Molly for a while. He didn't want a one-night stand, although he couldn't help glancing periodically at the woman, who was periodically glancing at him.

After about fifteen minutes, Andy waved Chris up to the stage and opened the second set with an a cappella version of "We Shall Overcome," which, by the third verse—"We shall live in peace...some-day-ay-ay"—had even quieted down the old men at the bar. It was a tested trick from their touring days, the plaintive, familiar melody tending to command people's attention, although what exactly two white guys from the San Fernando Valley had had to overcome was unclear. *More than you might think*, the brothers would have replied.

However, ten minutes later, after they'd finished their third song of the set, they had lost everyone but the woman from Shiranuka, and Chris said into his microphone, "Well, you've been a lovely audience, but this will be our final number for the evening."

Andy looked surprised, then shrugged.

"It's a little thing called 'The Psychics Are Crying,' and we'd like to dedicate it to all the people in Kushiro who missed out on tonight's performance."

"Shitty idiots!" the owner called out in English from behind the bar.

"Indeed," Chris said. "However, as the saying goes, 'You pays your money, so you takes your choice.'"

Andy coughed. "I've never really understood that saying."

"If I'm honest, neither have I."

From the audience, Jamie Ed, who had been drinking beer after beer, called out, "'Free Bird'!"

"Sorry, Jamie Ed," Chris said. "No requests tonight."

Then the brothers launched into "The Psychics Are Crying," with Chris taking a ten-minute solo at the end of the song that even he felt would never end. As the high C ringing from his guitar finally faded into silence, the woman from Shiranuka clapped louder than anyone else.

"Thank you, Kushiro," Andy said, "and good night."

After they had stowed their guitars in their cases, Andy made one more attempt with the mystery woman on Chris's behalf. Again, he pulled his brother by the shirtsleeve to her table and then, rather hard, pushed Chris into one of the chairs.

Chris glared at Andy but smiled politely at the woman. "I don't believe I caught your name."

"Akemi."

"That's a beautiful name. And what do you do in...in Shia—"

"Shiranuka."

"Right. Shiranuka."

"I run a brothel. Mostly for local fishermen."

For a moment, Chris was stumped. Then he muttered, "Sounds like interesting work."

"Very. Unfortunately, we have to wash all the linen every night, or the place smells too much like salted herring."

"I see."

Akemi smiled, which revealed two big dimples. "I am kidding. I own a small restaurant. Specializing in seafood, of course."

"Of course."

"I am not asking you back to my house tonight, by the way. I only invited you to visit sometime."

"Ah, oh right, right. I assumed as much."

"But you seem very nice, Chris."

"I am. I think. But...have you ever seen the movie *Annie Hall*?"

Akemi shook her head.

"Well, it's a Woody Allen movie, and I know he's been canceled, but at least in this one he's not dating a seventeen-year-old. So, in this movie, in *Annie Hall*, he references a joke by Groucho Marx, and it's, 'I would never want to join a club that would have someone like me as a member.'"

She looked at him as though he were speaking Martian.

"I guess what I'm saying is, I'm underconfident." Without thinking, he added: "For a rock star."

"For anyone," she said.

Chris laughed. "That's totally accurate."

Akemi stood up and reached out her hand, which Chris shook. "I must go now. Perhaps I will see you at another time?"

"I'd like that, but we're traveling all over Japan, usually only for a single night. I think we end up in Kyoto, but I'm not sure exactly when."

"Well, good luck on your tour."

As he watched her walk out of Dizzy Coltranes Jazz Nite Social Club, Chris felt a pang of regret, and then he felt Jamie Ed's meaty hand on his shoulder. "Struck out, huh?"

"Basically."

"Why don't you come back to our apartment and join me and Shiori for a nightcap?"

"I don't know. I'm pretty beat."

"Your brother said the same thing. Party poopers."

"We're old."

"Not that old. But listen." Jamie Ed reached into a bag. "I brought you a gift bottle of sake. Hakkaisan. It's good."

"Thank you, thank you very much," Chris said, accepting a green bottle with what looked like a hand-painted label.

"Time to go!" Andy called, holding up an envelope—presumably full of yen—and the four of them headed outside, walking together for several blocks. After they parted with the couple—Jamie Ed loudly proclaiming his love for the band, and Shiori nodding in agreement—Andy and Chris made their way back toward their hotel along a walkway beside the Kushiro River. It had rained, and the bricks were dotted with puddles. Streetlights shone on the river, which was broad and placid. Just north of the Nusamai Bridge, highlighted in blue spotlights, a sign consisting of six-foot tall stand-alone letters read "KUSHIRO." The word "cool" in cursive was stacked atop the "K," and instead of an "O" at the end, there was a bright red concrete ball.

The brothers took turns posing by the sign and sending the photos to Fumiko for posting on their social media. Afterwards, they walked to the car, swapping out their guitars for their luggage, but bringing the bottle of sake. They headed to the hotel and took the elevator up to their room. It was smallish but clean—in tones of brown and white, of course—and looked out on the river.

"Well, that was a night to be forgotten," Chris said, unpacking his toiletries.

"Your lady friend notwithstanding," Andy said. He was sitting on his bed, with his laptop open. "I got an email from Daisuke." He showed it to Chris.

"Does this look okay?" Daisuke had written. "Just let me know, and I will post it tonight."

"Should we just say, 'Yes,' and go to sleep?" Andy asked.

"Let's at least read it first," Chris said.

Chris sat next to Andy, who clicked the link in the email. Chris poured them each a water glass of sake as they settled down in front of a neon-themed webpage with flashing kanji in the margins. Chris looked over Andy's shoulder, and they began to read.

THE FAIRLEY BROTHERS
IN JAPAN (PART I)

The following interview was recorded at the Lake Akan Folk Festival shortly after the Fairley Brothers' well-received performance on the afternoon of Tuesday, August 9, 2022. The interview has been lightly edited for clarity and is available in Japanese here.

DAISUKE HAYASHI: So, the Fairley Brothers. Welcome to Japan!

ANDY FAIRLEY: Thanks, Daisuke, although I live here now.

DH: That's right, of course. In Kyoto, if I remember?

AF: With my wife Fumiko, yes.

DH: And you're a full-time musician?

AF: Actually, I teach English. At International Languages Japan.

DH: ILJ—that's a big corporation. How does it feel to be a folk-rock icon working for "the Man"?

AF: The people there are very kind, and I've made a lot of friends among the teachers, and, if I'm honest, among the students, too. Though we're not supposed to socialize with students.

DH: Because then they'd be getting their English lessons for free?

AF: Exactly.

DH: And you, Chris, do you also work for a huge Japanese corporation?

CHRIS FAIRLEY: Afraid not. I live in Los Angeles. I'm retired.

DH: Retired from music?

CF: That, and the Los Angeles Department of Water and Power.

DH: You also stepped back from playing?

CF: Our career, such as it was, basically came to an end after our fourth album, *What the Folk?* It didn't sell very well.

DH: That was back in 1988, if memory serves. I, personally, love that record, but, and I have this somewhere on my phone, a critic for *Rock Folk Magazine* called it a "'fairley' average offering."

AF: We got a lot of those bad puns.

DH: Well, the album title invites puns, doesn't it? *(Laughs.)* Still, I always thought the record held up well in comparison with other late '80s folk albums. Say the first Tracy Chapman album. Or Billy Bragg. Current 93, although I guess you'd call them more psychedelic folk.

CF: You know a lot about American music.

DH: I was born and raised in Greenwich Village. My father worked for the UN. My mother translated American poetry into Japanese, and vice versa.

CF: Interesting. How did you end up back in Japan?

DH: My family is Japanese. It's where I want to be. But this is *me* interviewing *you*, remember? So, let's go back to the start of the Fairley Brothers. I realize this will be well-trodden ground for hardcore Fairley fans—

CF: If there are any.

DH: There are many, I'm sure. You were both born and raised in Los Angeles?

AF: Tarzana. In the San Fernando Valley.

DH: And your parents were...

AF: Mom was a nurse. Dad...he kind of worked off and on.

CF: Mostly off. Our mom raised us.

AF: Our mom raised us, yeah. She worked hard. Double shifts, the whole nine yards.

DH: What was Tarzana like?

CF: When we were growing up in the '60s and '70s, it was pretty much working class. We had a very small two-bedroom, one-bath house. It was on this tiny, weirdly shaped lot. I think the developer hadn't planned on putting a house there, but then at the last minute they figured they could squeeze one more in.

AF: It was suburban, but definitely not the fashionable part of LA.

CF: Because our mom was always working, she couldn't be around a lot of the time, so we learned to take care of ourselves. Fix our own meals. Do the laundry. Do our homework.

AF: There was no maid service at the Casa de Fairley.

DH: Is there anything else you remember about your childhood?

AF: Good Christmases.

CF: Yeah, Mom tried her best then, whatever else was happening.

DH: Was music always a part of your life?

CF: Basically. I'm four years older than Andy, and when I was in my early teens, some of my friends started getting into trouble—

AF: "Trouble with a Capital T," Mom called it.

CF: Petty theft, breaking and entering—that sort of thing. Andy and I had always been into music, and Mom said she'd buy us both guitars if we stayed away from "the bad kids." These guitars were really cheap, I might add. Global guitars.

DH: A Korean brand, from the '60s and '70s.

CF: I did not know that. In any case, they weren't great. They went out of tune all the time. And we had these two tiny, extremely trebly amplifiers. Not a good sound.

DH: What sort of music did you listen to back then?

CF: Whatever was on the radio. Elton John. Billy Preston. The Chi-Lites.

AF: Cat Stevens. Jim Croce. Alice Cooper.

CF: I remember being transfixed by "American Pie." It seemed like a Russian novel to me—not that I knew what a Russian novel was at the time.

AF: Dad had left behind some folk albums before he took off, so give him credit for that. New Lost City Ramblers. Fairport Convention. The Kingston Trio. The New Christy Minstrels.

CF: Tom Paxton. The Weavers. We wouldn't have been caught dead by our friends listening to those albums, but Mom pretty much forbade us from having people over, so we were kind of protected from peer pressure when it came to liking folk.

DH: Obviously, those artists had a huge influence on the music you ended up making yourself. But I believe you first went through a punk rock phase?

CF: When Andy was thirteen, and I was seventeen, this kid, Jimmy Agile, moved in next door. He had a drum kit in his garage, and naturally we were intrigued. But Jimmy couldn't really play anything except that really fast punk beat—quick doubles, snare drum backbeats, open hi-hat, that sort of thing. So, we just sort of adapted the songs we'd started writing, which were mostly folk, for the drummer.

AF: Our dad had a job for a while at the GM plant in Van Nuys, and he bought us both Stratocasters and some better amps.

CF: To piss Mom off mostly, I think.

AF: Yeah. But it was fun. And suddenly we sounded okay. I don't think we ever would have had any songs on the radio if we hadn't been willing to stretch our wings and find out what rock and roll was all about.

DH: And how long did your punk experience last?

AF: About a year, until Chris went off to college.

CF: I went to Northridge, which is only about seven miles away, but it felt like a million miles, it was so different from our neighborhood in Tarzana. But I was still living at home—we couldn't afford the dorms. I was double majoring in English and music and picking up a lot of lyrical things that we later used in the band.

DH: And you, Andy?

AF: I was at home, playing guitar, playing records. Our little punk band broke up, but I played around the Valley with other kids when I could. Mostly house parties, that sort of thing. By this time, Mom had given up on keeping me from doing what I wanted to do.

DH: And how did the Fairley Brothers, the band as we know it, come together?

AF: For a while, we weren't really connected. Chris was going to Northridge, and I was working nights at a grocery store, and after I graduated from high school, I took a class or two at Pierce College—that's a community college near our house. Chris and I would play together occasionally, like every month or two—he was always writing new songs—and, like I said, I was gigging when I could, mostly in cover bands. But we didn't see that much of each other.

CF: I think we both just thought of music as a hobby. Something we'd do in the evenings after we got real jobs.

AF: Totally. But then one night this band I was playing with had a gig at a restaurant on Ventura Boulevard in Encino.

CF: Emil's Café.

AF: That's right, Emil's Café. It's long gone now, but it was a place where entertainment people used to go when they felt like slumming a bit, but not too much. The food was not wonderful, but it definitely had that fading LA glamour that a lot of people love. And they had an okay stage, and a pretty good sound system. Anyway, the other three guys in the band were in a car together and got pulled over on the way to Emil's. Somebody had a bag of weed, and somebody else had some shrooms, so they all got hauled in. I called Chris on the restaurant's pay phone and begged him to come over and play with me, and he did. And Bobby Tiryaki just happened to be in the audience that night.

CF: One of the great folk-rock impresarios.

DH: A legend.

AF: Absolutely. Chris didn't know the songs my band was going to play—this was obviously long before you could dial up the chords to any song on your iPad—so we just played some songs he'd written, and which I knew pretty well. The material we'd been doing off and on for years.

DH: And that was it?

AF: I mean, Lana Turner was discovered in Schwab's Pharmacy. Why couldn't the Fairley Brothers be discovered at Emil's Café?

CF: Just to put things on pause here—this interview is running longer than I thought it would. *(To Andy)* Are we going to have time to drive down to that next place and be ready for our show?

AF: It's a two-hour drive and we don't go on until ten, so, yes, we've got lots of time.

DH: Thank you. That's good news for me. I was actually thinking of this as the definitive Fairley Brothers interview, so I'm happy we have more time. So, this is 1983, am I correct?

AF: That's right.

DH: And how old are the two of you at this point?

CF: I was twenty-three, about to graduate from college—on the six-year plan. And Andy was nineteen. And suddenly we had a record contract.

AF: We went from losers to winners overnight.

DH: Can you describe the process of recording your first album?

CF: Well, I had written something like a hundred songs that felt finished to me, so it was mostly just sifting through those and picking out the ones we liked best.

AF: And the ones Bobby Tiryaki thought had commercial potential.

CF: Yeah, that was important, obviously. We were a brand-new group, and if we blew this, it was back to Nowheresville.

DH: You were accompanied by studio musicians.

CF: Sort of second-tier talent, and I mean no offense to the guys who played on our record. Second-tier in LA is superstar just about anywhere else.

AF: You have to remember that in the early and mid-eighties, folk rock was not a big thing. When we were recording, the big albums were like Michael Jackson's *Thriller* and Men at Work, and the *Flashdance* soundtrack.

CF: *Meet the Fairley Brothers* still sounds a little cheesy to me, a little over-produced. But we didn't have much choice if we wanted to see it in record stores.

AF: Back then, you didn't have the same number of options you have now to get your music heard. Nowadays, you can record in your living room and sound almost as good as we did in the eighties. And then you can distribute your own music on SoundCloud and Spotify and Apple Music and whatever else. It didn't work that way when we signed our contract. There were these big record companies, and they controlled everything.

CF: But if you did have a hit, it was heard by a much broader audience. Things weren't so sliced and diced into these micro-categories: Medieval folk-rock, math rock, Vegan straight edge, pirate metal—whatever.

AF: I think those are real subgenres.

CF: Probably.

DH: Maybe we should get back to the album's release. In my notes here, it says it went to number 36, which was quite respectable, I gather, since, as you've just said, at the time folk wasn't especially popular.

AF: We were happy.

CF: We ended up getting a couple of songs on college radio, which was a big deal.

DH: I believe one of them was "I'll Love You Longer Than a Bob Dylan Song."

CF: That's right.

DH: I've always loved that lyric: "I'll love you longer than a Bob Dylan song / Even the one about that boxer / Or the love that went wrong—"

AF & CF: *(Singing)* "It goes on and on / And on and on / And on and on and on / It just goes on and on / And on and on / And on and on."

DH: You still harmonize wonderfully.

AF: Thank you, Daisuke.

DH: And the other one? On college radio?

AF: "Simple Soul."

DH: That's right. "I am just a very simple soul / Cannot find my ass with both my hands."

CF: I think college kids liked to sing the word "ass."

DH: Generally, the album was well-received, am I right?

CF: Mostly. I'm not sure everyone knew what to make of us. We were kind of oddballs, with these sardonic lyrics and pretty melodies.

DH: Along those lines, I have a snippet of a review that I wanted to run by the two of you. After *Meet the Fairley Brothers* came out in early 1984, one rock critic, Jerry Dimgarten, compared you to the Everly Brothers, though he said—and I quote here, though I completely disagree with his judgment—that your harmonies were "nowhere near as sweet."

CF: Harsh. And, yes, I do remember that review. It was in *Creem*, right?

DH: Yes. Dimgarten goes on to say that you were more like the Righteous Brothers, who weren't, in fact, brothers at all. Chris, in this telling, you have Bill Medley's bass baritone, while Andy, you sing with a voice similar to Bobby Hatfield's tenor.

AF: That's a very specific comparison.

DH: Another song I love on your first album is "The Crazies and Me."

AF: I don't think that's a song we would perform now. "Crazy" is kind of insulting if you're mentally ill.

CF: But that was a cry of solidarity, from my perspective. I felt mentally shaky myself. So it's: "Say hello to the crazies and me / Sometimes we take a walk down to the sea / We shout our names into the sea air / And it shouts right back that it doesn't care."

AF: Fumiko is not "crazy" about that song.

DH: So, you won't be playing "The Crazies and Me" in Japan?

AF: *(Simultaneous with CF)* No.

CF: *(Simultaneous with AF)* Yes.

DH: It sounds like your set list is still in flux.

CF: I suppose so.

DH: Quick question. I know from your Instagram account that Lake Akan was the fourth performance on your current tour. You were very well received at that venue. How were the previous three experiences?

CF: ...

AF: You know, they were kind of quirky.

CF: I was thinking of "head-spinning."

DH: Really? What happened?

CF: We did a wedding, where they wanted us to play the same song over and over. We played at a sculpture garden where they forgot to tell people we were performing. We sang in the back of a souvenir store on a flower farm. I mean, are you telling me—

AF: I'm thinking we should stop there. *(To CF)* I think we ought to be grateful for what we've been given.

CF: Yeah, but—

AF: And we still have a long drive ahead of us.

DH: But this all sounds so interesting. And I was hoping we could do more.

AF: Thank you for your time, Daisuke. Thank you very much.

And with that, Part One of my interview with the incredible Fairley Brothers came to an end in a small restaurant in Lake Akan. I very much look forward to Part Two.

Andy, always the faster reader, made sure Chris was finished, then he closed his laptop. "Well, there's us," he said. "At least through 1984."

"Ends on kind of a sour note."

"It's accurate, though."

Andy held out his glass. "Could you pour me a little more sake?"

Chris picked up the green bottle. It was empty. "We drank it all." He closed and opened his eyes, then shook his head as if he were a swimmer trying to empty his ears of water. "Jesus, I feel kind of drunk."

Andy looked again at his empty glass. "Me too. And, hey, sorry, I cut you off there at the end. I just didn't want to hurt Fumiko's feelings about the gigs. She's doing the best she can."

"I get it. My bad. But *is* there a part two to this interview? No one told me about that."

"Me either. But what do you think? Should Daisuke go for it?"

"Can't hurt. Tell him to publish."

LIVE CAFE TUNEFULNESS (CANCELED)

Muroran
Wednesday, August 10

Andy sat on the toilet seat in the tiny bathroom, its walls just wide enough to accommodate his acoustic guitar. He quietly fingerpicked the strings, softly singing, "Bury me beneath the willow / Under the weeping willow tree." It was a tune that brought back a memory of their family together in their cramped living room, the two boys playing three-chord songs while their parents looked on, smiling, not fighting. When in the world might that have happened? Andy asked himself. Or was it just a false memory he'd conjured up to paper over the pain?

His head was throbbing from the late-night sake, and he left the bathroom to shake out a couple of ibuprofen from the plastic bottle on his bed stand.

Chris opened his eyes, rubbed them with both fists, then turned to the TV playing without sound.

This time four people—two men and two women—were standing at podiums in front of an eye-popping yellow-and-pink background. They appeared to be dissecting a text message. A woman in a deep-blue dress seemed particularly upset about the content of one line, which was highlighted in red.

"Communication problem?" Chris asked.

"Huh?" Andy asked, then turning back to the TV. "Oh yeah. It's some celebrity misfire. Somebody dissing somebody else, I think. Anyway, you're awake."

"More or less."

"So, I've got some good news and some bad news."

"I'm still reentering the world," Chris said. "Hit me with the good news first."

"You know how you've been saying that you feel like we've been rushing from place to place?"

"Yeah?"

"Today you don't have to worry about that."

"I assume that's also the bad news."

"Afraid so. Our gig in Muroran got canceled."

"Okay." Chris rubbed his eyes. "Was that a good one?"

"Live Café Tunefulness. From what I gather, it's definitely the most happening place in that part of Hokkaido."

"Not exactly Carnegie Hall."

"The Carnegie Hall of Iburi-shichō," Andy said.

"Okay, I don't even know what that means."

"It's a district in Hokkaido."

"Why did we lose the gig?"

"They hadn't sold enough tickets."

"Based on our gig last night, I'm not surprised."

"Doesn't matter. I've got some fun things for us to do instead."

Chris sat up in bed and smoothed back his hair. "Is that right?"

"Definitely. There's a famous marsh. And a crane sanctuary. And then I thought we could see the National Ainu Museum in Shiraoi."

"Sounds busy."

"But fun, right?"

Chris nodded noncommittally and went to the bathroom to take a shower.

Andy turned his attention to the television, which he unmuted. An elderly man in silk pants, a Joaquin Phoenix *Joker* shirt, and a Lakers cap answered, with great seriousness, questions from two well-dressed presenters about his latest film. Andy pondered the scene as though it were a koan.

Chris emerged from the bathroom, drying his hair with a towel. "You know, I've been thinking. I realize Fumiko has done a lot of work getting us these gigs, and I really appreciate it—honestly, I do—but I'm wondering if Hokkaido is really the best place in Japan to play music?"

"She got us that gig at the Lake Akan Folk Festival, and she just kind of worked backwards and forwards from that. We'll be going south tomorrow, and we do have gigs in big cities. Two nights from now we're in Tokyo. And later in Nagoya and Osaka and Kyoto. The biggest cities in the country."

"So, this is just kind of a warm-up for better things to come?"

"You could think of it that way. Or you could think of it as a chance to hang out with your brother and see a part of Japan that a lot of people, even a lot of Japanese, never visit."

Chris drew in his breath and nodded.

Andy's phone rang. He answered in Japanese and spoke to the caller for several minutes. When he rang off, he said, "That was Daisuke."

"The interview guy?"

"Yeah. He's here in Kushiro, and he wants to continue the interview."

"Oh, man. I don't know. That was pretty draining, reliving all that stuff."

"I know, but he said his post from last night already has more than three thousand views."

"For *our* interview?"

"I told you he was a popular journalist."

"Too bad he didn't post it before our gig got canceled. This trip is just one lousy thing after another."

Andy's neck began turning red. "You know, fuck you, Chris. I'm really working hard on this. I can't control everything."

Chris put his hands up in a gesture of conciliation. "No, no, I totally get it. Sorry. I haven't had my morning coffee yet."

"Well, pack up, and we can go downstairs and have breakfast with Daisuke and tell him some more of the Fairley Brothers' magnificent story."

After the brothers checked out at the registration desk, they wheeled their suitcases to the hotel's large restaurant, which smelled of miso and vinegar and sesame oil. Scattered pods of businessmen leaned over their food and spoke in low voices, emitting a sound that was both comforting and conspiratorial.

Daisuke was waiting for them, along with an ample spread of food. "I hope you don't mind," he said, "but I ordered for all of us."

The brothers thanked him and sat down while Daisuke pointed to each dish on the table. "Rice. Miso soup. Tamagoyaki—it's an egg thing. Grilled mackerel. And Japanese pickles."

"Looks delicious," Andy said.

"Totally," Chris said. He cleared his throat. "So, you followed us down here?"

"More or less, I suppose. I didn't feel as though we'd finished yesterday."

"You didn't come to our gig last night?"

"No, I'm sorry. I was editing the interview. How was your show?"

"Epic," Chris said.

"Actually," Daisuke said, "I'm friends with the bartender. He said it was rather lightly attended."

Chris said, "It's the shitty idiots of Kushiro."

A businessman at the next table looked over his shoulder and glared.

"I mean, according to your friend. Personally, I love Kushiro."

Daisuke tweezed a piece of fish between his chopsticks, put it in his mouth, and nodded approvingly. "Do you know the story of the high priest Shinran?" he asked.

Andy and Chris shook their heads.

"He was in charge of the Yamashina Temple. A very important place. Then one day, he felt he must spurn the world, so he left and moved into a hut in the countryside. He was happy for a while, but then people from a nearby village noticed his purity of heart, and they began to venerate him. Shinran hated that, so he moved up into the mountains, and he was satisfied for a while—meditating, living hand-to-mouth—but then the people found him again. They worried about how he would survive the winter, so they built him a new hut. But he couldn't stand their passion for him, so he left again, disappearing into a distant city, where he died, unnoticed by everyone except one person from his home village who happened to be passing through and recognized his corpse lying in the dusty street."

There was a long pause. "Wow," Andy said. "Heavy."

"An intriguing story," Chris said. "But is it supposed to have some relevance for our situation?"

"Possibly," Daisuke said.

Chris held up his hands. "We can't even get a gig in...where was it again?"

"Muroran," Andy said.

"Exactly. If we're supposed to be this priest..."

"Shinran," Daisuke said.

"Right, Shinran, then we've already disappeared from sight. And nobody's looking for us."

"They may be someday."

"After they read your blog posts?"

Daisuke shrugged. "Maybe."

"If that happens," Chris said, "I'm definitely going to turn to your story for advice and run away up the mountain."

"For me," Daisuke said, "the point is that whether we want to be venerated, or we want to leave the world behind, we all end up the same way."

"Lying dead in a dusty street?" Chris asked.

"Alone," Daisuke said.

"Anyway," Andy said. "Maybe we should get started with the interview?"

Daisuke nodded, flipped to the voice memo app on his phone and touched the "record" button.

The breakfast went unfinished. After fifteen minutes, Chris halted the interview. Nearly every other patron was staring at their table.

"Are you sure?" Daisuke asked, shaken. "We could—"

"Positive," Chris replied, looking around the restaurant, embarrassed.

"Intense," Andy said, wiping a line of sweat from his brow.

"Not all memories are worth reliving," Chris said, standing up and pulling out the retractable handle on his luggage.

Andy stood up too. "Well," he said, noncommittally.

Daisuke said, "I will stay here a little longer and go over my notes. Have fun on your journey today. Maybe I will see you again?"

"Are you fucking serious?" Chris said.

"You know what we say in Japan: Even monkeys fall from trees."

"I'm not going to even ask," Chris said, wheeling his suitcase toward the lobby door.

Andy followed, opened the back of the Aqua, slowly punched some kanji into the car's GPS, and pulled out of the parking lot.

"Not talking to me?" Chris asked as they left downtown Kushiro.

"That scene in the restaurant was totally unnecessary."

"As was Daisuke's line of questioning."

"I don't have anything else to say. Let's just zip it for a while, shall we?"

Andy said through gritted teeth.

What was the point of doing anything with his brother, when he was such an unholy asshole? Andy fumed as he followed the GPS north out of town. Why even bother trying to show Chris Japan when he was still living in the past?

Nevertheless, Andy kept driving. The two-lane highway, with purple and white flowers blooming on the side of the road, wound past farms and then cut through a broad marsh.

It's not my fault, Chris was thinking. Whatever happened, it wasn't my fault.

The road wound through a pine and birch forest, and a half hour after they'd left the hotel, they pulled into a parking lot below what looked like an observatory perched atop a modest hill.

Chris said, "I know it's the middle of the day, but are we going stargazing?"

"Nope, we're walking through the Kushiro Marsh." Rain pattered on the windshield. "Better bring your parka."

They slipped into their raincoats and stepped out onto the slick asphalt. The air was heavy with humidity, and cicadas screeched from the surrounding trees. The signs were all in Japanese, so Chris followed his brother, who walked up a set of stairs, then down a concrete path that went past the red-bricked observatory and ended at a long wooden staircase that descended into a forest.

"Looks slippery," Chris said.

"Yeah. Don't fall on your ass," Andy snarled.

Andy, in flip-flops, led the way down the stairs, while Chris followed in his running shoes, both brothers stepping carefully to avoid falling. The air was warm and wet, though the broad leaves of the trees kept most of the rain off them. They crossed a cable footbridge over a creek, then began ascending a hill. The stairs were crooked and warped and occasionally missing planks.

"Watch yourself," Chris called ahead, but Andy didn't answer.

At the top of the hill, they reached an observation platform that looked out over the marshland they'd driven through. Great stands of trees alternated with swaths of open land. Andy dropped a one-hundred-yen coin into an optical binocular viewer and bent down to look through the lenses.

When he didn't comment, Chris said, "Looks like the Serengeti. Not that I've ever been."

Andy still didn't answer, and Chris said, in a voice deeper than he'd intended, "Look, little brother, I realize I might have said some things during that interview that I regret. But a lot of shit happened back then, and it wasn't all on me. Far from it, in fact."

Andy turned and shook his head. "That was thirty-seven fucking years ago. A lot of people don't live that long. Let. It. Go."

"I'm trying."

"Without success."

Andy stalked off down the trail, which seemed to head in the general direction of where they'd parked the car. As they went down another set of rickety wooden stairs and then back up a hill, the rain grew heavier, then just as quickly diminished again. Everything was green and damp.

Chris looked down and noticed that the backs of Andy's legs had turned a pulsating gray. They were covered with mosquitos. He ran to his brother and began slapping at his calves and thighs.

"Whoa!" Andy yelled. "What the fuck?"

Chris kept slapping at Andy's legs. "You're covered with mosquitos!"

"You can't—" Andy began, but as he looked down, a cloud of them swirled around his head. "Jesus," he yelped, "let's get out of here."

The brothers trotted, as fast as they dared, along the slick steps, finally emerging in the clearing below the observatory. They made their way back to the Aqua, shucking off their parkas and stuffing them in the trunk.

"That was intense," Chris said.

"It was," Andy said, wiping the raindrops from his forehead as he started the car. "And for some reason it made me think of that monk Daisuke was talking about. Shinran. I think I learned a little lesson out in the woods."

"What lesson is that?"

Andy glared at his brother: "After he disappeared, Shinran wasn't missed."

Andy steered the Aqua out of the parking lot and then south down the two-lane highway. After a while, Chris said, "Are we still going sightseeing?"

"We don't have to," Andy grunted.

"I mean, I *want* to," Chris said. "I think you mentioned something about cranes?"

Andy nodded slightly.

"Let's go then."

Andy's grip on the steering wheel relaxed somewhat as he headed toward the Kushiro City Crane Reserve. During the twenty-minute drive, as they left the marsh behind and drove through a vast patchwork of rice paddies, neither brother spoke a word.

They pulled off the highway into a large, mostly empty parking lot. Andy was about to get out of the car, when Chris put his hand on his brother's shoulder. "This is just ridiculous. We were asked some questions about our lives, and we gave some uncomfortable answers, but that doesn't mean we have to do the rest of this tour in silence."

Andy paused before speaking. "I couldn't agree more, man. It's just that you said some pretty hurtful things this morning."

"And you *did* some pretty hurtful things back then. It still stings."

"I get that. But, as I said, it was a very, very, *very* long time ago. We've both been married and divorced. I got married again. There's been so much water under the bridge, the bridge itself washed away—decades ago. But the way you were talking this morning, it sounded like it all happened yesterday."

"I was wrong to get so upset," Chris said. "All right? How about this? We let it go for now, and we don't check and see if Daisuke has published the interview until tonight. Then we'll look at it with a little distance and a cold hard eye. Sound fair? I mean, why ruin the rest of the day? It's not like I'm going to be in Japan forever."

Andy shrugged. "All right. Okay."

They left the car and walked toward a visitor center that looked like a two-story log cabin. Inside were stuffed cranes in glass cases and photographs of cranes hanging on the walls. All the signs were in Japanese, and Andy read to his brother: "The red-crowned crane is a symbol of good luck, faithfulness—I think that's what that means—and longevity."

Chris said, "Perfect emblem for the Fairley Brothers." Andy gave him a sour look, but Chris held up his hands. "I'm serious. Here we are, playing together, decades past our prime, but lucky enough to have recorded a jingle for a Honda commercial."

"Sounds sarcastic to me."

"I know it *sounds* sarcastic. But it isn't. Believe me."

They paid the entrance fee, then wandered outside to a series of fenced-in enclosures. The spaces were more like paddocks than zoo cages, with trees and little ponds and a stream running down the center of each pen. They were big birds, mostly white, save for black tail and neck feathers and a splash of rust red on top, just behind their eyes. A few cranes sheltered in the background, but most of them were near the front, plodding along on their long, awkward legs, pecking at the grass and mud.

A light rain blew in from the north, then stopped suddenly.

"Well," Andy said, when they reached the end of the reserve, some of his old enthusiasm returning. "That was interesting."

"Certainly not something you see every day," Chris said.

"If you look around, their images pop up all over the country. Longevity—the Japanese really crave it."

"And why is that?"

"They think a long life is a good life."

"That seems like an open question to me."

"Yeah? You don't want to live a long time?"

"I honestly don't know," Chris said. "I mean, Mom and Dad? They died before they got really old, I know, but they were both in pretty bad shape at the end. Can you imagine if they'd lived another ten years? That would have been torture for everyone, don't you think?"

"Maybe. But I really love life. I'd never give it up willingly."

One of the cranes seemed to be looking at them. Chris gave it a little wave, and the crane stuck its beak back in the mud.

Andy said, "And now it's back to the car, and onward to the National Ainu Museum."

"How far away is that?"

"About four hours."

"Can we at least get lunch?"

Before entering the toll road, they stopped at a Lawson for two bottles of melon-flavored Ramune sodas and two pork-filled Chinese steamed buns, which they warmed up in the microwave.

Then they were on the Dōtō Expressway, heading west, slicing through the green hills and mountains and over muddy rivers, spending long stretches of time in tunnels that were occasionally miles long.

As they drove, they played their third album, *Never Believed You Anyway*, the mention of which had caused so much consternation in their discussion that morning with Daisuke Hayashi. Occasionally, one or the other would sing along with a verse or chorus, but mostly they listened carefully, as if the explanation for the morning's acrimony could be found in their own songs.

For Chris, the key song from the album was the title track, with its Dylanesque delivery of insults—he'd been trying to channel "Positively 4th Street"—including, "You lie so much even you believe it's true" and "Your heart's as black as the roses you dye in tattoo ink" and "Your street-worn conscience can never be repaired."

For Andy, what most resonated was the chorus of "Except the Dying": "Except the dying, it's all right. / There's nothing harder than looking...for the light."

It was four thirty by the time they pulled off the expressway, paid the eighty-dollar toll, and followed the GPS to the sizable parking lot outside the National Ainu Museum.

As they walked toward the entrance—the weather overcast and misty—Chris said, "It feels weird not playing a gig today."

Andy nodded.

"Like are we even musicians when we're not playing music?"

"Is that some kind of existential riddle?" Andy asked.

"Not really. I just miss having a guitar in my hands."

A small person dressed as a white radish—little brown feet, white body, green top and hands, a smile stitched into its costume—wobbled across the ticket plaza and stood in front of them. "Konnichiwa," Andy said, and the radish bowed.

"Yeah, konnichiwa," Chris repeated, then turned back to Andy. "Fumiko couldn't get us a gig here? At the museum? I mean, it wouldn't be the strangest place we've played so far."

"She's not a miracle worker," Andy said, "and she has a full-time job.

Plus, really? The Fairley Brothers at the National Ainu Museum? It's not a good fit."

"Oh, come on. *Nothing* could make the Fairley Brothers look awkward."

Andy's smile was weak, but he did smile. He turned to see what the radish thought of their exchange, but it had disappeared.

They paid and entered a huge new building. At the top of the escalator, floor-to-ceiling windows looked out on a small lake. The museum itself was spare and carefully curated, displaying colorful handwoven shirts, hand-carved bowls, jade necklaces, knives sheathed in engraved leather, baskets and rugs and spears and fishing rods. In the center of it all was a small stuffed brown bear, decorated with braided rope accented with red and blue ribbons. The dead creature stared impassively at the deeply buffed wood floor.

"Not to make everything about the Fairley Brothers," Chris said, "but this poor bear could be our mascot. All dressed up with no place to go. Ever."

"What about the white radish guy?"

"He was too cute."

Back outside, the brothers wandered the grounds, past four replica Ainu houses, and across a bridge to a theater, where they watched two short anime films about the Ainu spirit world—one in which a boy accidentally shot a god with his bow and arrow, the other focusing on a malevolent fox who stole the sun. When they left the theater, it was growing dark. Lights planted in the fields began to twinkle to piped-in ambient music.

"Cool culture," Chris said, as they entered the gift shop.

"Almost completely destroyed or assimilated by the Japanese."

"So, the Japanese are not a perfect people?"

"I never said they were."

"But better than Americans?"

"That goes without saying."

They browsed the shelves of mementos: coffee mugs and tote bags decorated with intricate Ainu patterns, silk scarves and ties, engraved wooden plates, ceramic bowls, and lacquered boxes. Everything was very expensive.

Chris paused in front of a bear with a hook emerging from its back. "Is that a Christmas ornament?" he asked.

"Maybe," Andy said. "Maybe just a decoration."

"Is Christmas big in Japan?"

"Kind of. But you don't see a lot of Christmas trees, outside of depart-ment stores, at least. You going to buy it?"

"I would have bought it for Mom," Chis said. "But now...I mean, why?"

It was night when they reentered the tollway and drove southwest for thirty minutes, the lights of small coastal towns occasionally appearing in gaps in the hills. They exited the tollway and drove down a long, desolate stretch of coastal road: a few shuttered factories, lots of warehouses, vacant lots, the occasional ramshackle house—a landscape lightless and forlorn. Other than the drivers in the other cars, no human beings were present.

The Aqua's GPS directed them to a parking lot in front of a square eight-story hotel. "Courtesy of the Live Café Tunefulness," Andy said as they car-ried their bags into the lobby, the featured color of which was a dark brown.

"I must admit it's pretty cool how these venues put you up at night, even when you're not playing."

"Give credit to Fumiko. She negotiated every one of our gigs."

They checked in and took the elevator up to the third-floor room. It was small, but new and clean, and, like the rest of the hotel, very brown. Towels, desk, bedspreads, carpet, wallpaper—a little white here and there, but mostly a symphony of brown.

As Chris unpacked, Andy checked his phone. "Well, Daisuke has posted part two of our interview. You want to read it now?"

"Let's get something to eat first. I'm starving."

They left the hotel and headed for what their phones indicated was downtown. They crossed the parking lot, took a right down a dark street, then a left down an even darker street and across a bridge above a small dark river.

"It's weird how no one's around," Chris said. "Or maybe everyone is hiding, waiting to jump out at us. If we were in the States right now, I'd be watching my back."

"Yeah, but we're in a small town in Japan, so that just means everyone's inside after work, watching TV."

They made their way to what Andy called an izakaya, "a pub with food," and settled in at the counter. At the lone table, an elderly couple—the only other customers—quietly ate their meal while openly staring at the Fairley Brothers.

The brothers ordered large Sapporos, which came in frosty mugs, and they gobbled up the bar food ordered by Andy: edamame, sashimi, chicken wings, skewers of fried vegetables, and meats of uncertain provenance. As they ate, a small spider wandered across the sticky tabletop, stopping periodically, as if to check some internal GPS, then heading off in a different direction.

"What do you think about this for a haiku?" Chris asked. "Little spider, / how does it taste, / the dried soy sauce?"

"Classic," Andy said.

The brothers ate the edamame quickly, almost competitively, each one sucking the beans from the pod, dropping the husk on a plate, then snatching up another one.

"Sex and violence," Andy said, when the edamame was finished.

"Pardon me?"

"I was reading this book, and the author said that's what all music is about: sex and violence."

"How does he figure?"

"It's been a while, but I remember he was talking about birds, that they use songs to attract a mate, or warn off a competitor. And when they're in a flock, their songs are trying to scare away predators."

"People aren't birds," Chris said.

Andy tweezed a mouthful of rice and continued: "The idea is that song is this primal thing. Like us, for instance. When we're talking about our set list, we're really specific and kind of banal. What songs are we playing? What keys are they in? How does the chorus go again? But deep down, we're calling out for mates, trying to frighten away predators."

"In that regard, I have to consider myself a failed musician."

Andy shook his head, mildly annoyed. "The author, he also talks about the different sounds wind makes against, say, marsh reeds and dry grasses, or different kinds of trees."

"Do you want to incorporate a forest into the act?"

Andy looked down at the table and rubbed his left temple with his thumb.

"Kidding," Chris said. When Andy didn't reply, he asked, "Headache?"

"Long day," was all Andy said.

Outside, Chris asked, "Are you curious to see it? The Café...whatever?"

"Live Café Tunefulness? I don't know. Maybe. Do you want to go check it out?"

"This town seems so dead. It's hard to believe it has a venue for live music."

Andy took his phone from his pocket and typed the club's name into Google Maps. "It's just a few blocks away. Why not?"

They walked past warehouses and dimly lit apartment buildings and shops that were either closed for the evening or were out of business altogether. Cicadas sang their shrill song into the warm night air. At the corner of two empty streets was the shuttered venue. "Live Café Tunefulness," read a sign above the door. "Music, Foods and Drinks."

"The Carnegie Hall of Muroran," Andy said.

"When you have been rejected by Live Café Tunefulness," Chris said, biting his lower lip. "Well, that hurts."

They stood there for a while, as though if they waited long enough, someone might open the place up, come out, and invite them inside to play. But the night was still, the only sounds the cicadas and the distant horn of a train.

"Their loss," Chris said, finally.

As they retraced their way across the river, the edge of the fat summer moon poked out from behind the massive rectangle of their hotel, causing them both to look up in alarm.

"Another haiku?" Andy asked.

"I'm fresh out."

They bought two more large Sapporos from a vending machine in the lobby and took them up to their room. Andy sat down on his bed and opened his laptop. Chris sat down next to him.

"You *could* look at it on your own computer," Andy said.

"I prefer yours."

Andy sighed, and they began to read.

THE FAIRLEY BROTHERS
IN JAPAN (PART II)

The following interview was recorded on the morning of Wednesday, August 10, in the restaurant of the Hotel Maximum Kushiro, the morning after the Fairley Brothers' appearance at the Lake Akan Folk Festival and their evening performance at Dizzy Coltranes Jazz Nite Social Club. The interview has been lightly edited for clarity and is available in Japanese here.

DAISUKE HAYASHI: Hello, Andy and Chris! Did you ever think we'd meet again so soon?

CHRIS FAIRLEY: No.

ANDY FAIRLEY: It's always a pleasure, Daisuke.

DH: Yesterday, at Lake Akan, we only heard the first part of your story, about your rise in the music business and your very first album, *Meet the Fairley Brothers.* This morning I'd like to hear about the rest of your catalog, beginning, of course, with your hit album *Dark as Dark Can Get.* Can you talk to me a little about the transition from being big on college radio to actually having two hit singles widely played not just in America, but around the world?

AF: To my mind, there wasn't ever really a clear transition. A lot of the time, we were out there on the road, playing gigs, doing more or less the same thing night after night. It felt kind of like we were off the temporal grid, like we weren't part of the way that time normally moves.

CF: Very philosophical.

AF: You know what I mean, Chris. It wasn't like suddenly someone came up and said, "Now you're going to have a much wider audience."

CF: No, you're right. I mean, we had Bobby Tiryaki behind the scenes, making connections for us, greasing palms probably, making sure his fifteen percent was worth taking.

AF: Chris started writing the songs for *Dark as Dark Can Get* while we were out promoting *Meet the Fairley Brothers*. So, of course, you're going to get some road songs.

CF: And, let's face it, what really did it for us was having "Whenever I Hit the Road" on MTV. Otherwise, I don't think we'd be sitting here talking to you.

DH: That was such a fun video! Was it as much fun to make as it was to watch?

CF: Debatable. The director of the video was Chris Gabrin, who directed John Mellencamp's "Pink Houses," and he sort of reused some of the same imagery from that earlier video: a car driving down a country road at sunset, a freight train, the two of us playing guitar in the middle of a field, a car pulling into a small town at night and the only place open is a little diner.

AF: I think we still put our own Fairley Brothers stamp on the video.

CF: Totally. Our song, it wasn't as popular as Mellencamp's.

AF: You know what I mean, Chris. Our song, well, *your* song, really, is more—you're going to laugh—"subtle."

DH: Absolutely agree. One hundred percent.

CF: Death by faint praise.

AF: Come on, big brother, we're talking about the apex of our career right now. You don't have to be so cynical.

CF: Okay. Fine. I'll save it for later.

DH: To shift the conversation a moment. I'm wondering if you would call what the Fairley Brothers were doing at the time "Americana"?

AF: Kind of. I think we were always more a rock band, though. The term "folk rock" seemed to fit us, the way it fits the Byrds. Or Richard and Linda Thompson, or maybe even The Band.

DH: And of course there are current...what you might call "folk-rock stars" who claim you as influences. Marcus Mumford. Colin Meloy of the Decemberists. Chris, what are your thoughts on the genre question?

CF: I was just writing the songs I heard in my head at the time. I'd be fooling around on the guitar, and I'd put two unlikely chords together, and then a couple more, then I'd try and make them all harmonize into a song that people might want to sing.

DH: So, the music was first?

CF: Mostly. I've always felt like you need to know your backdrop to write a decent lyric. The way a poet might have a certain meter or form in mind. In a way, it's a lot looser in popular music, of course. You can slur words or draw out a syllable over five or six beats. But at least in rock and folk, you're always working against, or with, the rhythm of the song, so your choices about what you can say—and how you can say it—are limited.

DH: What was it like having another album in the Top 40? And two Top 40 singles? "Whenever I Hit the Road" and "Take Me Till Tuesday."

AF: It was pretty head-spinning for a couple of boys from Tarzana. Although, honestly, if you grow up in LA, you're always kind of thinking you're going to end up being a star. At something. Don't you think, Chris?

CF: Mm.

AF: We were on *Austin City Limits*, which really expanded our audience, maybe even more than MTV and the radio songs. And we met a lot of great people.

DH: Some beautiful women among them, I assume?

AF: Well, I mean, yes. Sure. All I know is that was probably the greatest year of my life.

CF: You would say that.

AF: Wouldn't you? I mean, you were making a lot of money off those songwriting credits, in addition to whatever we made as a band.

CF: It's not all about money, Andy.

AF: I know that, Chris. Better than you, I think.

DH: I'm sensing a reference to a long-ago conflict here.

CF: Damn right, you are. My brother stole my girlfriend. The love of my life.

AF: Oh, come on now, that's just ridic—

CF: Is it? Is it "ridiculous"? I don't think so.

DH: Is this the mystery woman who appears in so many of the songs on your next album *Never Believed You Anyway*? The woman Jean-Paul Escoffier in *Rock & Folk* referred to as "l'équivalent des Fairley Brothers de la Dame noire de Shakespeare"?

AF: I'm not sure what that means, Daisuke, but I *can* assure you that my brother is making a mountain out of a molehill. This is just something he likes to dwell on when he's irritated with me about something else.

CF: You know what, man. You're an asshole, Andy. And this interview is over.

With that, Chris left the table, and thus ended Part Two of my interview with the Fairley Brothers. While our conversation came to a rather abrupt conclusion, I am optimistic we can pick it up again later in the Brothers' Japanese tour. Stay tuned!

Andy shut his laptop, and Chris got up and lay down on his own bed.

"Well," Chris said, "that's pretty much how I remembered it."

"Yeah."

"It says it's available in Japanese also. How does he translate it so fast?"

"I don't know—Google translate? Plus, he's bilingual. And our conversations aren't exactly about rocket science."

"Whatever. I don't want to talk to that nosy asshole again. Okay?"

"Hold on," Andy said. He was reading a text on his phone.

"What is it?"

"Fumiko got us a gig tomorrow."

"Wait, what?"

"The owner of a club in Sendai. He was reading the blog, and he got in touch with Daisuke, who put the guy in touch with Fumiko."

"Where is Sendai? Like, on the other end of Japan?"

"It's actually between here and Tokyo. The perfect spot."

"Is it in Hokkaido?"

"No, northern Honshu."

"So, back to the Big Time."

"We never left it, big bro."

"No, it just left us."

BAR BLUES

Sendai
Thursday, August 11

Once again, Chris opened his eyes to a muted television program, though this time there was a soundtrack, Andy strumming his guitar and softly singing, "I don't give a damn about a greenback dollar, / Spend it as fast as I can." On TV, a young Japanese golfer was bent over her putter. She swung her club smoothly, but the ball fell just short of the hole. The camera went to a close-up of her face: She looked as though she might die on the spot from shame.

Chris rubbed his eyes. "Frustrating sport."

"Have you ever played?"

"No, have you?"

Andy shook his head. He was packed and dressed, his hair still wet from the shower. "We probably ought to get a move-on. The Shinkansen from Hakodate to Sendai is a three-hour trip, and it's a three-hour drive to Hakodate."

"What time is it?"

"It's six thirty, but if we leave now, we should be able to catch the ten o'clock train and see a little of Sendai before the gig."

"God, you've got a lot of energy for a fifty-eight-year-old man."

Andy put down his guitar and stood up. "I'm still curious about the world. And I think you are, too."

They filled the Aqua at a full-service ENEOS station—washed the windows, checked the tires—and bought breakfast at a 7-Eleven—smoked salmon and cream cheese sandwiches and Demon Slayer energy drinks—then got on the Hokkaido Expressway.

Chris drove, and—after Andy informed him that he'd never known anyone who'd been pulled over for speeding in Japan—Chris drove fast, 130 kilometers per hour, weaving in and out of traffic, the kudzu-covered hillsides blurring into valleys and low mountains, each scene of verdure

periodically broken by a long stretch in a two-lane tunnel, the lines of whiz-
zing cars separated only by fluorescent red road separators.

"Maybe take it easy in the tunnels," Andy said. "There's not much between us and oncoming traffic."

"Kind of a metaphor, wouldn't you say?"

"Let's just keep it a metaphor, okay?"

In less than three hours, they paid sixty-seven dollars to exit the expressway—"You could go broke driving in Japan," Chris said—and followed the
GPS past warehouses and fields of corn and rice to the Shinkansen station
northwest of the city. They filled the car with gas again, then returned it to
the Toyota Rent a Car across the street from the station.

There was just time to buy their train tickets, two bento boxes, and
two large Sapporos before boarding. As they settled into their seats, the
Shinkansen came quietly to speed, and soon it was in the thirty-three-mile
Seikan Tunnel, racing through darkness under the seabed.

"I'm going to kind of miss the Aqua," Andy said.

"It's a great car. Too bad they don't have it in the States."

"Well, Japan keeps all the good stuff for itself."

Back on Honshu, the train zipped along, through tunnels and over rivers
and highways, passing small towns and stopping in the larger cities: Ao-
mori, Hachinohe, Morioka. Passengers, quiet and serious, got on and got
off. Chris, accustomed to Southern California's dry landscape, stared out
the window at the rice paddies and the green hills and valleys, while Andy
played Grindstone on his phone.

A little after one, they disembarked at Sendai station, and as they were
wheeling their luggage down a staircase toward the hotel Fumiko had
booked for them, one of the wheels on Chris's suitcase split in half.

"Jesus!" he yelped, as a piece of plastic went rolling down the steps.

"Don't worry," Andy said, "we'll get you a new one at the Donki."

"The what?" Chris said, as his suitcase thumped and wobbled behind
him.

"Don Quijote. It's a big store, like a Walmart gone crazy. There's one in
every city."

A few blocks later, after Chris had dragged his suitcase up the boule-vard like someone manhandling a drunk and uncooperative friend, they were checking into the Comfort Hotel. Fumiko had booked them each a room of their own, Andy explained, both because the rooms were cheap and she thought the brothers could use a "mental health break." This had been Andy's suggestion, though he did not tell Chris. Agreeing to grab some food after quickly settling in, they took the elevators up to their sep-arate rooms, each white and unadorned and barely large enough to squeeze in a queen-sized bed.

After fifteen minutes, they met up again in the lobby and walked a few doors down to a Turkish restaurant in the basement of a building.

"I'm famished," Andy said.

"Me, too," Chris agreed. They hardly spoke as they stuffed themselves with tabbouleh and fried calamari, lamb kebab, and something called "Sul-tan's Delight."

When they were done, Andy looked at his phone. "It's just two. The gig's not until nine, and I've never been to Sendai. Do you want to go do something?"

"I suppose so."

"How about Sendai Castle? I'm trying to go to every castle in Japan."

"How many are there?"

"More than a hundred, though it depends on how you count them. Most of the castles have been rebuilt, and some are just stone foundations. It's more just an opportunity to visit different places."

"We didn't see any in Hokkaido."

"There's only one, and it wasn't on the itinerary."

"How many have you visited so far?"

"Thirty-eight. Sendai will be thirty-nine."

They agreed to get the suitcase first, as a Don Quijote store was just a few blocks away, down a wide street of mid-rise office buildings.

"Welcome to Donki," Andy said stepping across the threshold. Vid-eos blared, neon lights flashed, blazing red signs dangling from the ceiling featured a blue penguin, his eyes on fire, announcing, "HOT SELLER!!!" The narrow aisles wound through mountains of merchandise that seemed to have no organizational principle. Cans of shaving cream were stacked atop mini-refrigerators, smoke detectors hung next to packages of ramen, rolls of toilet paper leaned precariously against karaoke machines. K-Pop blasting from hidden speakers competed with screeching videos for false eyelashes and eyelash curlers, wrinkle creams and hair dryers. A few feet from a section for sex toys hung a row of rubber chickens.

Andy led the way up several escalators, past storage buckets overflowing with makeup and shampoo and disposable razors. He paused in front of shelves of KIT KAT bars to point out the various flavors—yam, wasabi, apple vinegar, baked potato—before heading further up, floor after floor, past toothbrushes and sunglasses and costume jewelry, three-hundred-dollar bottles of sake and Balenciaga and Louis Vuitton baseball caps, deeper into the cacophony of electronic music and high-pitched come-ons from the video screens, until he exited the escalator and, miraculously, a wide assortment of luggage awaited their inspection.

"This place is *intense*," Chris said.

"That's what it's famous for. Let's get you a new suitcase and get out of here."

They bought a suitcase more or less identical to the broken one and dropped it off at their hotel. When they emerged from the lobby, rain was pouring down. Andy handed the umbrella he had brought from his room to his brother and slipped on a clear plastic rain parka.

"Always prepared," Chris said.

Andy's smile was less than friendly. "One of us has to be."

They sloshed three blocks through the empty streets to the nearest subway station, where the rain cascaded down the stairs. It was a small metro, with only two lines, and after boarding their train, they exited ten minutes later at International Center. The rain had stopped, and the humid air clung to their bare arms and legs. The wet grass and soil had a peppery smell, and cicadas shrieked from the underbrush. The brothers, sweating heavily, followed signs up a hill toward the castle, the road narrowing and the grade becoming steeper.

Past the ramparts, at the top of the hill, they bought cold bottles of water from a vending machine and drained them in one swallow.

"I'm getting old," Chris said.

"Me, too." Andy wiped the sweat from his forehead and deposited his empty bottle in a recycling bin next to the vending machine, pointing at Chris to do the same thing: "Not a lot of public trash cans in Japan."

"I've noticed. Why is that?"

"1995. The Tokyo sarin attack?"

"Remind me."

"This group, I forgot their name, but they believed the apocalypse was coming, and they were in charge of getting it started. So they released sarin gas into the Tokyo subway trains during rush hour. Some people died, a lot of people were injured. It's a big thing, almost like 9/11."

"What does that have to do with trash cans?"

"They're good places to stash sarin gas."

"Okay, maybe, but that was a long time ago."

"Japanese have long memories."

"I have to ask: How do you even know all this stuff about Japan?"

"I teach conversation classes for a living, remember? When I first got here, I had all the same questions you have, but I just asked my students, and they did their best to answer in English. It's a pretty useful way of getting to know a country."

They followed the road a hundred yards further to the Sendai Castle site, which was crowded with picture-takers and dawdlers, families and courting couples. "It's Mountain Day," Andy said, "a national holiday."

"And it honors, what? Mountains?"

"To the best of my understanding."

"Is Sendai Castle considered a mountain? It certainly has a good view."

That was true. Andy led his brother around the low parapets along the site's perimeter. To the east, he pointed out the downtown skyscrapers and the Pacific Ocean in the far distance. On the southwest corner, they crossed a small fence and edged through a stand of pines and maples. It was hazy in the distance, but Andy said, "Over there is Fukushima. Where they had the earthquake and the tsunami and the nuclear meltdown."

"Is it safe now?"

"Safer."

"That might be kind of interesting to visit. I mean, in a grim sort of way."

"Sorry, big bro, I don't do disaster porn."

"No, no, no, of course not," Chris said. "That's a stupid idea. I think this heat is scrambling my brains."

As they wandered the grounds, three men in their early twenties seemed to be following them.

Chris gestured over his shoulder. "Did you clock those guys behind us?"

"Sort of."

"What do you think they want?"

"I don't know. Let's just keep moving."

The ruins of the castle itself were not much—what looked like a parking lot with white lines connecting a series of flat stones. Nearby was a statue of a samurai warrior on a horse, and a monument commemorating those who had died in a nineteenth-century earthquake.

Outside a small temple, little pieces of paper were looped around wires strung between two red poles. "What's that?" Chris asked.

"Omikuji. Fortune slips. If you get a good fortune, you take it home with you, but if you get a bad one, you tie it there, and you avoid whatever was in store for you. Do you want to try? It's five hundred yen."

"Actually, no. Why risk it?" Chris squinted at a small sign off to the side printed in Japanese and English. "Also, there's this." The English version read:

CONTENT DISCLAIMER

All the contents written and suggested on the papers
you select are for the purpose of entertainment and
not backed up by scientific evidence. They don't
guarantee to improve your luck even if you follow the
suggestions. Please note that you and we shall not be
responsible for any troubles caused by your actions.

"Forewarned is forearmed," Andy said.

They strolled into a large air-conditioned souvenir store, lingering out of the heat amid wooden dolls and waving cats, tea sets and lucky charms. The three young men lingered inside as well.

Eventually, the brothers found a food court where Andy ordered them two Cokes and two plates of grilled rice balls. As they ate, the three young men came up to their table. One of them bowed. "Are you Fairley Brothers?" he asked from behind his face mask.

"We are," Andy said. "Hello."

"And hello to you," said the spokesperson. "We follow your music and read about you from Hayashi Daisuke."

"You like Daisuke's website?"

"Very much. Fairley Brothers. Mumford and Sons. Of Monsters and Men. Also Avett Brothers. You two are real brothers?"

"We are," Andy said. "I'm the younger, he's the older. But he pretty much writes the songs."

All three bowed at Chris.

"Very good songs. We will be at your show tonight. At Bar Blues. Can we take picture?"

Chris shrugged, and Andy said, "Of course."

Suddenly, the three young men became animated. In the span of a couple of minutes, they took dozens of photos, posing at different angles behind the brothers, flashing V-signs.

At some unspoken signal, the photo session abruptly ended. The spokesperson said, "Thank you. Thank you very much." The three bowed deeply, then disappeared from the food court.

"I told you Daisuke was good for the band."

"Pretty soon we're going to have to hire a bodyguard," Chris said, plucking a rice ball with his chopsticks and stuffing it into his mouth.

Eventually, the brothers retraced their steps, trudging through the impossibly humid air, and took the subway back to their hotel. Chris insisted that they be early for their nine o'clock show, and by eight they were showered and dressed in fresh clothes and standing in the lobby of the Bar Blues, a smallish club off a crowded downtown alley. Inside was a big Wurlitzer jukebox and a vintage ad for Camel cigarettes.

The manager quickly came up, bowing. Andy spoke to the man in Japanese, and he led them to a small but adequate stage. The walls were hung with oil paintings of blues greats: Muddy Waters, B.B. King, Buddy Guy, Big Momma Thornton, Bessie Smith, Etta James with her blonde hair and drawn-on eyebrows, Robert Johnson with his long fingers and an unlit cigarette between his lips. The lighting setup was extensive, and the PA impressive.

"No sound check at this place either?" Chris said. "I'm surprised."

"Actually, they wanted us to come in at six, but that seemed kind of ridiculous to me."

"*Really?*" Chris shook his head. "I mean, just once, couldn't we behave like professional musicians?"

"It's just the two of us, and I didn't want to sit in a bar for three hours. It'll be fine. I already made this clear: I told Fumiko that was one of the conditions of our playing. We weren't going to sit around backstage all night before the gig."

"That's probably cost us some decent shows, though, hasn't it?"

"I don't know. Maybe. I don't care. I wanted to go traveling with my brother."

"Well, your wish has come true."

They set up their guitars and mounted their iPads on their stands. They played a few uninspired verses of "Greenback Dollar" until the man at the mixing board gave them a thumbs-up. Then they went to the bar and ordered a round of beers, and another. As they were discussing the set list, someone tapped Andy on the shoulder. He turned around to find Daisuke and the three young men from Sendai Castle.

"Daisuke!" Andy said. "Great to see you."

"Are you stalking us?" Chris asked, frowning.

"Just here to catch one of my favorite bands playing live."

"We, too!" said one of the young men.

"You interview them again tonight?" another asked.

Chris shook his head. "No, sorry, fellas. Our last interview did not end well."

"All the more reason," Daisuke said, "to try again."

"Actually, that makes sense to me," Andy said.

"It doesn't to me," Chris said.

Daisuke said, "Do me one favor, and I promise not to pester you for an interview tonight."

"What's that?" Chris asked.

"Would you play that song—I believe it's new—about parking the car in the kitchen?"

"If that means no interview, then, yes," Chris said. "In fact, we'll open with it. Okay with you, Andy?"

"Sure. Why not?"

From the end of the bar, the manager made a signal that it was time to go on.

"I believe you're in Tokyo tomorrow?" Daisuke asked, and Andy nodded. "I'll be there myself. Maybe we can connect then?"

"Don't count on it," Chris said, and headed for the stage.

"Don't worry about him," Andy said to Daisuke, sotto voce. "Just text me, and I'll try to set something up." Andy bowed to the three young men, and they clapped in delight and bowed in return.

The manager introduced the brothers in Japanese, then Andy spoke a few sentences in Japanese before saying, "Hello, Sendai!" The bar, about three-quarters full, said "Hello" back. The response was polite rather than raucous, with the exception of the three young men, who hooted loudly as they took selfies with the Fairley Brothers in the background.

Andy said, "We're going to start tonight's show with a new one by my brother: 'Car in the Kitchen.' I hope you like it."

They strummed their guitars in unison, and Chris sang:

I suppose it's an old tale
Guy ends up in the loony bin
Still it's a tad unusual
Parking a car in the kitchen again

Several members of the audience clapped and laughed aloud, and Chris sang on:

I parked the car in the kitchen
Kind of run into the kitchen sink
But the refrigerator's still working
So I'd best get me another drink

When the song was over, there was a big round of applause. Andy said, "I think we'd better keep that one, Chris."

Despite himself, Chris flashed a big grin.

The rest of the set met with approval, though slightly less enthusiasm. As always, people joined in on "Whenever I Hit the Road," and some knew the chorus to "Take Me Till Tuesday." The three young men from the castle, however, were practically part of the band, singing along to "Simple Soul" and "Turpentine" and "I'll Love You Longer Than a Bob Dylan Song." They even knew the words to "Nine Pound Hammer."

An hour and a half after they began, the Fairley Brothers concluded with "Dark as Dark Can Get." As the lights came up, the audience looked suddenly shy, turning away whenever one of the brothers tried to make eye contact. Even the three young men from the castle had gone quiet, slipping outside before the brothers had packed up their guitars.

Daisuke, however, remained. "Tomorrow," he said, after they had collected their money and were walking toward the door. "Tokyo. If you want it."

FISH 4 DINNER

Tokyo
Friday, August 12

Although he had been divorced for years, after four nights with Andy, Chris felt odd waking up in a room by himself. He turned off the alarm on his phone—7 a.m., Andy's itinerary had them up early again—and went to the miniature bathroom where he clambered into the tiny shower.

Down in the lobby, Andy was texting his wife. No, he kept reassuring her, Chris wasn't driving him crazy. In fact, he felt like the tour was bringing them closer together, even if his older brother had a propensity for making things more difficult than they needed to be. Chris was, of course, driving Andy crazy, but Fumiko didn't need to know that, at least not yet.

When he saw Chris emerge from the elevator, wheeling his new suitcase, Andy slipped his phone into his pocket. "Big bro," he said, "you ready for Tokyo?"

"The real question," Chris replied, "is whether Tokyo is ready for me?"

In less than two hours, the Akita Shinkansen—speeding past small towns and midsize cities, baseball diamonds and walled cemeteries, parking garages and electrical pylons, rice paddies and the occasional sliver of forest—delivered them back to Tokyo Station.

"What now?" Chris asked, as they descended the escalator from the tracks into the bowels of the station with its swirling rush of people.

"Let's store our luggage here. We have a meeting at eleven."

"A *meeting*? What? Please don't tell me it's with Daisuke."

"Nope. Honda."

"Why do they want to see us?"

"I'm sure they'll tell us when we get there. Come on," Andy said, weaving through a stream of salarymen in black suits and ties, travelers steering their wheeled suitcases, mothers pushing strollers, stylish young women staring at their phones, shoppers weighed down with bags. "I see a couple of open lockers right over there."

They stowed their luggage, then boarded the Marunouchi subway line, changing for the Ginza line at Akasaka-Mitsuke Station. On board were ads for SOYJOY Fruits & Cheese and Pocari Sweat.

"What the hell is that?" Chris said, pointing at the latter ad.

"Believe me, it tastes as bad as it sounds."

Honda's corporate headquarters was a gleaming white building in the swank Tokyo ward of Minato. When the brothers emerged from the Aoyama-Itchome metro station, its angled front entrance stood before them like the prow of a ship, with the brothers like two sailors who had run aground on some hostile shore.

"Do we really have to do this?" Chris asked. "It feels both groveling and pointless."

"It can't hurt. Fumiko thinks that if we make a good impression on them, they might keep the commercial running a few weeks longer. Maybe a month. Our song as a jingle is about to hit its expiration date, but apparently one of the ad execs reads Daisuke's posts and thinks our tour might be generating enough buzz to keep it on the air a little longer."

"By 'buzz' do you mean the fact that we're not playing to completely empty houses? Because I don't feel a lot of buzz."

Andy made a buzzing sound like a bee, then playfully gave his brother the finger.

It was hot, and they immediately began to sweat as they made their way across two broad boulevards and into the "welcome plaza." A robot stood before a video screen, speaking in Japanese as the company's history flashed behind it: founder Soichiro Honda, a humble mechanic in the 1930s, tinkered with cars, which became more modern as the years zoomed by him. Soon, Soichiro was wearing a coat and tie and opening a new factory, and then another. The names and images of the vehicles sped across the screen—the Dream, the T360, the 1300, the Civic, the Accord. Then it was the present, and there was the Pilot and the Passport and the Odyssey—cherry red and bright blue and silver—and then the CR-V itself, with a five-second blast of sound, an amped-up, synthesizer-heavy tagline: "Whenever I hit the road!"

"Cool," Andy said. "The Fairley Brothers are now officially part of the historical record."

"That's one way of looking at it."

Andy walked over to the long front desk and told the receptionist the Fairley Brothers were here. She pushed some numbers into her office desk phone, spoke briefly with someone, then asked them to wait by a brightly painted race car protected by gold stanchion posts and elegant red ropes.

In a few minutes, a man in his early thirties with horn-rimmed glasses and long bangs walked over to them, bowed, and introduced himself as Mr. Kinoshita. "You are pleased to come up to my office?" he asked. "Honda has several gifts which we will bestow on you."

"We never turn down gifts," Andy replied.

Mr. Kinoshita bowed, and said, "No. That is wise."

The brothers followed him into the elevator, which they rode up to the sixth floor. They went down a corridor past glass-walled offices and open workplaces, where everyone wore masks and plastic face shields. Each person was bent over a computer, dressed in formal office-wear. It was quiet except for the occasional phone call or muted conversation and the sound of fingers flying across keyboards.

Mr. Kinoshita led them into his own small office, which looked down on a busy avenue and a hint of the city park. He indicated that they should sit in two wingback leather chairs.

He bowed and sat at his desk, behind which was a red accent wall with the Honda logo. He told them: "Your song 'Whenever I Hit the Road' has been most successful for our spring and summer 2022 campaigns."

"We're happy to hear that," Andy said.

"Of course, every sunrise must have a sunset, and we will be concluding this advertising campaign at the end of the month, as stated in your contract. As you may have read in the automotive press, this fall we will be discontinuing sales of the CR-V here in Japan. We knew that you were both in our country, and we wanted to tell you personally. As a courtesy."

"We appreciate that," Andy said.

"Is there any chance the ad might be extended?" Chris asked. "Maybe you could hook it up with a different model other than the CR-V? If you read Daisuke Hayashi's website, you'll know we've become quite popular here in your country."

"Yes, Hayashi-san, yes. Very good blog. But are you drawing big crowds? In the thousands?"

"We tend to count our audiences in terms of their enthusiasm for our material," Chris said. "In which case, yes, you can definitely measure their enthusiasm in the thousands."

"I'm afraid I don't understand," Mr. Kinoshita said.

"My brother's just pulling your leg," Andy said. "We haven't really had the opportunity to play in the larger arenas."

"But you will be playing in Tokyo tonight?"

"We hope so. There seems to have been a last-minute snafu."

"There has?" Chris said.

"I'll tell you about it later. But if not an arena tonight, then soon. And tomorrow we're in Nagano. Then Osaka and Kyoto."

"Nagano is very beautiful. But I think it is approximately two hundred and fifty kilometers away, so I will not be able to attend."

"We'll miss you," Chris said.

"And I, you." Mr. Kinoshita bent down behind his desk and handed each of the brothers a package wrapped in bright red paper with a bright red bow. "Please," he said, with another bow, "I know it is not the normal custom, but I would like to see you open them."

The brothers untied the bows, pulled off the wrapping paper, and took from their boxes shiny red stainless-steel Honda travel mugs.

Mr. Kinoshita smiled for the first time. "From now on, whenever you hit the road, you will remember Honda."

"Very thoughtful," Andy said.

Chris looked around the office, as though surely another gift was forthcoming, but when it wasn't, he stood up, and Andy followed his lead.

"It's been a great pleasure," Andy said. "Thank you so much."

"The pleasure is mine," Mr. Kinoshita said, and led them back down the hall to the elevator.

As they descended to the lobby, coffee mugs in hand, Chris said, "That was distinctly underwhelming."

"I guess so."

"And what's the deal about tonight's gig?"

"Nothing. Don't worry. We got bumped by a bigger act at Isolde, so Fumiko found us another gig. She's just ironing out the details. Our share of the gate, that sort of thing."

"Well tell her not to haggle too much. I don't want to miss playing in Tokyo. Unless it's like in a gift shop, or something."

"No, no gift shop. It'll be good."

They walked across the lobby, out of the air conditioning, and into the hot, humid air. Andy pulled his phone from his pocket, read a text, and said, "Daisuke wants to meet. To finish our interview."

"What's the point, Andy? It's not going to do our song any good with Honda. We just heard that from Mister...Whoever."

"I, for one, actually *like* Daisuke. Everything he's done has been to our benefit."

"Or his. I mean, I can't believe people are actually interested in reading about us, but apparently they are. We're just clickbait to him."

"Okay, the Fairley Brothers are *not* clickbait. That's stupid. Plus, Daisuke lives over in Arakawa. It's supposed to be a very chill neighborhood. He says he'll buy us lunch, and what else have we got to do?"

"You're telling me there's nothing in Tokyo worth seeing except Daisuke's house?"

"I'll tell you what. We'll get off at the Ueno Park stop and walk from there. Ueno Park is kind of like the Central Park of Tokyo. Lots to see."

"I'm kind of at your mercy, little brother."

"I know that."

The brothers returned to the subway, depositing their coffee mugs in the station's lone trash can, and took the Ginza Line to Ueno Park. The other passengers, masked and mostly glued to their phones, studiously avoided eye contact with Andy and Chris. The recorded voice announcing the stations sounded like a flirting teenage girl.

They exited the station and walked away from the rumble of trains toward a big concrete plaza. Chris said, "Not a lot of grass for a park."

"There's a zoo."

"Okay."

"And a bunch of museums."

"I'm not really in the mood for either of those."

"Let's just walk then."

Chris wiped the sweat from his forehead, then took out his phone. "It's ninety-four degrees."

"Feels like it," Andy said.

They walked past elderly couples hunched over and inching along in the heat. They walked past children pulling away from their parents' hands, and businessmen toting their leather briefcases past gaggles of teen boys and girls who were laughing and sharing the screens of their phones. Parents pedaled e-bikes, their children in seats on the front. Older women in bright kimonos of purple and green and blue walked in thick wooden sandals slowly and with dignity up and down the shaded paths. A few demented joggers struggled through the thick air. Nearly everyone wore a mask.

People stared at them—two tallish blonde Americans in a sea of Japanese—but whenever one of the brothers met someone's eyes, that person would quickly turn away.

"Do you ever get the feeling," Chris asked, "that we're simultaneously the most bizarre sight in Japan and yet entirely invisible?"

"I have that feeling just about every day."

They bought bottles of water and moved among the sweltering crowds until they came upon the Ueno Toilet Museum, which turned out to be a restroom. The concrete exterior was painted with the white silhouettes of animals—a lion and an elephant—and people—a mother and her baby— with one wall showing the path from the mouth down the esophagus to the twisting intestines and out to the anus. "The theme of the Toilet Museum," a sign read, "is 'Excretion and Environment.'" Above the urinals was a mosaic of birds amid a scattering of foliage. Andy walked into one of the stalls, closed the door, then came back out. "There's a panda in here," he said, ushering Chris toward the stall. In another, there was a giraffe. In a third, a penguin.

"Best toilet museum ever," said Chris, taking a photo of the giraffe.

They continued walking northeast, to the Tokyo National Museum.

Outside the ticket counter, Chris crossed his forearms in an X. "Like I said, I'm not really a museum person."

"I know. Just half an hour. We're still early for lunch with Daisuke. And good job with the Japanese nonverbal communication, by the way."

"I'm not totally without observational skills."

Despite Chris's protests, Andy bought tickets, and they walked past a long rectangular reflecting pool that led to a massive concrete structure with curving Japanese tile roofs. Inside, a wide marble staircase went up to the second floor. Chris, still dripping with sweat, did his best to follow Andy, who was taking the stairs two steps at a time.

They meandered down quiet corridors, past elaborate multi-panel screen paintings of birds and flowers, mountains and waterfalls, warriors and courtesans.

"I actually kind of love these," Chris said, "but why is there so much empty space in some of them? Just huge areas of gold?"

"The artists don't want you to get distracted from the main focus of the painting. They're giving you room to breathe."

They walked down another hall, which was full of glass cases containing long swords and fierce helmets and elaborate samurai armor.

Chris said, "From what I've been reading, for most of Japan's history, fear and violence were pretty central to keeping order. But now, I mean, the Japanese seem so polite. What happened to all that...aggression?"

"It's still there, somewhere, sublimated in work and codes of conduct and, I don't know, baseball?" Andy looked at his phone. "We'd better go. It's almost time to meet Daisuke."

They exited the museum near a sign that read, "Annoying acts such as skateboarding are prohibited in this park because they may disturb others." Then they were beyond the museum's garden and past a walled cemetery. They crossed a pedestrian bridge over the railroad tracks to Uguisudani Station, where they negotiated wide and busy Kototoi-dori Avenue before slipping into the narrow streets of a tranquil neighborhood.

Though the traffic had vanished, the brothers could still hear it in the near distance. They walked down the middle of the empty, sidewalk-less streets between small, neat houses, following the Google map on Andy's phone to the vegan gyoza restaurant where they were to meet Daisuke.

Daisuke rose up from his table in the small restaurant. He looked older in the bright lights shining down from the ceiling, his goatee grayer, the lines extending from his eyes more pronounced. Everything in the establishment was painted white except the wooden tables and mint green metal chairs.

Daisuke bowed, then shook hands. "So glad to see the two of you. Is Tokyo hot today, or what?"

"Oh, man," Andy said. "I'm starving, though."

"Well, if you like gyoza, you're really going to like this place." He ordered three large bottles of Asahi beer and two plates of gyoza, while Andy told him about their unsuccessful trip to Honda. Daisuke said, "It's kind of outrageous, yet at the same time not surprising. The music of the Fairley Brothers is not some gimmick for a car company. It's art and it's important, for all sorts of reasons."

Chris picked up a pair of disposable wooden chopsticks, took the paper wrapper off, pulled the chopsticks apart and put them back on the table. "You know, Daisuke," he said, "I appreciate that. I really do. Thank you." Chris took a sip of beer, then added, "Although I still don't understand why our little duo is so special to you."

"'When I looked back, / the man who passed / was lost in the mist.'"

"What?" Chris said.

"It's a haiku. By Shiki."

Chris said, "I'm not even going to ask for an interpretation."

"That is probably for the best."

When the food arrived, Andy put a dumpling in his mouth and practically sang. "This is *amazing!*" He read the printout that had come with their meal and turned to Chris: "Each color is associated with a particular food and flavor. It's all soy meat, of course, but then the dark green is celery, and the light green is green pepper, and pink is pickled cabbage, and purple is ginger miso, and this kind of peach color is eggplant miso, and yellow is—"

"Okay, okay, Andy, I get it. It's very clever."

Andy ate the purple dumpling and smiled. "The fact that you eat it without any soy sauce is just so *thoughtful* because soy sauce just drowns out the taste of everything, if you ask me." He tweezed the light green dumpling into his mouth. "I could eat here every day for the rest of my life."

"I'm pleased you like it," said Daisuke. "It's good food to eat before an interview."

Daisuke's house was two short blocks away, a gray two-story beneath tangles of overhead wires. A pair of unlocked bicycles was parked in front of a small patio where pink and white and red geraniums spilled from window boxes. A bird flew from a balcony to a tree limb and let out a whistle.

Chris pointed to the two bikes. "If you don't mind my asking, do you have a partner?"

"I'm divorced. It's my daughter's bike when she visits."

"No locks on the bikes," Andy said. "It's like living in a small town."

Daisuke nodded and opened his front door. "A small town in the middle of the biggest city in the world."

The boxy first floor of the house combined both the living and dining rooms. An enormous flat-screen TV hung from one wall, a Pokémon screen saver bouncing across its pixels.

Daisuke brought three bottles of mineral water from the refrigerator and gestured for the brothers to sit on the couch. He placed his phone on the coffee table between them and turned on the voice memo app. He walked over to a stereo on a stand and, at a very low volume, turned on Brian Eno's *Music for Airports*. Then he sat across from them in a low chair with a leather back and nodded.

In the quiet of the little house, with the soothing wash of synthesizers and the simple repeating piano figures as their soundtrack, the story of the Fairley Brothers spilled out from them as though they had been waiting years to tell it, which, evidently, they had.

After they had talked their way through the band's breakup—accompanied now by Eno's *Apollo: Atmospheres and Soundtracks*—with Andy aimless and unemployed, and Chris settling into his comfortable but boring job at the Los Angeles Department of Water and Power, Chris held up a hand. "That's enough for me. The rest, as they say, is history."

"You did mention a trip to Ireland five years ago."

"Maybe we can leave that story for the Irish to tell. What do you think, Andy?"

"I would agree."

"Well, all right then." Daisuke leaned over and pressed the "stop" button on his app. "Tonight you'll be at Isolde, in Chiyoda ward. It's small but very well established. A prestigious gig. I imagine you'll have a pretty receptive audience."

Andy shook his head. "Actually, no."

"That's what's on your website, and on Instagram and Facebook and Twitter."

"Isolde bumped us for somebody else," Andy said. "Evidently, they don't read your blog, Daisuke."

Chris said, "But we do have a gig, right?"

"Yeah, but it's a last-minute deal, obviously. Some kind of restaurant."

Daisuke was looking at his phone. "Your wife hasn't updated the tour schedule."

Andy hesitated. "Yeah, she actually thinks we probably don't want a lot of people to attend. It's not really in keeping with our new image."

"Well, what sort of restaurant is it, exactly?" Chris asked.

"I guess we'll find out when we get there."

Fish 4 Dinner was in a mall in Shinjuku. Its oddity and its attraction were that diners caught their own meals from a three-foot-deep glass-walled tank that surrounded a large boat, atop which was a small stage.

"You have got to be fucking kidding me," Chris said.

"I don't know," Andy said. "Let me text Fumiko."

After some frantic flying of his thumbs, Andy confirmed: "This is it. The pay is really good, though. It's two hundred thousand yen, plus five percent of however many fish are caught during our two-hour show."

"*Two* hours? Really? *Here?*"

Andy scratched his chin. "We could do something goofy like at that flower farm. Play fishing-related songs."

"I cannot think of a single fishing song."

"What about Taj Mahal's 'Fishin' Blues' and John Prine's 'Fish and Whistle'?"

"That's two."

"We could also do songs about the sea."

Chris shook his head, then rubbed his temples and sighed. "All right. I guess I can picture that, though I'm not happy about it. At all. One thing: no songs by the Fairley Brothers, okay? We'll just be this anonymous band playing background cover songs."

"Deal."

The brothers waited for the manager, a young woman who spoke American English, to take a horse mackerel off someone's line, then they were led up to the stern of the ship, where they plugged in their guitars and set up their iPads on their iPad stands. The manager—whose hair was striped blue, like all the female workers in the restaurant—gave them the Wi-Fi password, and they set about choosing twenty-five songs that felt appropriate for the venue.

When they had shared their lists with one another, Chris said into his microphone, "Hello, fisherfolk! I'm the Incredible Mr. Limpet, and this is my brother, Nemo. We're here to make your dining experience a memorable one."

They played "Fishin' Blues" and "Fish and Whistle" and also the Nitty Gritty Dirt Band's "Fishin' in the Dark." They played "Brandy" and "Sloop John B" and "Margaritaville" and "Yellow Submarine" and "Sitting on the Dock of the Bay" and a very rocky version of "Wipeout" and Neil Young's "Captain Kennedy" and Weezer's "Across the Sea" and "Under the Sea" from *The Little Mermaid*, which was so popular that they played it twice.

All the while, the people below bent over the man-made river with their tiny poles, jiggled their baited hooks, and caught red snapper and sea bream and flounder. Others scooped up netfuls of clams, shrimp, and sea snails. It was noisy, with a ringing bell and shouts of glee whenever someone hooked a prize, the caught fish splashing and flapping in the aerated water. Periodically, someone banged on a drum to celebrate an especially memorable catch.

While it was possible to have your fish grilled or fried tempura style, most diners appeared to prefer sashimi, with the whole fish placed on a bed of ice, a wooden skewer plunged through its tail and head, and the flesh fileted into thin pieces and served with a bowl of soy sauce, grated ginger, and a dab of wasabi.

A snapper—half sashimi and half tempura—was brought to the

brothers, but they declined it, instead drinking cold mugs of Kirin, with the occasional shot of Japanese whisky.

After the final G chord of Jimmy Buffett's "Son of a Son of a Sailor" had faded and their two hours were up, the manager bowed, thanked them, and handed Andy a thick envelope of ten-thousand-yen notes. "The fishing was very good tonight," she said. "We hope you will be able to play for us again in the future. I especially love 'Under the Sea.'"

"Who doesn't?" Chris said.

The brothers packed up and emerged from the mall into the bright lights of Shinjuku. The air was humid and carried an aroma of cigarette smoke, soy sauce, and truck exhaust. The streets were shiny with recently fallen rain. Neon billboards flashed their kanji. Anime characters flitted across enormous digital screens. Clothing stores with their doors wide open blasted out J-pop hits. Down an alley, a Thai restaurant abutted a Thai massage parlor. Almost everyone among the pulsing crowds was masked, with most of the pedestrians staring down at their phones. Tinny music blared from every little shop. A panel truck drove by with a picture of the band Billion Players on its side, each group member holding a rose. "5th Single," it read. "Gravity of Love."

"This is how I imagined Japan," Chris said. "Lots of lights."

They paused near the Shinjuku station to listen to a kid in his late teens or early twenties playing acoustic guitar with a small speaker and singing nasally into the humid air. Two girls stood up close, watching him devotedly, while everyone else hurried by. "That could be us," Andy said, dropping a hundred-yen coin into the singer's guitar case.

"That *is* us," Chris replied.

"Not quite. I know we still have to get our luggage from Tokyo station and check into the hotel, but do you want to get a drink first?"

"Maybe."

From behind them came a voice, singing, "'I'm a-going fishing all of the time, my baby's going fishing, too.'"

Andy turned, smiling, "Oh my god, Daisuke! What are you doing here?"

"I didn't dare go to your show, but I did search Instagram and TikTok for a folk duo playing in Tokyo, and I came across #fish4dinner. Based on the comments I read, I don't think anyone recognized you, but people do love your version of 'Under the Sea.'"

"Maybe it'll be a B side for our next single," Andy said.

Chris said, "Just to pause a moment and put things in perspective, it's getting kind of creepy, the way you keep following us."

"Look, I just want to finish my interview. Like I told you back in Lake Akan, this feels like part of the historical record. I want to get everything down in your own words."

"We told you almost everything this afternoon."

"Yes, yes you did. But I would like to hear more about what happened after the band broke up, especially your tour in Ireland five years ago. And I am getting deluged with emails and texts. Everyone wants to know what happened to the mystery woman."

"She died, okay?" Chris said. "That's all you really need to know."

There was a long pause as the lights changed, and the three of them stood still while a mass of people moved across the intersection in all directions.

When the lights were red again, Daisuke said, "My apologies." He turned and steered them down a narrow alley hung with paper lanterns. People inside eight-seat restaurants were bent over big bowls with chopsticks; others sat outside on tiny wooden chairs, drinking beer. The smell of burning meat filled the humid air, as Daisuke pointed to a door partially hidden by crates of empty Kirin beer bottles. "I suggest you eat here."

"Are you going to join us?" Andy asked.

"I had some other work to do after you left," he said, "so I'm still editing our interview from today. I must go home, but the interview should be up by tomorrow morning."

"And you're just leaving us alone in this back alley in the middle of our endless tour?" Chris asked.

"As the poet Issa said: 'O snail / slowly, slowly, / climb Mount Fuji!'"

Chris snorted. "Good one."

"I can hardly wait to read the interview," Andy said, signaling for two beers.

"It's a story," Daisuke replied, "that must be told."

NAGANO CLUB ROCK

Nagano

Saturday, August 13

The TV was on, but Andy was studying his brother's sleeping face. With his wild graying eyebrows, white beard stubble, and frowning mouth, Chris looked a great deal like their father. But those eyes, even shut, were both hopeful and uncertain, and he knew them as his own.

Chris began to stir, and Andy turned away.

Chris awoke to a familiar sight. Andy was in the other bed in their small hotel room watching TV with the sound off. On the screen, a baby in a diaper slept on a tatami mat. The point of view changed to an exterior shot of sunrise over an apartment building. A splash of text covered the screen. The commercial was over.

Then an eyeball floated over a checkerboard. From either side of the screen, a cartoon frog and bunny bounced into the picture, evidently in the midst of a conversation. Text splash. The commercial ended.

A high school girl crashed through her front door out into the world, her teeth chattering. She walked in a stiff, ungainly manner down the sidewalk as a dog barked at her. Inside a city bus, she yanked so hard on the strap that the bus shook as it drove down the street. At school, she sucked down an energy drink from a plastic pouch, and her face became calm, her troubles ended.

"Are American commercials this weird?" Chris asked Andy. "From what you remember?"

"I don't know. I don't think so."

"What time is it?"

Andy looked at his phone. "After nine."

"Seriously? And we don't have to be someplace?"

"Not until eight tonight. Our gig is in Nagano, which is just a couple of hours away."

"Another fish restaurant?"

"No, Nagano Club Rock. We're the opening act for Bloodline Ampersand. They're pretty famous. Or they used to be."

"Folk-rock?"

"More rock-rock, I think, but Fumiko says the owner of Club Rock is a big fan of ours, so I assume we're a good fit."

The room's decor, like that of the hotel lobby, was brown and white, with the occasional splash of orange. Chris pulled back the curtains, and from their room on the thirty-first floor, he could see the twenty or so tracks entering and leaving Tokyo Station. The sky was wet and gray. Modernist steel and glass skyscrapers rose on either side of the tracks, though on the west side, the original Edwardian-era station, all red brick walls and cast-iron cupolas, opened out onto a plaza planted with rows of identical trees.

"What's the agenda?" Chris asked

"Maybe get breakfast somewhere, then head out to Nagano?"

After checking out of the hotel, they bought rice balls wrapped in seaweed and two bottles of Survivor Energy Drink, then they ate breakfast on a bench beneath the wide eaves of Tokyo Station, while rain swept up and down the streets.

They promised not to read Daisuke's latest post until they boarded the train for Nagano. At eleven fifteen, they were stepping onto the Hokuriku Shinkansen, and as soon as they found places for their guitars behind the last seats and stowed their luggage in the overhead rack, both brothers were on their phones, typing in Daisuke's website. As the bullet train pulled quickly and quietly out of Tokyo Station, they began to read.

THE FAIRLEY BROTHERS
IN JAPAN (PART III)

The following interview was recorded in the living room of my home in To-kyo on the afternoon of Friday, August 12, after a delicious lunch at Vegan Gyoza Yu. The interview has been lightly edited for clarity and is available in Japanese here.

DAISUKE HAYASHI: The last time we spoke was in Kushiro, one of the northernmost cities in Japan. And now here you are in the capital. A very different atmosphere.

ANDY FAIRLEY: We're just happy to be playing to people who want to hear our music.

CHRIS FAIRLEY: Mind you, there aren't a lot of them, but we appreciate each and every fan.

DH: That's a very positive attitude coming from you, Chris. Or am I missing a note of sarcasm?

CF: Does it surprise you that I appreciate the members of our audience?

DH: Not necessarily. But you must admit that you ended our last conversation on a less than happy note.

CF: Our conversation brought back some unhappy memories. But I'm ready to deal with them now.

DH: What's changed?

CF: Spending more time with my brother. He's a good guy. I've always known that. He wants to get this all down for the record, and I understand that. Who knows? We might never have another chance.

DH: Let's hope that's not the case, but I do appreciate your willingness to talk. So, let's go back to where we left off. You were riding high from the Top Twenty success of your second album *Dark as Dark Can Get*, and you were about to begin work on *Never Believed You Anyway*. This was the end of 1985 through much of 1986. Is that correct?

AF: Yep.

DH: I know from our last conversation in Kushiro that this is a touchy subject, but apparently there was a woman who caused some conflict between the two of you?

CF: You want to take this one, Andy?

AF: I mean, not really, but I will. Basically, Chris was dating this woman, Molly. I won't say her last name. They were pretty hot and heavy from the end of '85 until the next summer, when he went off to a cabin on Vancouver Island for about a month to write the material for our third album. And during that time, she got in touch with me, and, well, we ended up as a couple for about three months. Right up until the time we started recording *Never Believed You Anyway* in the fall of '86. She came into the studio one time, and we realized it wasn't going to work. Having her there, I mean. Shortly after that, she and I broke up.

DH: What happened to Molly?

AF: She exited our lives.

DH: Chris? Is that how you remember things?

CF: I think that is factually correct.

DH: But is it...emotionally accurate?

CF: From Andy's perspective, I believe it is.

DH: And from your perspective?

CF: I don't want to go too far down this road, but it was a very difficult time for me. I thought Molly was the love of my life. It turned out she wasn't.

DH: The lyrics on *Never Believed You Anyway*, starting with the title track, speak a lot about betrayal.

CF: I made a lot of revisions after I got back to LA from Canada.

DH: So, you were writing about Andy's relationship with Molly?

CF: I was.

DH: That would account for a lyric like, "Smash my heart into the ground / Stomp it, tromp it, mess it around."

CF: It would.

DH: Or, and this is from "Blue All Week Long": "Double Crossing Mama, it's all foul play / But for you it's just another working day."

CF: Another solid example.

AF: I think your readers will get the picture, Daisuke.

DH: You're right, you're right. But I wanted to run one more lyric past you, one I've always been curious about. It's from "West Hollywood in the Rain":

*I ran into you on La Cienega
About five days ago*

You stared at me like I was a ghost
Something you'd outgrown

Is that Molly?

CF: ...

DH: Andy?

AF: Could be. I didn't write the song.

DH: At any rate, the album came out in December of 1986. It seemed like it divided your listeners. True fans of the Fairley Brothers, and I would certainly count myself among that number, think it's your best record. "Turpentine" really rocks, of course. And the record still has lots of lovely melodies, like the first two albums, but it's edgier. We know why now: the mysterious Molly.

CF: Okay, enough of Molly.

DH: Yes. So, the album did not do as well as its predecessors, commercially. Is that fair to say?

AF: Unfortunately. I thought "West Hollywood in the Rain" would catch on. We made a video of it, as you probably know. Our only one from that album. In the video, Chris and I spend a lot of time looking moody and walking down Hollywood Boulevard in the rain.

CF: They had to use a rain machine, of course. It never rains in Southern California. They kind of blurred the focus, but if you look closely enough, you can see that the only thing really getting wet is me and Andy.

AF: We still had some juice from the first two albums, so we were booked as the opener for several mini tours. First, we opened for Dexys Midnight Runners. They were definitely on the downhill side of their arc by then, although people still loved "Come On Eileen."

AF & CF: *(singing)* "You in that dress, my thoughts I confess, verge on dirty."

AF: Then the Proclaimers. They were twin brothers from Ireland—

CF: Scotland. They were from Scotland.

AF: Maybe, I don't know. It was billed as the "Brothers Rock" tour. But they sang in these ridiculous accents that you could not understand at all, plus nobody in America had heard of them. So opening for The Proclaimers pretty much made us seem like losers.

CF: I remember one especially dismal night in Columbus, Ohio. The football or basketball team or something had just lost their game, and all these frat boys came into the club, heckling us, spoiling for a fight.

AF: Frat boys are way worse than punk rockers, by the way.

CF: Way worse.

DH: Was there a fight?

AF: Yeah, in the crowd, between the frat boys and a few of our poor, outmatched fans.

CF: We ducked out before the fight made it up to the stage. Very cowardly.

AF: A judicious exit, in my opinion. Finally, we toured with Lindisfarne. They were a really good band. Folk-rock legends. Great songs. Real professionals.

CF: That was enjoyable.

AF: But we were just filling in the tail end of their tour, so it was only like five shows in New England. But they were good shows.

DH: More than a year passed before your final album, *What the Folk?* was released in the spring of 1988. Were you touring a lot during the interim? Writing new music?

AF: After that first tour for *Never Believed You Anyway*, no, we didn't really do much touring. We played around LA, say once a month or so, and did a short tour of the Midwest, but mostly promoters were not booking us. In fact, of course, our label, and our manager, ended up dropping us after that album.

DH: Were you surprised?

CF: Yes, and no. Yes, in that I thought our music was still really good, and no, in that everyone knows the music business treats artists like shit, and you could get flushed down the toilet at any moment.

AF: Good simile.

CF: Thank you.

AF: But Chris kept on writing songs.

CF: It's a habit—I can't help it. I still do it, even if no one ever hears them.

DH: I'll bet you have some great songs in the vault.

CF: I don't know how *great* they are, though I do have a lot of them.

DH: "Car in the Kitchen"?

CF: That's one of them. But you asked about the songs for *What the Folk?* Frankly, I was kind of tired of the folk-rock gig and was itching to get back into more of a rock thing. I'd been listening to a lot of Velvet Underground.

AF: Never a good idea.

CF: Probably not. But I wanted to experiment, and of course experimentation is nearly always anti-commercial. Still, we had an album's worth of songs, and no place to record them.

AF: We signed with a very small label, Mother of the Groom Records, that was only around for about five years.

CF: They leased a studio on Lankershim in North Hollywood. A very funky place. They weren't out to make money, not really, so they pretty much let us do whatever we wanted.

DH: I think it's fair to say *What the Folk?* is an album that further divides the true Fairley Brothers fans from the true-*true* Fairley Brothers fans.

CF: By that time, you're slicing the pie pretty thin.

DH: Be that as it may, I still find *What the Folk?* to be a fascinating record. You have a piano ballad like "On Your Own" right up against a real rocker like "Pickled and Juiced," which to me is one of the really great songs about being drunk.

AF: I agree!

DH: I love that line "Getting briny on my hiney on a Saturday night."

CF: Genius poetry, for sure.

DH: One of your heavier songs on the final album is "If You Want to Rock (You Must Learn to Roll)." There are some absolutely Dylanesque lyrics in this one. I'm thinking of the first verse:

Carbon and diamond, gray atmosphere
Smokeless chimneys and a financier
Soft flames from the catbird's tongue
Quietly asleep on the lowest rung

Also:

> *Milk Street mama with crushed raisin eyes*
> *Innocent circle transmogrify*
> *The River Eden is all about the swirls*
> *Silver branches of a silvertip girl*

CF: It sounds kind of stupid now, doesn't it? When you just speak the words rather than sing them?

AF: I don't think so. They're just...enigmatic.

DH: There's a long solo after the bridge that has a very kind of psychedelic sound.

CF: That was played with an EBow, which is basically this little device you hold against a string, and it vibrates like crazy, so you get this continuous sustained sound, which, I gather, is similar to playing a violin.

DH: I've heard that REM's "E-Bow the Letter" is an homage to your solo.

CF: I've heard that, too. But never from anybody in REM.

DH: Did you tour in support of *What the Folk?*

AF: We tried.

CF: We opened for Fairport Convention at the Troubadour, but I don't think they realized how far we'd veered away from folk at that point. We kind of got booed off the stage. We did something in Reno, and in Redding, and we played at a redneck bar in Sonora, California, and that, also, did not go well.

AF: Until our brief jaunt through Ireland in 2017, our last show was at the Telluride Bluegrass Festival in the summer of 1988.

CF: Again, a gig we'd probably just as soon forget.

DH: Was there any interest from the people at Mother of the Groom in having you do another record?

CF: If we'd wanted to force the issue, I think we could have done another one. They probably broke even on us, or even made a little money. It didn't cost much to produce *What the Folk?* But I think Andy and I were both ready to call it quits.

AF: If I'm honest, I didn't really think we were ending the band for good. I thought we were taking a much-needed breather. But, yeah, I was ready for a rest.

DH: What happened then?

CF: I found a job at the Los Angeles Department of Water and Power. It may not sound exciting, and it wasn't, really, but the benefits were excellent, and the work was pretty easy.

AF: And I sort of took the opposite route. I stumbled around for a few years, then I got my TEFL degree, and since then I've been traveling all over the world teaching English.

DH: No music during that period? No performances?

CF: Nothing to speak of. Sometimes my ex-wife would talk me into bringing out my guitar at a party, but you could tell people weren't that interested.

DH: Andy?

AF: Not unless singing in the shower counts.

DH: What about *Saturday Night Live*? I've read in several forums that you were scheduled to perform on the show in the early '90s. Is there any truth to that?

AF: Yeah, but it's not what you're thinking.

DH: Could you explain?

AF: Well, you remember the comedian Chris Farley?

DH: Of course!

AF: Apparently, he was a fan of the Fairley Brothers, in part because in the mid-eighties, when we were semi-famous, people thought he was a member of the band.

CF: It was a line he used to get laid. If you can believe that: "Hey, I'm Chris Fairley."

DH: Chris Fairley, Chris Farley.

AF: Exactly. When the other Chris became uber-famous, he had this idea for an *SNL* skit. It would be set in the eighties, and the Fairley Brothers would be about to go onstage, and Chris *Farley* would kick Chris *Fairley* out of the band, and sing one of our songs. It wasn't a groundbreaking concept, or anything, but, you know, he could make *anything* funny, right?

DH: How did you feel about the idea, Chris?

CF: We were basically going to be lampooned to death, but I thought, what the hell, maybe it would get our career back on track, being on national television—even as a laughingstock. I guess I did still have some hope for the band.

DH: What happened?

AF: They actually flew us out to New York and put us up in a nice hotel, and we did a couple of run-throughs of the skit in the middle of the week, but Lorne Michaels didn't like it. He thought we were too obscure by that point to even be made fun of.

CF: So they flew us back to LA. End of story. End of career.

DH: Well, it would have been a golden moment in the history of the band, in the history of rock and roll.

CF: Daisuke, you are really given to hyperbole.

DH: Force of habit in the music journalism business, I'm afraid. Also, you've mentioned a trip to Ireland five years ago. I'd love to hear more.

CF: Better for that story to vanish into the mists of time.

AF: Sláinte to that! Amen.

And with that, my epic interview with the Fairley Brothers came to an end...or did it? Readers of folkrockjapan.jp, let me hear your thoughts. Do you want to know more about the apparently tragic story of the enchanting Molly? Are you interested in the long years when the Brothers stopped playing music? And how about their apparently ill-fated tour of Ireland in 2017? If you feel satisfied with what we've learned, we'll stop here. If not, our pursuit of the always fascinating Fairley Brothers may continue.

Andy waited for Chris to finish reading, then he said, "What'd you think?"
"Meh."
"What about that part at the end? Where he asks his readers if they want to know more?"
"I can't imagine that even his crazy fans would want to hear about my days in human resources at the DPW. Or your tutoring in Uruguay. Or wherever. No offense."
"None taken."

They looked at each other, then looked away.

The Shinkansen made its quiet, implacable way forward, flashing past houses and electric poles, farms and apartment blocks, factories and woods, warehouses and motorways, parking lots and canals. As it did so, Chris stared out at the passing scenery, imagining all the lives—big and little, important and insignificant—populating the landscape.

Andy tilted his seat back, shut his eyes, and thought of Molly Moore. He tried to focus on the three months they'd been together, starting when Chris had left to write his songs, right up to her disastrous visit to the recording studio, but it was a mélange of images, not a straightforward plot from beginning to end. Molly lifting a forkful of scrambled eggs to her mouth in a diner on Sunset, or possibly Magnolia. Molly laughing as he lifted off her bra. Molly yelling at him at Griffith Observatory as they looked at the city lights below—he couldn't remember what he'd said wrong.

So engrossed in their own thoughts were the Fairley Brothers that if the conductor had not come to remind them, they might have missed the brief stop in Nagano.

They grabbed at their overhead luggage, snatched up their guitars, and stumbled out of the train.

Across the street from the plaza in front of the station was a huge video screen with a camera trained on their corner of the street. A computer-generated snorkel appeared on Andy's face, and digital fish swam around his head. Andy put down his guitar and bag and waved and waved. "We made it, big brother. We're on TV!"

Chris tried to smile but couldn't quite manage it.

A little after one, they checked into the nearby Nagano Hotel Fine Sleep and went up to the room that had been paid for by Nagano Club Rock. The carpet was brown, the walls were white. The curtains were white, the drapes were brown. The comforter on the beds was white, the coverlets at the bottom were brown.

"Was every business hotel room in Japan designed by the same person?" Chris asked.

"I think the idea is that impersonality is kind of inviting. You could be in a room anywhere in Japan, so you don't have to worry about being in the right place. You're where you should be. Everything's okay."

"That almost makes sense."

They dropped their luggage and guitars next to their beds, and Andy said: "Show's at eight. Sound check at seven. Are you ready to go see Nagano?"

"And if I wasn't?"

"I guess I'd just go without you."

"I'm kind of weirdly tired, but this room doesn't exactly invite lingering. I'll go with you."

The brothers walked up the long straight incline of Minami Nagano Road, past bakeries and bars, ice cream shops and guesthouses, coffee shops and clothing stores. It had rained earlier in the day, but now it was just hot and humid, and Chris asked if they could sit down when they reached a line of wooden benches. On a stainless-steel panel were five interlocking rings: blue, gold, black, green, and red. "The Winter Olympics were held here," Andy said, reading from a plaque. "In 1998."

"Go USA," Chris said, unenthusiastically. "Where are we headed again?"

"Zenkōji Temple."

"And what's that?"

"I haven't been there, and I've only read a little bit about it, so we'll see."

They left the bench and kept walking up the long slope, past cafés and restaurants, souvenir stores and candy shops, apartment buildings and convenience stores.

When they finally reached the temple compound, a light rain began to fall, and they stood and let it run down their faces and necks and arms.

A middle-aged man with blue-tinted glasses, a white vest, a green armband, and a plastic face shield approached them. "Is this your first time to Zenkōji Temple?"

"It sure is," Andy said, enthusiastically.

"Very good. I am telling you many things about this place. It is for Mahayana Buddhism. Do you know this?"

"We don't know this," Chris said.

"I will tell you another time. This gate, you are looking at? See?" He gestured toward an enormous two-story gate. "Called Sanmon Gate. It is containing five hidden Buddhas and five hidden doves. But you will not see them."

"Why not?" Chris asked.

"They are hidden. Many are making a pilgrimage here. Very important place." He fumbled for a map in his pocket, dropped it in a puddle, picked it up and wiped off the rainwater, unfolded it, looked at it for a moment, then refolded the map and stuffed it back in his pocket. "Would you like to hear more?" the man asked.

"I don't think so," Andy said.

"Very well. Then I am wishing you a pleasant trip to Zenkōji. And re-member: The Way is not in the sky. The Way is in the heart."

"Words to live by," Chris said.

As they left the odd guide and walked deeper into the complex, the con-stant shrill of cicadas grew ever louder. "Don't know if I've told you this," Andy said, "but I *really* don't dig their sound. It's like nails on a chalkboard all through the summer."

"Just Zen it out, man," Chris said, blank faced.

They paid a thousand yen apiece to walk up the steep wooden stairs of the Sanmon Gate. On the top floor, dusty golden Buddhas were crowded on shelves. A tatami-covered passage ran around the exterior, and through the bird netting they could see Nagano below them, with the Japanese Alps rising blue-green in the distance.

Though the weather remained unpleasantly hot and humid, the broth-ers wandered contentedly, past racks of wooden good luck charms in the shapes of houses, hearts, and teddy bears. At the incense burner—a large brass kettle with a dragon on top—Andy joined others who were waving the thick, healing smoke toward their faces.

Inside the main hall, a life-size wooden Buddha's face had been rubbed for good luck so many times that all the features were gone except the hint of a nose and a sliver of mouth. People shuffled across the stone floors in their stocking feet, angling their phones for the best picture of the gargan-tuan Buddha in the center of the temple.

"Why does he have such big ears?" Chris asked.

"The better to hear you, my dear."

Outside, a few of the maple trees had begun to turn gold and scarlet. On a grave marker, an orange cat slept soundly. Andy reached down to scratch it between the ears, and the cat purred before reaching out and casually scratching Andy's forearm. He recoiled and the cat hissed at him before disappearing behind a bronze bodhisattva.

"That hurt," he said. "Fortunately..." He pulled a small bottle of hand sanitizer from his pocket and, wincing, rubbed it into the two cuts. "Stings, but it should work."

They walked back to their hotel via a different route, passing through a nearly abandoned shopping arcade. The only businesses still in operation appeared to be noodle joints and gentlemen's clubs. Near the train station, a sign outside an establishment with frosted windows read: "Fun to amusement place. We love pachinko & slot. Welcome to our GOD."

"Any interest in visiting a pachinko palace?" Andy asked.

"None whatsoever, I'm afraid. Look, I know it's not even four, but do you want to get an early dinner?"

"Actually," Andy said, as they stood across from the ranks of taxis, "I would really, really love to see Nagano Castle. Would you indulge me?"

Chris said that he would, and they took a twenty-minute taxi ride south through a dull landscape of gas stations and convenience stores, beauty salons and small apartment complexes. Absent the kanji and distant mountains, it reminded both brothers of the San Fernando Valley.

The driver let them out, and they crossed an arched bridge over a moat, entering the grounds through a tall wooden gate between two stone walls. Inside the walls, the castle was mostly dirt and gravel, dotted with old broadleaf trees. "Wow," Chris said, sweat dripping down his forehead and the back of his neck. "This is really something."

"It's shit, I know, but at least I can cross it off my list."

"You can totally cross it off your list."

In fifteen minutes, they were back out in front of the castle. Their taxi driver was still there, though they had not asked him to wait. Andy said something in Japanese, and then translated for Chris: "He says there is nothing to see here so he knew we would be returning soon."

Back in Nagano, they ate bowls of glass noodles and fried shrimp and drank ice cold Kirins at the counter of a tiny restaurant near their hotel. At six thirty, Chris insisted they leave for the gig, although Google Maps said Nagano Club Rock was just a five-minute walk up Nagano odori Avenue.

With a duffel bag of gear in one hand and a guitar case in the other, they drew both quizzical and admiring glances from passersby as they made their way to the club. "I watched one of their videos," Chris said. "Bloodline Ampersand. It's basically just this six-minute black-and-white tracking shot of this dude walking down the street. Reminds me of our video for 'West Hollywood in the Rain.'"

"Or us walking right now."

"Two rock stars," Chris said. "Incognito. Everything taken care of at the club?"

"I just got a text from Fumiko. Backline ready to go. Line check only."

"There are some advantages to being the opening act."

Nagano Club Rock was on the fourth floor of a nondescript office building, but when the elevator opened, they were immediately and indisputably in a rock club. Posters of previous bands were plastered on the walls. The brothers edged through a crowd of patrons milling around in the lobby, most of them wearing black Bloodline Ampersand shirts, which featured a fanged ogre playing guitar. The concertgoers looked either uninterested or outright hostile.

The manager saw the brothers and waved them into a greenroom the size of Chris's hall closet. In broken English, the manager explained that there would be no need for a sound check, as the Bloodline Ampersand fans might cause trouble.

"So," Chris said, "they're not really looking forward to hearing us play?"

"You have fans here," the manager said.

"Really?" Chris replied. "Because I didn't see any."

"We sold some tickets to people who ask about you. And Bloodline supporters will listen. But maybe you play your most...*upbeat* songs."

The manager smiled and said he would send someone back with beer very soon.

"I'll bet Bloodline Ampersand has got a *huge* dressing room," Chris said.

Andy shrugged, gestured down the dark hall, and the brothers left the greenroom to peek at the stage.

Three truss bridges were hung with stage lights, and a welter of amplifiers cluttered the space. There were two microphones, but no stools. Hung at the back of the stage was a banner of an ogre eating a person, blood dripping from its toothy maw.

"I'm thinking that manager was right," Chris said. "Maybe trot out the rockers from *What the Folk*? 'Pickled and Juiced.' 'If You Want to Rock.' 'Ray Guns in the White House.' 'Dead Man's Last Tale.'"

"Totally. And some covers? Like 'Raw Power,' or that extended version we used to do of the Electric Prunes' 'Too Much to Dream Last Night.'"

"I wish we had electric guitars. And a drummer and a bass player."

"I've got two distortion pedals in my bag," Andy said. "I brought them just in case."

"So, you knew Bloodline Ampersand was not a folk act?"

"I mean, yeah. I guess so."

"And you still took the gig?"

"A gig is a gig is a gig. That's what you always said."

At eight o'clock, having shared three pitchers of beer and successfully rehearsed the cover songs they had not played in years, the Fairley Brothers, fairly drunk, took the stage of Nagano Club Rock. They plugged their guitars into the distortion pedals, and Chris called out: "Who's ready to get fucking pickled!"

There was some half-hearted cheering in response. The venue's overactive light show swung into action, and the brothers began barring the song's power chords to strobes and multicolor washes, bellowing the chorus as loudly as possible: "Pickled and juiced / Loose as a moose / Dancing in a tutu / Doing drug abuse!"

Though the Fairley Brothers had not played with that much punk energy since their high school days in Tarzana, the end of the song was met with applause from only one corner of the club. The rest of the space was silent.

Someone in the crowd yelled something.

Chris turned to Andy: "Did he just say, 'Free Bird'?"

"I'm afraid so."

Chris had long ago memorized the opening solo from "Free Bird" for occasions such as this, and as he began playing it, a great cheer erupted from the crowd. However, as he always did, twelve bars in, he let the final note trail, and then he began banging away at the Ramones' "We're a Happy Family."

A chorus of boos overtook the song, and almost immediately a chant went up: "Blood-line! Am-per-sand! Blood-line! Am-per-sand!"

Chris stopped playing. Andy strummed a few more unheard chords, then he stopped, too. "I thought Japanese audiences were supposed to be polite," Chris shouted at his brother.

"I guess they really want to see their favorite band."

But then something unexpected happened. Ten or twelve people in the back corner of the club began shouting: "Fairleys! Fairleys! Fairleys!"

"Oh my god," Andy said, squinting. "It's the dudes from Sendai Castle."

"With friends," Chris added.

While the two camps competed in a shouting match, in which the Fairley Brothers partisans were clearly outnumbered, a man exited the sound booth and made his way through the crowd, grabbing Andy's microphone. He was silver-haired and bespectacled, but his bare arms were muscled and tattooed, and everyone quieted when he began to speak.

He talked for nearly five minutes, and the longer he spoke, the more a blanket of shame seemed to settle over and muffle the audience. When his speech was over, he gestured at Andy and Chris, and said, "The Fairley Brothers." Everyone clapped politely, and the brothers began again.

Andy turned off his overdrive, Chris did the same, and they played, to a roomful of attentive listeners, the folk-rock numbers for which they had once been well-known: "Simple Song," "Take Me Till Tuesday," "Dark as Dark Can Get," "Blue All Week Long," "Whenever I Hit the Road."

When their set was over, they left the stage to the same measured applause and returned to the tiny dressing room. On a table were two cold bottles of water. The brothers drank them down, and Andy asked, "Do you want to stick around and hear Bloodline Ampersand?"

"No," Chris said. "Fuck them."

VENUS LINE PLAIN AIR
PARK & MUSEUM

Andy awoke when a slash of light pierced the closed drapes. He looked at his phone: 6:07. He looked over at his brother in the other bed, softly snoring. He reached for the remote control, his normal routine, then he put it down, slipped on his clothes, and eased out of the room. He took the elevator down to the hotel lobby and walked out into the humid Nagano morrning.

Something was bothering him, something about Chris, though he was still sleepy and couldn't pinpoint it just yet.

He turned right and, in a few blocks, came to a concrete path that ran along what a sign told him was the Susobana River. He walked north on the path. On his left, bushes and small trees grew along the riverbank, often obscuring his view of the river, though he could always hear it, rushing south, his phone told him, toward the Sai River, which joined the Chikuma River, which finally emptied out into the Sea of Japan. On his right were two- and three-story apartment buildings, anonymous and unlovely, with their blinds shut and their air conditioners humming, telephone and electric poles planted beside them.

Andy nodded to those he passed—joggers, women pushing babies in strollers, salarymen with briefcases on their way to work. He would be one of them again in a little over a week, back at International Languages Japan, "working for the man," as Daisuke had put it in their first interview, no longer playing music with his brother.

After a while, Andy left the path and went to sit down on the bank under a willow tree. He pictured the audience from the night before: angry at first, then simply passive. Then he was deluged by memories of Chris's face from the past week: grimaces, eye rolls, scowls, and sighs of disappointment and distress. Maybe this is it, he thought. Maybe this is the end of this misguided reunion of two brothers who no longer know one another.

Maybe I actually *want* to go back to work. He shook his head and watched as the shallow river ran around the rocks and over them.

But that wasn't quite right either. What really bothered Andy was having to carry the burden of the tour, of not having his brother as a full *partner*, the way that Fumiko had been his partner since he'd first come up with the idea of the Fairley Brothers in Japan.

Andy felt a headache coming on, and he picked up a rock and threw it hard into the river, then turned and stalked back to their hotel.

He made no effort to enter their room quietly, instead pulling the brown drapes open as loudly as he could and shaking Chris roughly by the shoulder.

Chris rubbed his eyes and looked around. "No TV?"

"Not this morning, big brother," he said between clenched teeth. "How are you feeling about things?"

Chris scratched the back of his head. "Wait. What things?"

"Our tour. Us."

"I mean, fine, I guess. Why are you asking?"

"Well, sometimes it feels like I'm pulling all the weight here. Not just on an organizational level, but emotionally. Like maybe you'd prefer not to be with me?"

Chris was wide awake now. "I never said that."

"You want to finish the tour?"

"Of course I do. Why wouldn't I?"

"Just asking."

"Okay, but you seem kind of weird this morning."

"I can't always put on that sunshiny face," Andy said. "Do you understand what I'm saying?"

"I think so. Yeah." Chris let out a deep sigh. "I'm sorry."

"All right then, Jesus," he said, still scowling but feeling his anger beginning to ebb. "So maybe take a shower pretty soon? It's almost seven and our train leaves at seven fifty. We're renting a car in Matsumoto. Our gig this afternoon is at one, and it's up in the mountains, so we don't want to be late."

"I'm on it, boss," Chris said, hurrying out of bed and heading for the bathroom. As he turned on the shower and stripped off his clothes, Chris muttered, "What a psycho," though for a moment he didn't know if he was referring to his brother or himself.

The train from Nagano to Matsumoto wended through a valley and then ascended into a low mountain range. The trip took an hour and a half, and though it was supposedly the express, the train stopped in a number of small country towns, where one or two people from each car would get off and one or two would get on.

In Matsumoto, Andy insisted that they each grab a coat from their luggage, which they left in two station lockers. They carried their guitar cases several blocks to a car rental office, where they rented a Honda N-BOX, a blockish compact that lived up to its name.

"Honda should pick this up," Chris said. "I mean the rental fee."

"If you want to call them, that's fine. Otherwise, hop in."

Andy drove east down narrow one-way streets through the unremarkable city until the houses and small businesses began to thin out and the road started to rise. As they ascended the mountains, the road twisted and curved, trees occasionally reaching out over the concrete berms that hugged the mountain side of the highway. They passed greenhouses and small restaurants with flags flapping in the wind. Chris rolled down his window, then quickly rolled it back up again. "It's cold out there," he said.

"Told you."

As the road became steeper, signs of human habitation began to disappear, and mist rose from the valleys, sometimes obscuring the view. His headache lingered, even after three ibuprofen, and Andy drove cautiously, slowing down each time a guardrail kept the road from veering off into empty space.

The clock on the N-BOX read 11:50 when they saw a tiny restaurant that appeared to be perched on the edge of a cliff. "Some lunch maybe?" Andy said, and Chris nodded agreement.

They pulled into the parking lot and got out. A fierce wind whipped their hair, and they each reached back in the car for their coats. The restaurant was a single room with two plastic tables, each with three mismatched plastic chairs. They were the only customers, and an elderly man insisted they sit down and have a bowl of his miso soup, which was simmering over a fire in an iron pot hung just outside the front door.

It was the best soup either of them had ever tasted, salty and savory and so hot they could barely swallow it.

The proprietor nodded continuously until they finished their bowls, then he served them each another bowl and refused to take any payment for his meal.

Back in the car, they followed a mountaintop road called the Venus Line until they reached a plateau that housed a building that looked like an enormous red-roofed Swiss chalet. Men in fluorescent green safety vests waved them into a huge gravel parking lot that was mostly full.

"Wow," Chris said when Andy turned off the car. "A lot of people."

"I don't think they're all here to see us."

"That's the kind of negative thinking I'd just as soon do without," Chris said, smiling, as he got out, opened the back door, and retrieved their guitar cases.

They walked to the building, which was, indeed, packed with people, although most of them seemed to be shopping for souvenirs. Andy pointed to a sign that read "Inquiries," and they bumped through the crowd with their guitars until they reached a desk where a smiling young woman spoke to them in Japanese. Andy answered, and she gestured toward a door painted shiny black with a kanji marking in the center that Andy whispered to Chris meant "Number One."

Andy knocked on the door, and a young woman showed the brothers inside.

Sitting behind a huge oak desk was a balding middle-aged man who clearly felt himself to be important. He took a few moments after the door closed behind the brothers to look up from some paperwork.

"Mr. Andrew and Mr. Christopher, I presume," he said in British-accented English.

"That's us," Andy said.

"Good. Venus Line Plain Air Park and Museum is very much looking forward to your performances today."

"Was that a plural 'performances'?" Chris asked.

"The Venus Line Plain Air Park and Museum, as I'm sure you know, contains more than three hundred and fifty sculptures on thirteen hectares by artists from around the world. What we are thinking is that you will do different songs by different art exhibits. Fifteen songs total? Miss

Sugiyama," the man behind the desk, who had not given his name, gestured to the woman who had opened the door, "will follow you around to
take the video, then she will be posting it to social media, TikTok, and so
forth. What do you think? We have portable audio equipment, and Mr.
Taniguchi," he pointed to a slight young man who stepped from the shadows and bowed, "he will carry this equipment from one statue to the next
one and be your, how do you say...'sound man.' Good promotion for you,
good promotion for us."

Chris looked at Andy. "Do you mind if I clarify?"

Andy shrugged.

"So, there's no audience, per se?" Chris asked. "There's no venue?"

"The venue is the museum. The venue is all outdoors."

"And when will we receive our payment?"

"When you have finished your performances. Is that satisfactory?"

Chris looked at Andy, who shrugged again. "Okay," Chris said.

Miss Sugiyama led the way out of the office, across a bridge over the
entrance road, and into the open-air sculpture park. There were no trees
to impede the view, and hundreds of sculptures, many of them brightly
colored, were scattered like toys across a hill.

One of the first pieces they encountered was a group of six plastic zebras
with iron poles for legs and no heads. "It's called 'Zebra,'" Miss Sugiyama
said. "Do you want to play here?"

Andy said, "Maybe a different one," and they walked to a swirling ab-
stract concoction of red steel bars and shiny pipes held in place by guy wire.
"It's called 'Distillations,'" Miss Sugiyama said. "Maybe play from inside?"

The brothers crouched beneath the lowest pipe, with Mr. Taniguchi
following with two microphones, stands, and a portable amplifier. He set
up the equipment, but the wind kept blowing over the microphone stands,
so Miss Sugiyama, who was standing outside the sculpture with her phone,
suggested that they stand in the lee of the wind while they sang.

"Miss Sugiyama," Andy said, "I'm afraid that the wind is so strong up
here, you're not going to get much audio from our performance."

"It's okay," Miss Sugiyama muttered, clearly exasperated. "Just do the
fifteen songs."

"Which song?" Chris asked Andy. "'Whenever I Hit the Road'?"

"Just follow my lead," Andy said. He struck a C chord, over and over, and sang:

Whenever I wanna go
To Wadatogenono
I always have to say
Girl get out of my way

Girl get out of my way
My way!
Girl get out of my way
No way!

Andy stopped playing, and two extra C chords later, Chris stopped too.

A bitter mountain wind howled down the hill, shivering the grass and the tiny yellow and purple flowers sprinkled across the landscape.

Miss Sugiyama hit the "pause" button on her video camera and looked annoyed.

"What song is that?" she asked.

Chris asked, "And what is 'Wadatogenono'?"

Andy said, "According to my phone, Wadatogenono is the name of this little village, or wherever this is. And the song is some piece of shit that I'm making up on the spot so that none of our real songs come out sounding like 'Symphony for a Tornado.'"

"My uncle says we need fifteen songs," Miss Sugiyama called from outside the circle of steel and wire. "Doesn't matter what the songs are."

"Can I please, please, please go back into sarcasm mode?" Chris said. "Just for the duration of our performance? Because it seems like you're already there."

"Yeah. Why not."

"Good. So let's just ham it up to your Wadadata-whatever song fifteen times, and have fun. Like the Beatles in *Hard Day's Night*. It'll probably make for better social media videos, and we get paid no matter what."

Over the next hour and a half, the Fairley Brothers performed their new

song, which Andy entitled "Wadatogenono Blues," in the proximity of fifteen works of art. They played in front of what looked like a giant lipstick
resting in a giant cage. They mugged for the camera in front of a giant metallic foot with a giant metallic cicada perched on the foot's bulging vein,
and they draped their arms around a sad-looking man in bronze, singing
a cappella to his ruined face. They strummed their guitars behind a low
sculpture of three blindfolded heads.

They went inside a castle that looked as though it was built to host children's birthday parties, but when they opened the door at the top, the wind
almost blew them off the parapet, so that was a no-go.

Instead, they held their guitars in the air and ran around the ceramic
pylons of an exhibit that combined elements of Ancient Egypt with futuristic Japan. They played beneath a moving sculpture that bore more than
a passing resemblance to a Zipper carnival ride. The wind blew the alumi-
num poles and panels up and down and around, and the clouds rushed
overhead as though the sea were calling the clouds, and they were late, late.

"What do you think, Miss Sugiyama?" Chris asked, after they'd finished taping the final segment in front of a concrete gnome biting off the
head of a fish.

Miss Sugiyama did not reply.

"Totally stunk?" Andy asked her.

She raised her eyebrows in mild agreement.

"You know, Miss Sugiyama," Chris said, "the thing about the Venus Line Plain Air Park and Museum is that a lot of the sculptures are
pretty cool. But then some of them are really lame, so you start to question
whether the ones you thought were cool are actually total shit."

Miss Sugiyama's face remained impassive, but she said, "I did not want
to have Fairley Brothers. I wanted Billion Players, but we cannot afford
Billion Players, so we have Fairley Brothers instead."

"Not to worry, Miss Sugiyama," Chris said. "While no one can gainsay
the Billion Players' undeniable cuteness, I believe history will ultimately be
kinder to the Fairley Brothers. Isn't that right, Mr. Taniguchi?"

Mr. Taniguchi gave Chris a thumbs-up, and they all proceeded across
the windswept sculpture garden back to the enormous faux chalet, where
the Fairley Brothers collected their money and returned to their car.

Andy retraced the winding, narrow two-lane highway back down the mountain, but before they had gone too far, he noticed a pullout and parked the car in a rudimentary gravel lot.

"What's up?" Chris said.

"How about a hike? I feel like we've been to all these beautiful places, and we haven't really dragged our asses out of the car."

"What about our guitars? You can see them through the window."

"This is Japan. No one's going to steal our guitars."

They had two mostly full plastic bottles of water from the Venus Line Plain Air Park and Museum, but they were otherwise unprepared for a hike. Nevertheless, Andy identified a trail on his phone, and they headed up the mountain, periodically crossing a highway that switchbacked across the mountain's flank.

When they at last were away from the highway, they encountered a big brown sign with a yellow warning triangle containing a silhouette of a bear and an exclamation point. Most of the sign was in Japanese, though the English was plain enough: "Warning Bear Habitat." There was also a "date of verification" showing the most recent bear sighting, which had occurred on the fifteenth of July, less than a month earlier.

"Maybe we should turn back," Chris said.

"I heard that as long as you make a lot of noise, they won't bother you," Andy said, picking up two fallen branches from the forest floor. He knocked them together. "See?"

Chris picked up two fist-sized rocks and smacked them together. "I can always throw these," he said.

"I mean, you were always good at Frisbee golf," Andy said, "so why not?"

They hadn't traveled a hundred yards before Andy halted. At his feet were muddy prints that seemed fairly fresh. "Another hiker?" Andy asked.

"With claws? Should we wave the white flag and ditch?"

"I don't know. I've always wanted to go hiking in the Japanese Alps," Andy said. "It could be a long time before I get another chance."

"It could be forever if a bear eats you."

"We just need to make a lot of noise."

"Man," Chris said. He took out his phone and set the timer to go off every five minutes. As they made their way toward the top of the ridge, a brisk wind blowing the fog in, then blowing it on its way, periodically the "Playtime" alarm would ring, a descending scale that sounded like the beginning of an eighties electropop hit.

"Do you think a bear will be scared of that ringtone?" Chris asked.

"Depends on what kind of music he likes."

When they reached the spine of the ridge, they found a weathered, lichen-covered Buddha atop a cairn, and a sign, which Andy translated from the Japanese, indicating there had once been a village here, with several taverns for overnight stays for those traveling across the mountains from Edo to the Sea of Japan.

"Can you picture that?" Andy asked. "Traders and soldiers and pilgrims huddled by a fire in a stone tavern, swapping stories, writing haiku, while the innkeeper served them sake and the wind roared around them in the dark. It must have been magical."

"Mostly right now, I'm just thinking about bears."

"I think there's a better view up there," Andy said, pointing further up the ridge.

"This here is good for me," Chris said.

"Come on, big brother, don't be a chicken," Andy said, as Chris's ridiculous phone alarm sounded once again.

They continued hiking up the mountain, past more cairns, and the occasional tiger lily in gorgeous orange bloom. When the ridge began to slope back downhill Andy stopped, and they gazed out on an ocean of spruces and firs and pines as far as they could see.

"It's like a giant Christmas tree farm," Chris said.

Andy nodded.

Chris's alarm went off. "This is stupid," he said, pulling his phone from his pocket and turning off the alarm.

They drank from their almost empty water bottles while the clouds raced past, and the tall grass whished in the wind.

Then, from not far down the hill, came what sounded like an old man clearing his throat. A pause, then there was a low growl, and a snort.

"Jesus motherfucking Christ!" Chris yelped and grabbed his brother by the shirtsleeve, dragging him away from the noise and toward the path they'd just hiked up.

The brothers stumbled down the muddy trail, running as fast as they could without tripping over roots or rocks.

When they reached the first highway crossing, they stopped and turned around. Nothing was behind them.

"Probably our imaginations," Andy said, without conviction.

"Yeah. Or a bear."

Andy drove them back down the winding road to Matsumoto where they retrieved their luggage and parked their car in a lot across from their hotel.

After they checked in and dropped their luggage in their room, Chris said, "Time for a nap?"

"Actually, Matsumoto Castle is just a couple of blocks from here." Andy pulled out his phone. It's quarter to four, and it closes at four thirty, so I thought I'd zip over there real quick. It's supposed to be one of the best."

"I'll go with you."

"You don't have to. If you're tired."

"I'm tired, but I don't want to be the nay-saying stick-in-the-mud you were making me out to be this morning."

"You know what? I was just tired. You've been a real trooper today."

"You're making me sound like I'm ten years old," Chris said. He added, "Maybe I am."

They left the hotel and walked down the street and around the corner. They crossed a moat, paying their entrance fees, and practically loped through the gatehouse into the grounds. "Hey, wait up," Chris called as Andy hustled down a path lined by bamboo fencing, moving with great focus toward the castle's entrance.

The castle—six stories, mostly black with white trim—was in classic Japanese form: a low base rising to a narrow keep, vaulted ceilings, rectangles stacked atop one another, the sun—hot again in Matsumoto—flashing on the ceramic roof tiles.

A guard stood in front of the massive wooden doors, handing out plastic bags to cover patrons' shoes, which were tucked into a series of shelves. In their stockinged feet, the brothers went up the steep steps into rooms with polished wooden floors.

It was even hotter inside, and Chris moved from window to window to bathe in slightly cooler air as Andy studied the exhibits of armor and swords and guns and scrolls.

They moved upwards on a series of stairs that felt more like ladders until they reached the "moon viewing room," the only such room in the country, according to a sign, other than the one in Okayama Castle.

"Have you done Okayama?" Chris asked.

"Of course."

A bell clanged, and the docents began calling out, "Closing now!" in Japanese and English.

The brothers made their way down the ladders, several times almost slipping on the slick rungs and floors.

Outside the castle, Andy insisted they pose for a selfie, and Chris, with the longer arms, took the picture. Unshaven, their hair damp with sweat, a bit sunburned from the mountains, they nevertheless both smiled—Andy more widely than Chris, but no more genuinely. They looked like nothing so much as two brothers on a trip to Japan, enjoying themselves.

"I'm starving," Chris said when they were back on the streets of Matsumoto. Andy took out his phone and located a restaurant a block from the castle that was open and that served traditional Nagano cuisine.

Outside, the sign and menus were only in Japanese. Inside, the other patrons, all Japanese, took quick, appraising non-looks at the brothers as their waitress showed them to a table, then went off to find bilingual menus, which apparently had not been requested for some time.

When she finally returned, with two Asahi beers—unasked for but appreciated—the brothers scanned their menus.

"Hmm," Chris said. "I'll try the boiled bee larvae as an appetizer, but I'm not eating the raw horse tongue. Are you?"

"No, I'm not eating the raw horse tongue."

"What are you going to have?"

"I think I'm going to go with the steak carp boiled in soy sauce and sugar. How about you?"

"Probably the deep-fried bony chicken on a skewer with spicy marinade sauce."

"Sounds like a winner."

"You know," Chris said, taking a long swallow of his beer, "going back to this morning."

"Do we have to?"

"Am I really that bad?"

"Is that what you got out of it? That you're 'bad'?"

"I get that you're frustrated with me, that I'm not pulling my weight, and I want to say that I do appreciate how you and your wife have set everything up. It obviously took a shit ton of planning."

Andy nodded, sipped his beer, and said nothing.

"It's just...man. It's hard for me to do things that aren't part of my regular routine. It's like I used up all my spontaneity back in the eighties when we were touring, and now I'm this drudge who can't figure out how to have fun. It's why Larissa left me, but it's also why I was so good at that Department of Water and Power job, doing the same thing, day after day, year after year." Chris took another long pull from his beer. "But I'm *really* trying to break out of that. You have no idea how hard I'm trying."

Unexpectedly, Andy felt a tear well up in his right eye. He reached over and patted his brother on the hand, as though Chris were not a child, but his father, or grandfather—some much older person who needed comforting. "It's all right, man," Andy said. "Don't worry about it. Let's talk about something else."

When they had eaten and finished two more beers, they paid and went back outside. It was dark now, though still very humid.

From the direction of the castle came what sounded like a recording of traditional Japanese music. They walked in that direction and noticed that the lights leading back toward the castle were all red now.

In a park in front of the moat, a square stage had been set up with paper lanterns hanging from the roof trusses. Red and white bunting decorated the base of the stage. A woman chanted as drums and chimes were struck in a slow, ceremonious rhythm. At the edge of the stage, dancers in long kimonos moved in a circle to the percussion's tempo. They took two steps toward the middle of the stage, then two steps back. One step to the left, then one step to the right. Turning to face the back of the person in front of them, each dancer raised one arm, then the other, and took three steps forward. Then the process repeated itself, the circle advancing unhurriedly, but with comforting uniformity.

Outside the stage, audience members had formed their own much larger circle and were mimicking the moves of the professional dancers. There was plenty of open room, and Andy walked over and became part of the circle. He gestured for Chris to join him, but Chris shook his head and sat on a concrete curb beneath a pine tree, watching the ritual, whatever it was, move at its appointed pace.

HAPPYLAND JAPAN RESORT

Chris woke to the soundless TV cutting relentlessly between shots of various boy bands on stage at what appeared to be a boy band festival. Their dance moves were slickly choreographed. The audience, in the tens of thousands, waved glow sticks as a young woman in a box in the upper-right-hand corner of the screen gesticulated enthusiastically.

"Ever get the feeling we're in the wrong genre for this country?" Chris asked Andy, who was clipping his fingernails.

"We have our audience, too."

"That may be the case, but to be fair, they have largely been absent from our shows."

"We had some fans in Nagano."

"Who were getting booed down by the fans of Bloodline Ampersand."

"So?" Andy said, exasperated. "Should we just quit now? I'll take a train back to Kyoto, and you fly home to LA?"

"No, no, no, no, I was just blowing off steam. Come on, now."

"*You* come on now. I know you said yesterday that you're trying, but I told you that I'm sick of this negative shit."

"Okay, I understand. Let me get in the shower and get a cup of coffee. I'll be right as rain."

Andy shook his head and sighed. "Maybe you'd be happier if you looked at our social media. We have a thousand followers on Instagram now."

"Is that a lot?"

"Not necessarily, but it's better than the zero we started with. Plus, there are multiple posts from Akemi in Shiranuka. The lady at the Kushiro gig. Remember her?"

Chris nodded. Of course he did.

"She really likes your songwriting. And people who follow Daisuke's blog are posting on their own websites and social media, so we have a bit of momentum going. That's good, right?"

"Of course it is. I'm stoked, really." Chris moved toward the tiny bathroom. "What's today's gig?"

"Happyland Japan in Nagoya."

"I won't ask."

"Don't."

Chris paused as the boy bands disappeared from the TV screen, replaced by a weatherman with a long wooden pointer with a ball at the end. He stood off to the side of the green screen, pointing to a map of central Japan dotted by various cartoon images of the sun wearing sunglasses. "What's the forecast for Nagoya?" Chris asked.

"Thirty-five degrees Celsius."

"Is that hot?"

"Yep. Mid-nineties."

"Is it humid in Nagoya?"

"I would imagine so."

The train from Matsumoto to Nagoya ran southwest along tracks shadowing the shallow Kiso River, which tumbled over rocks and rushed past boulders. Chris thought that the low clouds moving in and out of the valley at times made the scene outside the window look like a painting from the Tokyo National Museum.

Occasionally, a northbound train would go past them at speed, and Chris would flinch back from the window. He was remembering a coworker from the DWP, Erica, who, after his divorce, had clearly indicated that she was interested in him. She was pretty and kind and funny, but she was not Molly or Larissa, and Chris had let opportunity after opportunity pass by until eventually Erica stopped talking to him altogether.

Andy sat with his eyes closed, his seat in the reclining position. He was envisioning what might have happened had the Fairley Brothers' third album been a bigger seller than their second. A few more radio hits, maybe a shift in their sound toward something more palatable to the masses, and they might at this very moment be lounging in a fully equipped tour bus with a tour manager and a suitable entourage.

Instead, they were on a train headed to a gig at an amusement park.

The Sex Pistols leaked from Andy's AirPods as he mouthed the words to "Holidays in the Sun."

Gradually, the valley broadened, then the river disappeared behind golf driving ranges, construction sites and love hotels, supermarkets and warehouses, and the occasional enormous factory complex.

Then it was all city: apartment blocks and office buildings, the glass and steel seeming to press against the train. Huge electronic billboards flashed corporate logos from the tops of buildings.

Nagoya station was crowded and confusing, and it took the brothers twenty minutes to find the left-luggage lockers, which were tucked in the basement at the end of a long zig-zagging corridor.

With their suitcases stored, they walked with guitars in one hand, equipment bags in the other, following signs toward the Aonami Line. Everyone looked at them curiously, then turned away immediately when Andy or Chris managed to catch someone's eyes.

It was a thirty-minute ride south to the harbor, during which time, Andy made a song list on his iPad using his phone as a hot spot. They emerged into an un-air-conditioned station, and the heat slapped them across the face and chest.

"My God," Chris said. "This is intense. I hope we're not playing outside."

When Andy didn't respond, Chris said, "Are we? Outside?"

"I don't know."

Chris put his guitar and gear bag down and opened his weather app. He looked at Andy. "It says ninety-one degrees. Feels like one hundred and six."

Andy shrugged.

From the windows of the station, all that could be seen was heavy industry: container terminals and warehouses, factories and smokestacks and giant cranes.

"Doesn't seem like a very happy land," Chris said.

Ignoring him, Andy looked up from the Google Maps app on his phone. "Follow me," he said.

They walked along a pedestrian overpass that led to a vast parking lot where a series of sprinklers sent out blankets of mist that brought the heat down a few degrees. Past the parking lot, back out in the heat, they followed signs for Happyland Japan Resort down a spiral ramp to the theme park's entrance. The park's name was written in sparkling letters, in English and Japanese, on a great arched gate, behind which was a row of restaurants and souvenir shops.

Panting, they stood in the shade of a building. Chris took out his phone: "Ninety-two degrees. Feels like one hundred and nine."

Andy took a water bottle from his bag and handed a second one to Chris. "It's hot. I get it."

Chris said, "I think we're going to have to pass on this one, don't you?"

"Let me just go find out what's what."

Andy disappeared into a door marked "Fun Center," and Chris slid down to the asphalt, resting his back against a metal plate that was mercifully cool.

A sprinkling of small children pulled their parents by the hands, but most people had evidently chosen to avoid Happyland on this particular day. "Torrid," Chris muttered to himself. "That's what this weather is: torrid."

Andy returned in fifteen minutes with a man in his fifties wearing a business suit.

"So?" Chris said, sweat dripping from his forehead.

"He wants us to play."

"Indoors?"

"There's a stage in the park. He says it's mostly shady."

"No. I mean, no way."

"At least give it a look. It's six hundred and fifty thousand yen. That's like five hundred bucks. For thirty minutes of work."

"Is the money up front?"

"We get paid after we do our half hour."

Inside the park, a tame-looking roller coaster ran its route, mostly devoid of passengers. A miniature train circled the grounds. A giant mechanical octopus waved its two front tentacles, flashing lights where the suction cups should have been. "Enter the Octopus," a low voice said in English, "if you dare."

As the brothers trudged through Happyland, Chris continued mumbling descriptions of the heat: "Sizzling." "Oppressive." "Stifling." "Suffocating." People in anime costumes moved slowly in the sun, bending down to shake a child's hand, then quickly seeking shade. "See," Andy said. "It could be worse. You could be in a Godzilla suit."

"That's just inhuman," Chris said.

"Japanese are tough."

They made their way past a talking robot and an out-of-order dragon to a very large stage, with two microphone stands and an impressive array of loudspeakers. Overhead was a fabric stage cover, but the sun was shining from an angle, directly onto the stage.

"I don't see any shade," Chris said.

"It's only thirty minutes," Andy said, almost pleading.

Chris took out his phone and swiped to his weather app. "It's ninety-three degrees. Feels like one eleven."

Andy took his duffel bag and his guitar to the back of the stage, removed his guitar from the case, retrieved his iPad and its stand from the bag, placed the strap around his neck, and walked up to the microphone. "This is me not caring how hot it is," he said.

Then he tapped on the mic, which was live, and said, "Hello, Happyland Japan Resort! You're all looking mighty happy out there, and we're going to make you even happier." He gestured toward Chris. "If I can get my brother to help me out. What do you say, people?"

Someone in the shade clapped politely.

"That's what I thought. Hop on in, Chris, the weather's fine!"

Chris followed his brother's lead and was soon set up. "What's the Wi-Fi password?" he whispered to Andy.

"happyhappyhappy. All lower-case, three times in a row." Andy pointed to a song on the list he had prepared earlier. "Let's start with this one."

Soon the Fairley Brothers were singing *The Partridge Family* theme song: "Come on, get happy! We'll make you happy!"

Then it was the Turtles, "Happy Together," and the Ramones' "Gimme Gimme Shock Treatment"—"Happy happy happy all the time / Shock treatment, I'm doing fine"—and Elvis Costello's "I Hope You're Happy Now."

All the while, the sun blazed down on their faces and bare arms. Their skin grew clammy, sweat streamed down their foreheads and backs. Chris was visibly wilting, barely making an effort to keep up with his brother.

A park employee had given them each a liter bottle of water, and they took long gulps between songs, but the day kept getting hotter and more humid, the light growing brighter and more unbearable.

It was during the third verse of the Rolling Stones' "Happy," Andy doing a passable version of Keith Richards, that Chris dropped his guitar and collapsed unconscious to the stage.

For a moment, Andy stood there, staring down at his brother as though he were pulling some childhood prank, then he muttered into the microphone, "That's all, folks," and he bent down and splashed what was left in his water bottle on his brother's face. Chris opened his eyes long enough to utter, "Shade," then he closed them again.

Andy looked around, heat-besotted and desperate, and then, suddenly, like a character out of a comic book, Daisuke Hayashi bounded onto the stage.

Daisuke yelled something in Japanese, and two security guards hustled out of the shade. One took Chris under the arms, and the other grabbed his legs. They carried him into an air-conditioned room with a large couch, on which they set him down, rubbing their backs in relief when the job was done.

After a large bottle of water, and ten minutes of frigid air, Chris began to revive.

"How are you?" Andy asked, gripping his brother's hand.

"I've been better, but I'll live."

Daisuke and the park manager were arguing about something.

"What's he saying?" Chris asked.

Andy said, "He doesn't want to pay because we didn't do the full half hour."

Daisuke added: "He says you're foreigners. You should be used to the heat."

"That's pretty harsh, considering I just passed out on his stage. I could have died. Not a happy thought at all."

Daisuke turned back to the park manager and argued some more. After a few minutes, the park manager looked cowed. He bowed to Daisuke and left the room.

"What'd you say?" Chris asked.

"I told him: Pay up or face the wrath of Daisuke Hayashi."

Chris sat up on the couch, ready to leave, but Daisuke insisted that he remain in the room and drink another full liter of water.

Before they left, Chris went to the toilet. His urine was reddish yellow.

The three of them walked back to the station, Daisuke carrying Chris's guitar and gear bag. As they sat on a metal bench waiting for the train, Daisuke said, "I'd like to do one more interview to complete my profile. The Fairley Brothers from their official breakup in 1989 to today."

"I guess we owe you that," Chris said, "after the big save there at Happyland."

"Just one request: I'd like to do the interviews separately."

"Why?" Andy asked.

"I loved hearing from the two of you about when the band was together—all that back and forth, and kidding around was great—but, let's face it, when the band split up, you mostly went your separate ways. That's right, isn't it?"

Andy nodded. Chris shrugged.

"So," Daisuke continued, "it only makes sense that you'd each need your own time and space to tell your individual stories. How does that sound?"

This time Andy shrugged, and Chris nodded.

"If your online tour schedule is still accurate, then you have tonight off, and you're playing in Osaka tomorrow."

"That's right," Andy said. "I'm leaving the train in Kyoto to spend the night with my wife. I've booked a hotel for Chris in Osaka."

"You have?" Chris asked. "I mean, I'd like to meet Fumiko."

"You will. Tomorrow. I just need a little break, okay?"

"I get it, sure." Chris turned away. Of course they needed a break from one another, so why did that fact feel so painful?

Daisuke said, "How about this as a plan? I'll join you both on the Shinkansen and get off in Osaka with Chris. My sister lives there, and we can have a traditional Osakan dinner at a great place I know—on me.

We'll do the interview afterward. Then tomorrow morning, I'll take the train back up to Kyoto and interview Andy. Then Andy, Fumiko, and I will come back to Osaka for your gig at Music Club Infinity."

"Sounds complicated," Chris said.

"But it's not," Daisuke replied.

The Aonami Line train pulled into the station.

Andy said, "It's okay with me, if Chris is on board."

Chris sighed. "Whatever works."

The Shinkansen eased almost noiselessly into Nagoya station as the brothers waited patiently in line. Passengers exited in an orderly fashion, while those entering boarded with slightly less decorum and a little more bustle. Two minutes later the train was moving out, toward Kyoto, with Andy and Chris in one carriage and Daisuke in another.

"Kind of weird how Daisuke keeps turning up," Chris said, lowering his seat back.

"Lucky for us, though, I'd say."

"I guess so. I'm still kind of baffled by his obsession with the Fairley Brothers. We must represent something more to him than just, you know, *ourselves*."

"Probably, but I doubt he'd tell us what. That sort of honesty would be inconsiderate on his part. How are you feeling, by the way? You look a lot better."

Chris's face was no longer red, but he still felt physically and mentally depleted. "I don't know. The whole thing kind of felt like a dream." Chris patted the duffel bag between his legs, wishing he'd taken the time to buy a beer. "So, are you looking forward to seeing Fumiko?"

"Of course."

"Tell her I said, 'Thanks.' For all she's done."

"You'll meet her tomorrow. You can tell her yourself. Oh, and I got us some tickets to a baseball game."

"Sounds fun. In Kyoto?"

"No, they don't have a team. It's the Orix Buffaloes. They're based in Osaka, but the game's in Kobe. We can meet at the stadium. It's easy to get to. All the signs are in English. I'll text you the directions."

The landscape—parking lots and canals, gas stations and warehouses, rivers and highways—rushed past them, and thirty-five minutes later the train pulled into Kyoto Station. Andy patted his brother on the shoulder, retrieved his guitar and luggage, and exited down the aisle without a word. "Text me!" Chris called out. Andy appeared to nod, but he didn't turn back. Chris peered through the train window and gave his brother a weak wave, but Andy was already disappearing down the stairs.

Then the train was moving again, zipping through an almost entirely urban landscape, pulling into Shin-Osaka Station in less than fifteen minutes.

Chris trundled through the door with his guitar, suitcase, and duffel bag and stationed himself behind a pillar until the mass of exiting passengers had made their way down the stairs. His phone pinged in his pocket, and he took it out and opened a message from Daisuke. "Meet me at the taxi stand," it read, and "I'll put you in a cab to your hotel."

Chris followed the yellow signs to the taxis, where he found Daisuke waiting for him in the sultry evening air, a small, wheeled suitcase at his side.

"How does it feel to be in Japan without your brother?" Daisuke asked.

"Honestly, it feels a bit weird."

"Andy texted me all the details. He's booked a room for you for two nights in a place that's just a few blocks from your gig tomorrow in Namba. Your hotel is a short walk to Dotonbori, where there are some pretty cool restaurants. Do you still want to have dinner tonight?"

"Definitely. Thank you. I appreciate your...competence."

"All right then, I'll just give your taxi driver directions to your hotel, and then I'll text you the address of the restaurant."

"Was it as bad as you thought it was going to be?" Fumiko was asking her husband as she prepared dinner in their small kitchen, sprinkling dried tuna flakes and kelp into the stock she had emptied into a cast-iron cooker atop a gas burner.

"It's kind of hot for nabe, isn't it?" Andy asked from the tiny table wedged into a corner of the room.

"I just felt like it tonight. It's food for home."

As the broth came to a boil, Fumiko emptied a small plate of sliced cabbage and white radishes into the mix. "So, was it? Bad, I mean?"

"Sometimes. Mostly not. He's an odd duck, my brother. I think he wants to be generous and kind, but there's some weird personality quirk that keeps getting in the way. He says he's not able to have fun, and I can see that."

"Is he depressed?"

"Maybe. Yes. And lonely. He's still funny, though. He's got a crack about everything, even if it's usually a downer." Andy shook two ibuprofen from a small bottle in his pocket.

"Still having the headaches?"

He smiled. "Whenever the subject is Chris."

Fumiko retrieved small containers of mushrooms, diced onions, and bean sprouts from the refrigerator, took off the plastic tops, and emptied the contents into the boiling stew. "I'm not sure I'm ready to meet him," she said.

"I'm not doing a very good job of describing him. He has this monster musical talent—he really does—but he basically just gave up on it and did a desk job for thirty years. He's underconfident, in some ways, but in others, I think he expects people to recognize his talent, and when he's ignored, like we have been for all these years, he's just like, 'Fuck it, I don't care.'"

"Well, I am looking forward to seeing *you* play your music, live and in person," Fumiko said, as she stirred the hot pot with chopsticks. "And the two of you have done a lot in just a little over a week. That's something to be proud of, and I want to hear all about it."

"It was all thanks to you," Andy said, getting up and pulling Fumiko toward him. "My beautiful, beautiful wife."

Raindrops fell on the Dotonbori Canal as Chris stood under the awning of the restaurant where he had agreed to meet Daisuke. Along the canal were innumerable neon signs lighting up the night. Above a seafood restaurant, a giant plastic crab. Above another restaurant, a giant plastic octopus. Next to the octopus was a giant billboard of a cartoon cat eating what looked like a corndog. Another billboard, three stories tall, showed a woman in an expensive-looking overcoat holding a cat. The tag was "Life is a Challenge."

People surged through the wet streets. Chris was thinking how infrequently one umbrella ever touched another, when Daisuke tapped him on the shoulder.

"Hungry?" Daisuke asked.

"Very."

"Excellent. Tonight, we'll have some traditional Osakan food."

Just beyond a Kobe beef restaurant advertised by a demonic plastic cow eating a plastic steak, they entered a dark establishment, hung with dark-red banners, and were led to a booth with a grill in the center of the table. They sat across from each other, and a waiter appeared, placing wet napkins in plastic wrappers in front of them, along with two small plates and metal spatulas.

Soon a chef was standing in front of their table. He dropped some thin slices of chicken on the grill, and, as they began to sizzle, in a large white bowl he began mixing shredded carrots, chopped green onions, green beans, and strips of bell pepper.

"Okonomiyaki," Daisuke said. "It's a kind of pancake."

"Yes, I've had it before."

"Do you like it?"

Chris smiled noncommittally.

The server returned with a plate of skewered deep-fried vegetables along with a metal container labeled "kushikatsu sauce," with a second label, in bold, warning: "No Double-Dipping!"

"*Meshiagatte kudasai*," Daisuke said. "Please eat."

As Daisuke used his spatula to heap okonomiyaki onto his plate, Chris said, "You know, Andy and I have been zipping through this country, but I don't feel like I've learned much about Japan. You aside, Daisuke, my interactions with Japanese people have been pretty superficial."

"Japan is not an easy place to know. Even after a long time. On the surface, yes, you get it fairly quickly: the homogeneity, the traditions, the workaholism, the sexism. But of course it's much more than that."

"I've missed most of it."

"I think you're probably being modest. However," Daisuke said, taking his phone from his pocket, "if you don't mind, I'd like to turn on my voice memo recorder and ask you some questions."

"The final interview?"

"Just so."

"All right then."

For nearly an hour, they ate their food and drank their beer while Daisuke asked questions and Chris did his best to respond with candor.

When they had finished dinner, and the interview, Chris said, "Shit. That was heavy."

"But cathartic maybe?"

"Maybe."

"How about I buy you a drink as thanks? And no more interview."

Chris agreed, Daisuke paid the bill, and they left their air-conditioned haven for the humid summer night. The rain had stopped, and the neon signs shone clearly on the water of the Dotonbori Canal, down which motored a barge with digital advertisements featuring anime characters on hoverboards.

"Let's head over to America-mura," Daisuke said.

"What's that?"

"It's a kind of mock American neighborhood. But fairly trendy, as far as Osaka goes."

They followed a man in a blue T-shirt with a legend on the back that read "School Runned My Life." They passed smallish restaurants and tattoo parlors, shops full of women's shoes and stores with Westernish fashions—*What*, Chris wondered, *was a Red Cap Girl?* Many of them were closing up, although it was only nine o'clock.

Daisuke turned the corner into an alley, then paused. "There's a hidden bar up here," he said, pressing the button for a tiny elevator that took them up six floors. Next to the elevator buttons was a printed note that read: "No talking in the elevator."

The establishment had no signage, only black curtains covering the open door, which Daisuke pushed aside, ushering Chris in ahead of him. "It's called the Bar Times Nothing," Daisuke said.

"Unusual name."

"Appropriate, nevertheless. I always feel like a cipher when I'm in here."

It was a quiet, dark place with three people sitting on leather stools around a semicircular bar, all staring moodily into their glasses. As Daisuke approached him, a lone barman wiped the counter, his silhouette outlined by backlit rows of liquor bottles. The lights were low, and a tasteful jazz ensemble that Chris didn't recognize was playing on the loudspeakers at a just barely audible volume. Daisuke ordered two martinis, and they took a two-person table in the corner.

Chris said, "Sometimes I feel like the more I talk to you, the vaguer it all becomes. Even the concept of the Fairley Brothers just clouds up."

"Do you know the author Jun'ichirō Tanizaki?"

"Afraid not."

"He wrote an essay called 'In Praise of Shadows.' In it, he talks about how certain things, like a scroll, say, in the dark nook of a temple, are more beautiful because they can't be seen clearly. Lack of clarity, he says, creates a kind of harmony."

"And that's what you're trying to do with this interview?" Chris asked. "Create a 'lack of clarity.'"

"No, the opposite, of course. I'm trying to bring things into the light. But if that doesn't always happen, well, according to Tanizaki, maybe it's not such a bad thing."

"And if you were to sum up the importance of the Fairley Brothers in one sentence, what would it be?"

Daisuke put his chin in his cupped hand. "Interesting question. I think I would say, and no offense here, but your importance is primarily metaphorical. The Fairley Brothers are a metaphor for the fragility of co-creation. That is, especially in music, we see how essential collaboration is in the making of something magical, something transcendent, and yet our human egos are constantly at war with this transcendence. Just envision the extraordinary songs we would have now if John and Paul had reconnected as friends and songwriting partners and kept the Beatles together for another ten years...or five...or even another twelve months."

"Okay," Chris said, nodding, mostly convinced. "But there's nothing personal for you about the Fairley Brothers? No hidden reason why you've chosen us as your metaphor rather than countless other acts that have split up?"

Daisuke ate a handful of spicy rice crackers from a small dish and shook his head, noncommittally. "As Bashō said: 'A butterfly flies / in the meadow / only in sunshine.'"

The bartender brought their drinks over, bowed silently, and returned to his station behind the bar. One of the other tables was occupied by a couple who looked as though they didn't want to be seen.

Daisuke seemed to be staring at him, and Chris blurted out: "Are you gay?"

"No, I'm not, actually. Are you?"

"No sign of that to date."

"Why do you ask?"

"I don't know. I thought you were kind of gazing at me. And despite everything you've just said, I still can't quite figure out why the Fairley Brothers are so important to you."

"Yes, well. Who can say?"

Both were suddenly in a rush to finish their drinks, and soon they were outside again. Daisuke asked Chris if he wanted a taxi, but Chris shook his head. "No, thanks. I'll walk. I'll use my phone to find my way."

MUSIC CLUB INFINITY

Osaka
Tuesday, August 16

Fumiko had taken the day off work, and she and Andy were asleep in each other's arms on the two futons laid out side by side in their tatami room.

At first, the knocking on the door incorporated itself into Andy's dream, a swirling vision of music clubs and trains, hotel rooms and incense-shrouded Buddhas, unfamiliar voices calling out to him from the edge of darkness. Then he was lying on a plank of wood and a small, faceless child was pounding a mallet right next to his head. Andy reached out to swipe at the annoying youth, and suddenly he was awake and aware that someone was at his front door.

He threw off the comforter, tiptoed out of the tatami room, and padded across the tiny kitchen. He opened the door a crack to see Daisuke Hayashi.

"Daisuke? What are you doing here?"

"Our interview, remember? Yesterday in Nagoya, you told me to come by your house at nine."

"I don't remember that."

"No, I'm sure that's what you said. But I apologize. Obviously, I've found you still sleeping."

Andy shut his eyes tight, then opened them again, half-thinking he might be dreaming, but Daisuke was still there. "So," Andy said, "maybe we could do it tonight? I told my brother I'd take him to an Orix game this afternoon. They're playing in Kobe."

"I actually interviewed him last night. I just need to talk to you now, to sort of tie the story all up."

"Is there a rush?"

"I have other things coming up. I don't want to let this slide. My readers are really interested in the two of you right now."

"Strike while the iron is hot."

"In so many words."

They looked at each other. A crow landed on a power pole across the street. They both listened as it cawed, once, twice, thrice. Finally, Andy said, "There's a coffee shop down the street, Nishiyogoku Coffee. I can meet you there in half an hour."

"Sounds perfect," Daisuke said. "I'll see you then."

Fumiko was awake when Andy returned to the bedroom. "I heard," she said.

"I know. Annoying."

"But good publicity."

"That's why I'm going to take a shower and go over there."

"Don't take too long," she said, nodding, thinking.

When Andy emerged from the shower, Fumiko was already dressed. "I'm going with you," she said.

"Really? Why?"

"I feel like I should. So your side of the story can be told."

"I don't really have a side, per se," he said, toweling his wet hair.

"Of course you do. With that whole Molly Moore business."

"Ancient history. Who cares?"

"But your brother is probably making you out to be the bad villain. You're not."

"I doubt that will even come up. Daisuke just wants to know what we've each been doing since our final album."

"Well, you'll tell him. And I'll make sure you tell it right."

At Nishiyogoku Coffee, Daisuke, Andy, and Fumiko stood in line for coffee and pastries, then sat down at a table with three chairs by a plateglass window overlooking the street. Daisuke took the lid off his coffee and stirred in three packets of sugar before saying, "I'm so happy to meet you, Fumiko. I've heard a lot about you."

"I've heard a lot about you, too."

"I must say, though, I was expecting this to be an interview with just Andy."

"It will be. Mostly."

"Ah," Daisuke said.

"It'll be fine," Andy said, furrowing his brow and taking a sip of coffee.

"Okay then," Daisuke said. "I'll just turn the voice recorder on, and we can get started."

They spoke for an hour, Fumiko inserting herself more than Andy would have liked, but less than he had feared. Other than their earnest conversation, the only sounds were the baristas calling out orders, the clinking of forks on plates, J-pop on the shop's speakers—with the occasional sprinkling of well-mannered rap—and the periodic roar of the espresso machine. The other customers kept themselves to themselves, even when they weren't alone.

When they finished, Daisuke said, "Well, that should do it. I have some free time, so I may be able to post it today. I'll try and do it before your gig at Music Club Infinity. But no promises."

"Your questions were a little rough at the end, but Chris and I are grateful for the publicity you've given us, though, I must say, I'm still a bit puzzled as to why you've been so keen to map out the lives of the Fairley Brothers," Andy said.

"Who knows why we do the things we do? Fate, I suppose."

Chris woke at ten o'clock and looked over where he expected to see his brother in the adjoining bed. But there was no bed and no Andy.

The room felt eerily still without the television on, so Chris picked up the remote control, turned on the TV, and muted it.

On the screen were five well-dressed announcers, three women and two men who were all gripping the thumbs of their right hands with their left hands, then wriggling their thumbs, so that the right thumb appeared to be trapped in the grasp of the left hand. Suddenly, they all stopped and burst out into silent laughter that just as suddenly ceased. Immediately, the screen changed to a news story that seemed to be about someone who had drowned in an overflowing river. The next story was about an uncertain number of people who, despite the rain, had died in a house fire.

When the camera returned to the studio, the announcers all looked grim for a long moment. Then they grabbed their thumbs and once again erupted into soundless hilarity.

Chris switched off the TV, shaved, took a shower, then got dressed. It was the first time since he'd arrived in Japan that he would be spending a second night in the same hotel, and it felt like a luxury not to have to pack.

He took his guitar from his case and played a few songs he'd felt slightly shaky on at previous gigs. In the old days, he would have insisted that he and Andy rehearse every few days, even when they were on the road, but this time their pre-trip practicing and the gigs themselves had been sufficient. "Maybe you're getting less uptight," Chris said to himself aloud. "Good job." Then he put his guitar away and went out for an early lunch at MOS Burger before departing for the ballpark in Kobe.

It was after eleven when Chris boarded the Hanshin-Namba line at Osaka-Namba station, riding it west for ten stops. A change of trains was required at Amagasaki station, where he stepped into a carriage marked "Mildly Air-Conditioned Car" and rode for another eleven stops. The train was surprisingly crowded for midday, so Chris hung onto the strap, swaying with the car, glancing down at each stop to see if a seat might open up, pretending gamely that everyone was not surreptitiously staring at him.

At Itayado station, he changed for the final three stops. The train was even more packed, presumably with those going to the game, though he was surprised to see how few fans sported team jerseys.

When the train arrived, Chris followed the mass of people to a large brick-paved plaza outside Hotto Motto Field, where Andy had said they could easily spot one another.

Sure enough, there Andy was, standing next to a petite and pretty woman in her fifties with short salt-and-pepper hair. Her expression was quizzical and slightly amused. "Over here!" Andy shouted, waving.

Chris crossed the plaza and gave his little brother a hug. "Long time no see," he said.

"Long enough," Andy said. "I'd like to introduce you to my wife, Fumiko."

Chris bent down to hug her, but she stuck out a hand, which he shook. "My pleasure," he said.

"I've heard so much about you."

"Not all bad, I hope."

Fumiko smiled enigmatically.

"So, what's the plan?" Chris asked.

"First, we get dressed for the game. I brought you a hat," Andy said, handing Chris a cap with a blue brim and a brown front panel, on which were stitched the interlocking English letters "O" and "B." "Now you are a B's fan for life," Andy said.

"Go Buffaloes," Chris said, adjusting the strap until the cap fit snugly on his head. He looked around. "I noticed there weren't a lot of people dressing up for the game."

Andy said, "It's considered rude to do that until you actually get to the ballpark. You don't want to offend supporters of the other team."

"Wow. Very thoughtful."

"Yeah. Anyway, there's a Lawson over there. Most people stock up on snacks and beer before going into the stadium. It's also where a lot of people change into their uniforms."

The three of them went down a set of concrete stairs to the store, which was surging with people buying beer and energy drinks, corn dogs and plastic-wrapped rice balls, plastic tubs of salad and packages of potato chips, fried chicken and candy bars, and whatever else could be stuffed into a shopping basket. Barely audible above the hum of commerce was a Muzak version of "Let It Be."

Outside the store, people took their jerseys and caps from their backpacks and geared up for either the Orix Buffaloes or the Chiba Lotte Marines. After emerging from the store with four plastic bags of purchases, Andy and Fumiko joined the crowd and began changing into their Buffaloes regalia.

Once the two were attired, they all returned to the ballpark plaza, where they waited in a series of long wending lines, making small talk about the band's gigs, the Buffaloes' lineup, the hot weather, and the gathering thunderheads.

Before the first pitch, the public address system played the Buffaloes' theme song, a tune that combined J-pop with a martial theme. On the field, cheerleaders in white blouses and black shorts danced to the song, while in the stands, fans banged together mini baseball bats and plastic dumbbells in support of their team.

"Where exactly is Orix?" Chris asked, when everyone had settled into their seats and the game had begun.

"Nowhere, really," said Fumiko. "All the teams are sponsored by corporations."

"What about the Tokyo Giants?"

"You mean the Yomiuri Giants," Fumiko said. "They're owned by a media conglomerate."

Andy said, "Orix is a rental car company."

"Weird," Chris said.

"It's Japan," said Fumiko.

It was overcast, and light sprinkles periodically swept across the field. They were seated in right field, Fumiko between the two brothers. Andy and his wife joined in some of the well-rehearsed chants, bolstered by complex rhythmic clapping: "Let's go, let's go, Buffaloes, Buffaloes! Play, play, play, play, play!"

Meanwhile, Chris looked on, amazed at how civil everyone was being. No booing the umpire when he made a bad call. No taunting the opposing team's best hitter. People clapped, but no one seemed to be calling out the Japanese equivalent of "Come on, you bums!" Other than one section of the stadium that seemed to be exclusively devoted to cheering for the team, no one ever stood up, except, presumably, to go to the restroom or the concession stands. And when they weren't drinking beer or eating peanuts, all the fans were dutifully masked.

"It feels a lot more like a family sport here, don't you think?" Andy asked.

"Definitely. Kind of reminds me of those few times Dad would take us to a Dodgers game when we were kids. Dodger Dogs with lots of mustard. That feeling that you were sort of at a county fair." Chris took a sip of his beer. "Not that I've ever actually been to a county fair."

At one point, the right fielder for the Buffaloes missed a catchable ball in the warning track. A moment of silence, then a polite round of applause from the Buffaloes fans. "What was that for?" Chris asked. "He totally should have had it."

Andy said, "At least he tried."

Even stranger to Chris was the fact that the Chiba Marines had brought their own drum corps, which pounded out a complex rhythm each time their squad got a hit or made an out, both of which happened with some frequency: The Buffaloes were getting shellacked.

Beverage girls wearing plastic gloves and anime-style costumes in yellow, pink, blue, and red walked up and down the rows, their bangs plastered to their foreheads from the intermittent drizzle. Each carried a small keg on her back and squirted liquid from a plastic hose into customers' cups.

"What do the colors mean?" Chris asked.

"Pink is regular beer," Andy said. "Yellow is lemon sour. Blue is the expensive beer, and red is an energy drink." He waved over one of the girls in a pink costume and paid for three more beers.

"No tip?" Chris asked, after she left. "That's hard work."

"No tip," Fumiko said. "It's her job."

The clouds grew darker, and the rain began to fall with more regularity. It didn't take long before fans were struggling into their see-through plastic rain parkas, and umbrellas sprouted throughout the stands.

At the seventh-inning stretch, the Buffaloes theme song made another appearance, and then there was a fireworks show, somewhat premature in Chris's opinion, considering that the home team was down five to nothing.

Then it started pouring. The players ran off the field, and fans fled the stands for the safety of the overhang, some huddling together hoping the rain would pass, others moving quickly toward the exits, obviously believing the game would be called.

Rain still dripping off the bill of his Buffaloes cap, Chris asked: "What now?"

"We leave," said Fumiko, "before the subway gets crazy."

She was off then, the Fairley brothers trying to keep up with her rapid pace, as she darted between slowpokes and raced against those who were also in a hurry.

Andy had advised Chris to get a round-trip subway ticket, and Chris could see why, as those who weren't as prepared began to queue up in front of the ticket machines.

The three of them swiped their cards and headed down the escalator to the tracks, Fumiko still in the lead. On the platform, Fumiko nudged them toward the painted lines that indicated where a door would open, and in less than a minute a train entered the station. There was quite a bit of subtle, almost polite pushing and shoving as the car immediately filled up, and the doors closed. Out the window, Chris could see fans running toward the train, though it was already on the move, the passengers still masked and looking down at their phones.

When they reached Osaka Station, an hour and a half later, it was five thirty. Fumiko carried their wet baseball jerseys and caps in a plastic bag, which she held as though it were much heavier than it actually was. Andy had stowed his guitar in a locker, and while he went to retrieve it, Chris and Fumiko leaned against a glass partition overlooking the train platforms. Whenever multiple trains pulled in at the same time, there was a measured cacophony of electronic bird whistles, dinging, and competing announcements.

"How was your interview?" Fumiko asked. "With Daisuke?"

"All right, at first. Then I thought he was pushing too hard, was getting too intrusive. You mentioned at the ballpark that he came over this morning. Did you enjoy talking with him?"

"Not really, no. Too pushy. He is a difficult man to...what's the word? To *read*."

"I want to believe his intentions are good. So far, we've benefited from what he's written about us."

"Yes, probably," Fumiko said. "I am suspicious, though, of everyone. I don't know why."

Chris nodded: He could relate.

For a few minutes, they watched as passengers on one platform dashed for a train about to depart, while on another track an arriving train disgorged its passengers like agitated ants released from a trap.

Chris said, "I haven't really had a chance to thank you for all the hard work you did setting up our tour."

"I enjoy it, that sort of thing. Making plans, watching them work out."

"She does a good job," Andy said, joining them, his guitar case swinging in his right hand. To Chris, he said, "Shall we stop by your hotel and get your guitar?"

"Sounds good."

The rush-hour subway was packed, but they were back at Chris's hotel a little after six.

"The show is at nine," Fumiko said, when Chris rejoined them in the lobby with his guitar case. "Maybe we should eat dinner at the venue."

"I like your style, Fumiko," Chris said. He smiled at his brother: "Some people like to wait until the last minute to do things."

"Makes things more exciting," Andy replied. "Hey, remember when we used to play Rochambeau, loser carries both guitars?"

"I'm too old for that," Chris said. "Too bad we don't have any roadies."

"Maybe you will again someday," said Fumiko.

"I'm afraid that's wishful thinking. We've got, what? Three more gigs, including tonight? Then the tour's over and I'm headed back to LA."

"But what if you are suddenly stars?" Fumiko asked. There was a note of desperation in her voice. "I know I sent the Fairley Brothers to some small and odd places, and for that I apologize, but now you are here in the heart of Japan, where things can really happen."

"I must admit I was hoping Tokyo would be our big break," Chris said. "But you'll recall the gig was at a fish restaurant. Where people were catching fish while we sang."

Fumiko blushed. "I didn't realize what I was booking. I'm sorry. The pay was good, though, wasn't it?"

"I think so. But there weren't a lot of record executives sitting around trying to hook sea bream."

"I try, okay. I try!" she said, her English suddenly louder and rougher around the edges.

Several other guests looked over at the trio.

Chris set his guitar on the lobby's marble floor and held up his hand. "I'm not complaining, Fumiko, really I'm not. I just don't want to have unrealistic expectations. My plan is to enjoy these last gigs, then sail back into retirement, which was not bad for me, not at all."

But Fumiko wasn't ready for a truce. "You're saying you prefer to live by yourself in a lonely house? Not playing music? Not making the most of your life?"

"Realistically, what's the alternative?"

"Oh, come on, Chris," Andy said. "That's so defeatist."

"But maybe that's me," Chris said, feeling a weight growing in his chest. "Maybe that's all there is."

Andy turned away from his brother and stared at the little fountain burbling in the hotel lobby. It sounded so peaceful, so content—so unlike

Chris. Jesus, Andy thought, there is no winning with this guy.

Barely speaking, the three of them made their way along the broad boulevard of Yotsubashi-suji and then down a series of crowded narrow alleys
crammed with restaurants and bars, all brightly lit with flashing signage
and paper lanterns.

Music Club Infinity was on the second floor of a squat five-story building. Ten tables, each with three chairs facing the stage, dotted the floor
of the club. At seven o'clock, the place was half full with couples eating,
drinking, and quietly conversing. Elaborate lighting hung from the bat-
tens. The back wall was bare, except for twin stacks of amplifiers and trip-
lets of lights aimed at the stage. The Fairley Brothers were going to be well
seen, regardless of how many people were in attendance.

After checking in with the manager and performing a sound check
of "If You Want to Rock (You Must Learn to Roll)," Andy and Chris sat
down with Fumiko and ordered dinner.

They sat at a table silently sipping mugs of beer, waiting for their food,
when Andy said, "How about a reset?" Chris and Fumiko nodded vigorously in agreement. "Okay. Good. What'd you think of the game today?"
he asked Chris.

"Everyone was very polite."

"Is there something wrong with that?" Fumiko asked.

"Not at all. It's just different. Actually, I prefer the Japanese style. Being
jostled for nine innings by some drunk asshole with a giant cup of beer isn't
any fun."

Their meal began with miso soup, and as they cupped the bowls in their
hands, Fumiko said, "I don't mean to be nosy, but I would like to ask you
more about your life in Los Angeles."

"Is this part of the reset?" Chris asked.

"You don't have to speak about it if you would prefer not to."

"No, that's fine. I don't mind."

"You were married for some time, I believe?"

"That's right. Larissa was my wife. Twelve years. She left me for a money
manager."

"Were you happy?"

"I thought so. I was wrong."

"And, again, I'm sorry for asking, but I'm just very curious about my husband's brother. Have there been other women in your life since then?"

"A couple. Online things. They didn't work out."

"May I ask why?"

The waiter had brought skewers of yakitori, and Chris picked one up and pointed it at Fumiko. "Your wife, she asks a lot of questions."

"That she does."

"Well," Chris said to Fumiko, "I wonder if I'm just not made out for long-term relationships. I want too much, I give too little. At least that's what my ex-wife said."

They talked more about the baseball game—Fumiko was a big fan of the Buffaloes—until the next course was served. "Sukiyaki," said Andy of the beef simmering in a pot of soy sauce, onions, mushrooms, and tofu.

Their chopsticks were busy for a while, until Fumiko said, "Again, I hope I'm not overreaching, but Andy tells me he's seen you taking little yellow pills a couple of times during the tour. Is your health all right?"

Chris gave Andy a sour look, then reached into his pocket, took out a small black pill case, and opened it to reveal three yellows pills. "These?"

"I suppose so."

"They're Clonazepam."

"What's that for?" Andy asked. "Depression?"

"Anxiety."

"You have anxiety?" Andy asked, already knowing the answer.

"Doesn't everybody?" Chris replied.

"Well...no," Andy said.

Fumiko nodded sympathetically. "I think I have it. Very much so."

"You should try these," Chris said. "Very helpful."

"Medications like that are not so readily available in Japan."

Chris shrugged, slipped the pill box back into his pocket, and they turned their attention to the sukiyaki, with the brothers discussing the evening's setlist.

For dessert, the waiter brought a plate of red bean paste mochi and green tea cookies.

As he took a bite of his mochi, Chris said to Fumiko, "I don't know very much about Japan, obviously, but you strike me as being more outspoken than the average Japanese woman—or man."

"I probably am. My mother raised me that way. She spent a good deal of time in San Francisco, in the fifties and early sixties. She was born in Kyoto, but she was a full-fledged rebel. My grandparents cut off all ties with her. In fact, she was a character in Jack Kerouac's *On the Road*. A minor character, yes, but he deleted all mention of her from the final version of the manuscript at the insistence of his editor, Malcolm Cowley." Fumiko's neck was scarlet. She stared at Chris, clearly daring him to contradict her.

After several moments, he asked, "Why was she deleted?"

"Because she was Japanese, of course."

"Man. I thought Beatniks were, you know, progressive."

"You think they weren't racist against Japanese like every other American back then? And sexist? Please."

An awkward silence was broken by Andy: "These cookies are really delicious."

"No kidding," Chris said. "The whole meal. Boy." He turned to Fumiko. "And quite the interview session, too. You ought to work for Daisuke."

Fumiko nodded, as though she'd been seriously considering the idea.

"It's always a risk playing on a full stomach," Andy said, aggressively changing the subject once again.

"Why is that?" Fumiko asked.

"Farting on stage."

Chris grinned. "I just hit that E chord really loud, and nobody seems to notice."

By nine o'clock, all the tables at Music Club Infinity were full, as was every barstool. "All things considered," Andy whispered to Chris as they stood looking out from the wings of the stage, "you'd really have to call this Standing Room Only, wouldn't you?"

"As a matter of fact, you would."

"Do you see Daisuke out there?" Andy asked.

"I don't, no. He probably didn't want to show his face after those last interviews."

As the lights dimmed, the buzz in the crowd grew louder, and when the house manager shouted into the microphone, "Please welcome, from Los

Angeles, California, the Fairley Brothers!" the audience erupted in cheers. The brothers launched into their second biggest hit, and when they reached the chorus, everyone sang along: "Take me till Tuesday, baby, / Make the weekend last two more days."

By their fourth number, "Pickled and Juiced," it was clear that this was going to be their best show of the tour, by far, and as they dug deeper into their catalogue, enthusiasm for their set kept increasing. "The Psychics Are Crying," which, way back in the Sapporo wedding chapel, had elicited nothing but boredom, was met with shouts and fist pumping as Chris extended his solo into every variation on the E minor scale that he could think of.

When they finally finished after two hours, entirely exhausted, the roar for an encore was so insistent that they had to return to the stage. They had run through every song they'd rehearsed from their four albums, so Chris said, "This is a pretty new one. We premiered it about a week and a half ago in a flower store in Hokkaido."

"Hokkaido rocks!" a young man with a gleaming eyebrow stud yelled, and everyone cheered.

"It sure does," Chris said, "though this is more of a country song. Comic country, but nevertheless."

"'Car in the Kitchen'!" the same person yelled, and again the crowd hurrahed.

"That's right," Chris said. "How in the world did you know that?"

"TikTok!" the man yelled, and TikTok got an even bigger, drunker ovation.

"Well, then," Chris said. "Let's play it."

Somehow, the lyrics had leaked out into the world, so the audience knew when to join in on the refrain, "I parked the car...in the kitchen... again."

After a thunderous round of applause, and chants for "More! More! More!" Andy and Chris bowed, then left the stage for good.

When the house lights went up, there was a moan of genuine sadness and disappointment, but the Fairley Brothers were fairly buzzing with excitement as Fumiko met them backstage.

"I told you," she said to Chris. "Big stars. Any day now."

"I have to admit that felt good," he replied.

There was a knock on the greenroom door. A big man with a big red beard held out his arms, and Andy rushed over to give him a hug. "Jamie Ed! What in the world are you doing here?"

"I've been hearing about your tour. I wanted to come see you again. Great show, by the way, even though I had to stand in the very back."

"Thanks," Andy said, wiping the sweat from his neck with his hand. "You came all the way down from Kushiro?"

"Hell, yeah."

"Where's your girlfriend? Shiori?"

"Couldn't make it, I'm afraid. Y'all want to go out for a drink?"

Andy nodded, but Fumiko held up her phone. "We don't want to miss the last train back to Kyoto. We're going to have to hurry to catch it. I'm sorry."

"I'll have a beer with you," Chris said. And then to Andy and Fumiko: "And I'll see you both tomorrow."

Carrying his guitar case, with Fumiko squeezing his bicep, Andy slipped out the backstage door.

Jamie Ed gestured with his thumb. "There's a little place next door."

"Just one, though," Chris said.

In a tiny, dark bar hung with red lanterns, the two of them ended up talking about American politics over three beers. Jamie Ed turned out to be a true-blue Democrat, and he had nothing good to say about his state's politicians, especially Lindsey Graham, whom he referred to as Mrs. Lindsey Graham.

When Chris had had enough reminders of his country's dysfunction, he paid the tab and found himself wrapped in one of Jamie Ed's sweaty, all-encompassing hugs. "Wish I could be there tomorrow, but I teach in Kushiro on Thursday morning. I have to take a super early Shinkansen in the morning to get back by tomorrow night."

"How long is the trip?"

"Sixteen hours, give or take."

"Holy shit. You may be the Fairley Brothers' number one fan."

"I don't know. After tonight, I'd say you have quite a few number one fans."

Chris patted Jamie Ed on the back. "Well, thank you. It means a lot to both of us."

"Any time," Jamie Ed said. "Stay sane."

"I'll try."

Spent, happy, sitting in his bed, Chris opened his laptop to find an email from Daisuke indicating the final part of the interview had been posted.

Sitting on the couch in their apartment, drinking beer and watching late-night reruns of the day's high school baseball playoffs, Andy's phone hummed. He read Daisuke's email and texted the link to Fumiko, who was sitting next to him.

They all began to read.

THE FAIRLEY BROTHERS
IN JAPAN (PART IV)

The following interviews were conducted separately. Chris Fairley was interviewed in the Okonomiyaki Dotonbori Restaurant in Osaka on the evening of August 15. Andy Fairley was interviewed, with his wife, Fumiko Yoshida, in Nishiyogoku Coffee in Kyoto on the morning of August 16. I've combined their responses to my questions and done some light editing to omit duplicate questions on my part and to make the interview more conversational; I have not, however, omitted instances when the brothers are at odds about the interpretation of specific events. This is my final interview with the Fairley Brothers, whom I thank for their time and frankness. The interview is available in Japanese here.

DAISUKE HAYASHI: Toward the end of our last conversation, the Fairley Brothers had just performed at the Telluride Bluegrass Festival in June of 1988, and, unfortunately, the response was not what you'd hoped for.

CHRIS FAIRLEY: It was a disaster.

ANDY FAIRLEY: It wasn't that bad. I think people just needed more time to appreciate our new sound.

DH: Sadly, that was not to be. We know that Chris took a job with the Los Angeles Department of Water and Power. Meanwhile, Andy earned a Teaching English as a Second Language degree and began traveling the world as a teacher.

AF: A lot of fun for me, but Chris's work was also important, if unappreciated by most people.

CF: Human Resources: the great refuge of the mediocre and uninspired.

DH: I'm sure that's not true.

CF: Oh, but it is, it is.

AF: Also, we both got married. Chris much later, of course. Me in the early nineties, then divorced less than a year later.

DH: I didn't know that. Can you tell us more about the first Mrs. Fairley?

AF: It was a mistake on both our parts. She prefers to keep out of the lime-light, such as it is. And I've always honored that request.

DH: Was she a musician too?

AF: A kindergarten teacher. That's all I'll say. Anyway, I had some rough years, but then I started teaching abroad, and everything changed for the better.

DH: Where all have you taught?

AF: It's hard to remember sometimes. South Korea, Malaysia, Cambodia, Vietnam. Let's see, Russia and Kazakhstan.

FUMIKO YOSHIDA: Don't forget South America.

AF: That's right: a couple of countries in South America. Oh, and Côte d'Ivoire in Africa.

DH: Get a TEFL degree and see the world!

AF: And you really do get to know the people too. If, in some alternative universe, the Fairley Brothers had become a huge band, like, say, U2 or the Stones, or even Poor Ghost, and we'd toured the countries where I've lived, we would have just been zipping through them. Security guards would have been paid to keep people from getting close to us. No real interaction with other human beings at all. No thanks.

DH: Presumably you never would have met Fumiko?

AF: Exactly! The love of my life.

FY: I am lucky, too.

DH: Two lovebirds to be sure. Andy, one country you didn't mention in your list of places worked was Ireland. I know you and Chris toured there five years ago.

AF: We did.

DH: What was the experience like?

AF: Umm.

CF: Ireland was terrible.

DH: Why? What happened?

CF: It's more like what didn't happen. People didn't show up. Andy was working as a bartender in Dublin—he'd taken a little break from teaching—and he'd convinced me that Ireland was this bastion of folk music where the Fairley Brothers were practically revered as gods.

DH: But you weren't?

CF: Fuck no. Nobody had any idea who we were. In Japan, at least we have that car commercial to give us some kind of recognition. But in Ireland, we'd show up at a pub and people would *leave*. I mean, the average person, you're sitting there drinking a pint, listening to some music, and maybe you don't know the songs, but it's tuneful music, it's well crafted, so you'd just kind of hang around, right? But the Irish, they'd hear one song from the Fairley Brothers, and they'd just gulp down their Guinness and bounce.

DH: Did you ever—

CF: Dingle was the worst. Again, it's supposedly this haven for folk music, but if you're not playing "Danny Boy" or "Whiskey in the Jar" or whatever the fuck, people don't want to hear it. We actually got booed in Dingle. We're playing "Whenever I Hit the Road," our big hit, and people started booing: "Give us 'Carrickfergus,' or get off the feckin' stage!"

AF: My memories of Ireland aren't quite as bad as Chris's. It's true that overall we didn't have enthusiastic crowds, but we had a gig in Waterford that went really well. Granted, most of that particular audience was a tour group from America who happened to be about the right age to know our songs, but the Irish in the crowd, they were digging it, too.

CF: Andy had booked eight gigs, but after the fifth one—the one in Dingle—I just said, "Sorry, no more." I know that put him in an awkward position with the "promoters," I use that word loosely, of the final shows, but it was just a hard no for me. Period. The end.

AF: There was one incident, really bad, I admit. It was kind of a crisis, to be honest. Chris and I were standing outside this pub in Dingle, where we'd been booed. Our show had been cut short by the crowd, and the manager didn't want to pay us. It was a Saturday night, and there were a lot of drunks walking up and down the street, and we were just standing there with our guitar cases in our hands—Chris was telling me he was finished with the tour—and two drunk guys came up and started insisting that we play them a song.

I politely told them, no, we were through for the evening, but they got more and more in our grills.

Finally, Chris punched the more obnoxious one in the face. The guy fell back—boom. Out cold. So his friend comes around, and Chris hits him with his guitar case, and the guy kind of stumbles and Chris's guitar falls onto the pavement, and you can hear it *crack*. So Chris picks up the guitar by the neck and smashes it against the guy's head, and the guy goes down, but he's not unconscious. He just lying in the street, staring at us with this sort of disoriented menace.

And we just started running. We ran to our car, and we drove back to Dublin, though it was night and the roads were narrow and we were sure someone—the cops, the guys, their families—would be chasing us.

We drove to the Dublin airport and dropped off the car, then Chris got on a plane for America early the next morning.

I figured my time as a bartender in Ireland had come to an end. I kept waiting for a knock from the Garda, but it didn't come, and a couple of days later I had another teaching job lined up, and I was on my way to Kuala Lumpur.

DH: Amazing.

AF: I'm not sure I should have told that story. What's the statute of limitations on battery in Ireland?

DH: I have no idea.

CF: I do have one good memory. Andy and I were in Cork, sitting in a pub, waiting to go on. I knew it was going to be another lousy show, you could tell by how drunk and belligerent the crowd was. I said to him, "This isn't fun," and he looked at me, this serious look he used to get when we were kids, and he said, "It's fun being with you. I don't care about anything else." Just a moment of pure sweetness. I don't think I cried, but I felt like it.

AF: I guess Ireland seemed like the end of the Fairley Brothers. I was honestly surprised when Chris said he was willing to play in Japan. Albeit grudgingly.

DH: Why do you think he agreed?

AF: There's something about playing music with another person, or other people. It's just this different way of communicating that we humans don't have in any other context. I think he missed that.

CF: I came to Japan because I'm retired, and I didn't have anything else going on. And I missed my brother. I don't mind saying that.

DH: I know you'll want to push back on this, but I must ask again about Molly. I've since learned, from a little Internet sleuthing, that her surname was Moore.

AF: You wait until the very end to ask the hard questions.

DH: It's now or never.

CF: What about Molly Moore?

DH: We've learned from our previous interviews that you and Andy met her back in 1985?

CF: ...

DH: Initially, she was Chris's girlfriend, then she left Chris for Andy.

CF: ...

AF: So?

DH: And we know she died, but we don't know how that happened.

CF: ...

AF: Sadly, she committed suicide.

DH: Not to sound morbid, but can you tell us more?

AF: Chris had read her obit, which was cagey about the cause of death, but I had the number of Molly's sister, who found her. I got her number and gave her a call.

DH: How did Molly die?

AF: She cut her wrists. Vertical, from hand to elbow. The serious way.

DH: Had she been depressed for a while?

AF: I don't know. We'd been apart for a long time.

DH: So, you hadn't spoken to her about her depression?

AF: As I said—

FY: It's not his fault.

DH: I'm not implying that it was.

FY: It sounds like you are. She wasn't right for him. He's told me all about it.

DH: Really? What did he say?

FY: ...

DH: In your defense, Andy, she could have gone back to Chris, after the two of you broke up. It wasn't all on you. Why did Chris stay angry at you for so long?

AF: That's a question you'd have to ask him.

DH: Chris, why did you stay angry at Andy for so long?

CF: ...

DH: I never met the woman, of course, but she sounds unstable.

CF: You don't know what the fuck you're talking about, Daisuke.

DH: Then explain it to me.

CF: There are certain times in a person's life when good things can happen, despite everything being in league against them. There was a moment when Molly and I could have been good together, a real long-term couple. A partnership. I'm sure of it. But Andy came in and spoiled it. The infuriating part is he probably didn't even mean to. He was just casually charming, and he said *yes* when he should have said *no*.

DH: Do you think about her very often?

AF: No. Occasionally, but mostly no.

CF: I mourned her death at the time. I still do. In fact, I'll tell you a story that I've never told anyone before, not even my brother.

DH: Please do. I should say here to our readers that in my opinion the history of the Fairley Brothers is like a narrative Russian doll—one story nested inside the other. You have no idea when you'll reach the final tale.

CF: Do you want to hear the story, or not?

DH: By all means.

CF: Molly came to see me, not long before she died.

DH: *Really?*

CF: Really. This was in the summer of 1991, more than thirty years ago. I hadn't seen her since 1986, I suppose. It was before the Internet, so I'm not sure how she found me. I thought I had an unlisted number in the phone book, but maybe not. Anyway, somehow she found out where I worked, and she showed up at my office at the Department of Water and Power.

DH: That must have been a surprise.

CF: A shock, definitely. I was just getting established in my new job, and the receptionist shows in this woman I barely recognized. Kind of matted hair, too much mascara, pale and shivering. A scar on her neck.

DH: The years had not been kind to her.

CF: Rock and roll specifically, I learned after she sat down and started spilling out her heart, had not been kind to her. After me and Andy, she'd found her way to other not-so-famous musicians, each one less and less concerned about her welfare as a person.

DH: And what did she want from you?

CF: Why do you assume she wanted something?

DH: Did she not?

CF: Well. Yes. She did. Money, of course. Not a lot, and I wasn't exactly flush at that point, but I had my checkbook with me, and I wrote her a check for five hundred dollars. I asked her if I could see her after work. Meet her for a drink. There was a bar around the corner, on First Street, where DWP people used to go. Kind of a dive, but I told her I'd clock out early and be there in an hour to hear more of her story and see if there was anything else I could do. She got up and gave me a kiss on the cheek and left.

That kiss. I didn't feel anything. At all. I only felt the *absence* of everything I used to feel. And somehow that made me feel a whole lot worse, as though I had to resuscitate the memory of what she used to be, to keep it alive, to keep *her* alive.

DH: What happened? Did you meet her at the bar?

CF: I didn't leave when I said I was going to leave. I got cold feet. It was three hours, not one, before I got there. The bartender said she'd gone off with another guy.

DH: ...

CF: So that's the final chapter of the story of Molly Moore, at least as far as my part is concerned. I read about her death in the papers about a month later, a very short obit in the *LA Times*. I wouldn't have seen it if I hadn't been looking for it. But I didn't do anything. I didn't contact the family. I didn't go to the funeral. I just abandoned her the way she'd abandoned me.

She left a big hole in my heart, and when I got married to Larissa, well, she couldn't fill that hole. No one could.

DH: ...

CF: I don't think I've ever heard you speechless before, Daisuke.

DH: For some reason, I can't help thinking of that old Irish song, "Molly Malone": *(Singing)*

> *She died of a fever*
> *And sure no one could save her*
> *And that was the end of sweet Molly Malone*
> *Now her ghost wheels her barrow*
> *Through the streets broad and narrow*
> *Crying, "Cockles and mussels, alive, alive, oh!"*

CF: Except, of course, that wasn't her name. And that's a really tasteless comparison.

AF: Daisuke, I feel like up until this morning, you've given us a lot of mostly easy questions to answer. You haven't shied away from controversy, but you've been fair. More like a friendly biographer than a tabloid journalist.

But now? I don't know, it just feels like you've set a trap for me. For Chris, too, I assume. Like you're not the person we thought you were.

DH: And that feels unfair to me. I'm only asking the questions that need to be asked to wrap everything up.

AF: Well, I don't know.

DH: Let's switch gears, okay? You're coming to the end of your Japanese tour—three more concerts to go. What has the experience been like?

AF: I would have to give a shout-out to my lovely wife, Fumiko. She put the whole thing together.

FY: Andy is so talented. I wanted people to hear his music.

DH: And Chris? It's his music, too, right?

FY: Of course.

DH: How do you and Chris get along?

FY: I've never met him. I will later today, at a baseball game.

DH: What's your *impression* of Chris, based on what Andy has told you about the tour?

FY: His guitar playing is quite good.

DH: Anything else?

FY: A strong sense of melody.

DH: Anything more personal?

FY: ...

DH: What's your impression of Fumiko?

CF: I've never met her. But she's good at organizing things.

DH: That's it? Do you feel like she's interfered with the band at all? Is she the Yoko Ono of the Fairley Brothers?

CF: That's ridiculous. The Fairley Brothers wouldn't be playing at all if it weren't for Fumiko.

DH: And the tour itself?

CF: I've learned a lot about myself and my capacity for handling disappointment. It's greater than I thought.

AF: The tour has been a jumble of images, sights, sounds. Lots of great audiences, some unusual venues, which turned out to be a lot of fun. It's not over, though. Three more nights.

DH: Not quite over, no. I wonder how you imagine the people listening to your songs actually respond to them? Do they get what you are trying to do, or are they just humming along to the melody? What are they thinking, for instance, when they listen to "West Hollywood in the Rain"?

AF: That's impossible to know, isn't it? People's reaction to music is...mysterious.

CF: I imagine it's different for every person, depending on how well they know and understand the song, whether it calls up any personal associations—

DH: I believe music without personal associations is empty. Blank. Void.

CF: Okay. That's definitely a thought. Bottom line, though: I still can't believe that you, or anyone, could be so interested in the life and times of the Fairley Brothers.

DH: As I told you when we first spoke in Lake Akan, Japanese-language popular music begins with Happy End and folk rock. You are part of a great tradition.

CF: But all our songs are in English.

DH: It's the spirit that counts. Besides, in Japan, there's a subculture for everything.

LIVE HOUSE KYOTO NOCTURNE

Kyoto
Wednesday, August 17

Chris's phone alarm woke him at eight; he was supposed to meet Andy at Kyoto Station at ten. As he struggled into consciousness, fragments of last night's dream about Music Club Infinity were mixed with actual memories of the gig. Japanese fans, their arms raised in joy, were double exposed with images of Larissa joyfully copulating with a man whose face was a fuzzy blank.

Chris clicked the television on, and immediately hit mute. It was a piece about Shohei Ohtani, the phenomenal pitcher and designated hitter for the Los Angeles Angels. The Angels had been blown out by the Seattle Mariners, eight to two, but Ohtani had gone three for four, with two singles and a triple to deep left center.

When the camera cut back to the studio, the announcers—two female and one male—seemed to be ecstatic about Ohtani's performance, despite the Angels' loss. Chris was a Dodgers fan, of course, but he couldn't blame the Japanese for revering Ohtani, who might well be the best player in the world.

Chris went to the bathroom to shower and get ready. As he stood over the toilet, he saw that his urine was once again streaked with blood. He thought it looked like the color of the Angels' jerseys.

When Andy woke up and went into their apartment's tiny kitchen, Fumiko was dressed and drinking a cup of black coffee.

"I have to go to work," she said.

"But you'll be there tonight, right? At Live House Kyoto Nocturne?"

"I know where it is. I booked the gig, remember? And we agreed we put the money in our savings?"

"We're going to put most of the money in our savings. But you only live once. Some of my colleagues from ILJ are coming, and it's Chris's next-to-last night. I think a little drinks party afterwards would be nice."

Fumiko frowned, but Andy gave her a kiss. She patted his cheek, shook her head, then she was out the door.

Andy had texted Chris, "Meet me at the Raptor." Chris responded with "???" but Andy did not reply.

At Kyoto Station, Chris disembarked from his train and made his way past beverage machines and convenience stores and a lighted billboard for an ear, nose, and throat clinic with the English slogan: "Total Nose Support." He walked until he found the lockers, where he stored his luggage and gig bag in one locker, and his guitar in another. Then he followed the signs to the concourse, a futuristic fantasy of cascading escalators and polished steel and glass.

As he rode down an escalator, Chris was surprised how quiet the station was. Other than an electronic dinging and the occasional train announcement, it *sounded* almost empty, although he could see plenty of people below, scurrying to and from the tracks. On the ground floor, the main sound was the rumble of suitcase wheels being rolled across the tiles. Over the entry doors, a digital video showed a geisha bowing—apparently to departing passengers—then the screen filled with cherry trees before it faded to a series of temples set amid autumn foliage. In the air was a whiff of diesel, and possibly donuts.

Chris began looking for someone to ask about the Raptor's location, but everyone in the fast-moving crowd turned away as he approached, and the few who listened to his query either didn't speak English or had no idea what he was talking about.

He exited the station. Past the entrance plaza and across the street stood a white tower with a red observation deck near its top. Buses idled in a loop ahead of him. To the left was something called "Porta Dining," which sounded unappetizing, so Chris headed right and soon realized there was a small crowd of people congregating around a bench. Behind that bench stood a five-foot-tall statue of an upright raptor in a lab coat. Its wicked claws extended from its sleeves as though it were welcoming a patient for an experiment.

From behind, someone tapped Chris on the shoulder.

He turned and asked Andy, his hair still wet from the shower, "Does Kyoto have some sort of connection with raptors?"

"I wouldn't think so. I assume it's some kind of advertisement." Andy looked his brother up and down. "How you doing this morning? You look a little shaken."

"I'm fine, fine. What about you?"

"Okay." Japanese people flashed past, glancing at the brothers, then turning quickly away.

"So," Andy said slowly, "did you read Daisuke's interview?"

"Yeah. I take it you did, too."

"What'd you think?"

"I thought he made our lives post-1988 sound fairly grim. What about you?"

"Yeah. I mean, we just answered his questions, but I had this feeling during the interview that he was taking care of some unfinished business regarding the Fairley Brothers."

"I had that feeling, too," Chris began, when someone else tapped him on the shoulder.

He turned. "Are you Chris Fairley?" a pretty young Japanese woman asked.

"I am."

"I love your songs," she said. "Very relatable. And you too, Andy. Beautiful singing voice."

"Well, thank you," Andy said.

"I would come to your show tonight, but the tickets, they are sold out."

"They are?" Chris said, genuinely surprised.

She held up her phone. "But I still listen to you on Spotify." She sang, "Whenever I hit the road—the road! / Whenever I hit the road."

"Very nice," Andy said.

The young woman bowed, then walked a few yards away where she was met by two friends. She whispered to her friends, then pointed at Chris and Andy. "Rock on, Fairley Brothers!" the three of them shouted. They made devil horns with their hands, took pictures with their phones, and covered their mouths when they giggled.

Chris raised his eyebrows and Andy smiled. "Come on," Andy said, gesturing back toward the station. "I'm going to show you the most famous temple in Kyoto."

Andy bought two tickets at the ticket machine, and they boarded the southbound Nara line, disembarking at Inari station. Outside, they were immediately greeted with enormous vermilion torii with black tops and bases. A concrete pathway led up a gentle hill to a ticket booth and an enormous orange and white gate leading into the temple complex. Inside were crowds and shrines, incense and pines, bells and lanterns and booths selling talismans and amulets.

The brothers followed the crowds up the hill, where two stone foxes stood guard over a path that led to a densely packed line of much smaller torii that felt like entering a tunnel of orange and black, punctuated by the occasional lantern. A fine rain misted across their faces. "There's ten thousand of these gates," Andy said. "All of them donated by Japanese businesses. Those are the names of the businesses etched into the wood. Inari is the god of rice and of commerce. So, it's good luck to be part of this place, the Senbon Torii."

"Impressive," Chris said, as they huffed uphill, "but kind of discouraging. Like someplace this beautiful ought to be ruled by the god of music or poetry, not technology or...widgets."

"Some of my students say that business is like music and poetry. They call it the highest art form."

On and on they trudged. A new line of gates was even smaller, barely a foot higher than the brothers' heads. The crowds had become so dense it was hard to avoid stepping on the person in front or being stepped on by the person behind. A sign overhead said: "Please go right way." Almost everyone was wearing a mask, despite the August heat. At the top of the hill were more shrines, more incense, more people. A middle-aged man and his wife were staring at them. Andy gave a half wave, and the man yelled out, "Rock on, Fairley Brothers!"

"We're big in Kyoto," Chris said.

"Totally," Andy replied.

The rain began to pelt down through the pine branches in earnest and Andy took two plastic rain parkas from his backpack, handing one to Chris.

"I know this is going to sound spoiled," Chris said, slipping into the parka, "but is it possible to go someplace less crowded? I mean, a temple still, or whatever—it doesn't have to be so spectacular—but just not with so many people."

Andy pulled out his phone. "It's eleven. We can do that, but it might take a while. Are you okay with that?"

"Absolutely."

They pushed their way downhill through the rain-spattered crowds and rode the Nara line back to Kyoto station, where they took an escalator up to the bus station. While they waited for their bus, a digital sign in Japanese, English, and Korean spelled out a list of rules for passengers: "Please hold on to your luggage at all times in order to prevent them from moving around. Please do not wear your backpack on the train or bus. Instead, please hold onto your backpack with your arms. Please do not throw trash away at the bus stop. Do not lean on the bus stop or stand too close to the road. Please refrain from shouting or causing a commotion at the bus stop while waiting for the bus to arrive."

"Have you ever actually seen someone shouting or causing a commotion at the bus stop?" Chris asked.

"I think that one's for foreigners," Andy said.

Soon, the bus pulled into the station and was half filled with wet and silent passengers. It headed north, and before long, was lumbering loudly uphill. Their knees pressed against the seats in front of them, the brothers looked out the window, watching Kyoto go past: small shops and two-story houses, apartment buildings and restaurants, pedestrians sheltering under clear plastic umbrellas, a walled temple, the omnipresent tangle of overhead wires, a FamilyMart, a Lawson, a 7-Eleven, another FamilyMart.

They were the only non-Japanese on the bus, and each stop was announced in Japanese only. After forty minutes, Andy motioned for Chris to get off, and they were standing in front of a wooden temple gate, with a steep tiled roof and two large round windows.

"Genkō-an," Andy said. "Off the beaten path, but worth the trip."

As they walked into the small complex in a light rain, Andy said, "That last one, Inari, was a Shinto temple, this one is Zen Buddhist."

"What's the difference?"

"I mean, that's a question for somebody else, but I think Shinto is more focused on the spirits, the *kami*, and it's not so much about explaining the world. Just getting in touch and appeasing these local gods who can help you out. Zen—well, it's trying to find enlightenment, but coming at it from all these weird angles. Like, not overintellectualizing things. Neither one of them is similar to an American church, obviously. It's not like there's some preacher in the pulpit shouting at everyone." Andy wiped the rain from his forehead. "That's probably a horrible explanation."

"Sounds good to me."

They took off their shoes and padded quietly along the corridors of the temple. The air was humid, and the rain had turned to mist, lightly blurring the rock gardens and stone lanterns covered with lichen, the small pond and the Japanese maples, their trunks blanketed in moss, a few with leaves just hinting at yellow.

In one room of the shrine, a small sign on the wall instructed visitors to look up at the ceiling, a portion of which was covered with brown footprints. The sign indicated the ceiling had once been the floor of a ferocious battle, and it had been placed where it was to soothe the spirits of the dead warriors, whose feet had made the bloody impressions.

"Super soothing," Chris muttered.

In the main hall, a circular window on the left of one wall paired with a square window on the right. Andy picked up a leaflet lying on the mat floor. "The round window is called *satori no mado*. It's the Window of Realization, or Enlightenment. The square window is *mayoi no mado*, the Window of Delusion or Ignorance. The life of *samsara*," Andy said. "Human suffering."

"Pretty sure I know which window is mine," Chris said.

"Me, too. But that doesn't mean you can't strive for the circle."

"Or at least inch toward it."

Outside, as they put their shoes back on to leave, a sparrow flitted around inside a grove of bamboo, as though it were trapped. "We should go help the little guy out," Andy said, walking toward the bird. However, the moment the sparrow sensed Andy's approach, it burst out of the bamboo and flew over the temple wall.

"For some reason, that reminds me of a haiku," Andy said, "I think it's by Basho. It goes something like: 'In Kyoto, / hearing the cuckoo's cry, / I long for Kyoto.'"

"Kind of the human condition, maybe? Wanting what you can't have?"

"Except in this instance, the person actually does have what they want. But they want more of it somehow."

"Philosophy and poetry make me hungry," Chris said. "Can we find somewhere to eat?"

It was after two, and as they walked downhill on Takagamine Kuormoncho, they realized the few establishments serving food were all closed.

Finally, they discovered an open bakery, a tiny place with nowhere to sit. After Andy pointed to the items they wanted to purchase, the elderly woman behind the counter squinted her eyes and asked, "Fairley Brothers?"

Andy replied in Japanese, and she smiled and spoke at some length.

"What'd she say?" Chris asked.

"It's an honor for her to have us in her shop."

"That's all?"

"She expressed the sentiment elaborately and with some warmth."

They each bought a croissant, a bun dusted in powdered sugar, and a hot dog baked into a roll. "Bye-bye, Fairley Brothers!" the woman called as they left the bakery.

"I feel like we're the most famous people in Kyoto," Chris said.

"Thanks to social media, right now, that might be true."

The bakery sold no beverages, but there was a vending machine further down the block, and they washed down their food with bottles of cold water as they continued walking.

"What did they call this hot dog thing back in elementary?" Chris asked. "Remember, they used to serve it in the cafeteria? Pup in a bun?"

"No, no, it was pigs in a blanket."

"That's right." Chris swallowed the last of his food. "By the way, where are we going?"

"The Imamiya Shinto Shrine. We're almost there. It's very photogenic."

It was, indeed, with an impressive red and white gate outside. Inside were weathered stone statues of guardian dogs and lions, paper lanterns painted with kanji, bronze lanterns engraved with dragons. Incense smoke wafted picturesquely across the scene.

Andy led the way to a small shrine in which a stone the size of a football was placed atop two silk pillows on a wooden stand. "You probably want to rub that stone for good luck," Andy said. "Then touch any part of your body that isn't right."

"I guess that means I'll have to grab my dick."

"Really? Is that still an issue?"

Chris shrugged. "Can't hurt, right? I need all the luck I can get."

When Chris was finished, Andy reached in, rubbed the stone, then rubbed the top of his head.

"Problem?" Chris asked.

"Just a little headache. They've been kind of bugging me the last couple of months."

"Are you worried?"

"It's nothing," Andy said. "By the way, how are you doing? We've done a lot of walking. Are you done with temples and shrines for the day?"

"I don't know. It'll probably be a long time before I have a chance like this again. I could maybe do one more," Chris said.

"There's another one just down the street."

"Let's go."

They crossed Imamiya Dori and followed a street next to a low brick wall from behind which grew thirty-foot-tall bamboo stalks. They turned left down an unmarked lane and were soon inside the Daitokuji Buddhist temple complex, which, save for the inevitable chirping and clicking of amorous cicadas, was empty and quiet, as though everyone had moved out long ago.

In one of the temples, they paid an entrance fee to a monk who seemed to be about sixteen years old, then took off their shoes and wandered down a wooden corridor to sit and stare at a Zen rock garden. According to a flyer they'd received at the gate, the gravel, vigorously raked into what looked like waves, was meant to give the impression of rough seas. Jagged stones in the center conveyed "islands of energy." It was a small space, maybe fifty feet long and twenty feet across, but the longer the brothers sat there, cross-legged, the larger it seemed to become.

"I kind of get it now," said Chris. "That feeling of being transported out of this place by going deep inside the place."

"Very Zen, man," Andy replied, standing up. "Now that you've reached enlightenment, do you want to see my apartment?"

"The gig's at nine, right? And I still have to get my stuff from the train station and check into my hotel."

Andy looked at his phone. "It's just three thirty. We've got plenty of time."

On the two buses they rode from Daitokuji to Andy's apartment in the far southeast of the Ukyo Ward, they were recognized three times: by a teenaged boy, a middle-aged woman, and an elderly woman whom Andy referred to as "a grandma."

"How do they know us?" Chris asked. "It's not like we're on TV."

"Apparently, we're big on TikTok. Also, as you may have noticed, we're the only non-Japanese almost everywhere we go, so we're pretty easy to pick out."

"And Grandma looks at social media?"

"Maybe her grandkids do? Or she just likes the Fairley Brothers."

Andy and Fumiko's apartment was on the third floor of a building in a nondescript neighborhood of four- and five-story apartments. Wedged in a rectangle between the buildings was a rice paddy, green and thriving.

Andy unlocked the front door, took off his shoes, and indicated that Chris should do so as well.

Then Andy took his brother on a tour of the apartment, which lasted less than two minutes. He began by opening the door to the bathroom, with its small but deep tub. Then the brothers stood in the kitchen/dining room/living room area with its low couch and an even lower table, a microwave, and a two-burner stove. A large HDTV bolted to the wall had been left on and was showing the high school baseball championships at a very low volume. Someone hit a single, to the delight of fans and players, all of whom rhythmically clacked thundersticks together.

The bedroom had two armoires and a tatami floor, with two futons folded in half and leaning against the wall.

The third room was long and narrow and contained two desks, each with its own laptop computer, and a bookcase overflowing with books.

"That's it," Andy said, when they were back in the main room.

"Very cozy," Chris said. He took out his phone. "It's four thirty. I feel like I should check into my hotel and take a little rest before tonight's gig."

"I booked you a hotel right across from the station."

"That's nice. How much do I owe you?"

"It's all paid for from our tour proceeds."

"We must be making a fortune."

"I told you this tour was going to pay off," Andy winked.

"I'll walk you over to the nearest subway station so you can get to the hotel. Try to leave for the gig by seven. There's a cab stand in front of the train station. I'll text you the club information and address in Japanese, and you can just show it to the driver."

"Sounds easy." As he was leaving, Chris stopped in the doorway. "I've been wondering...that thing Fumiko said about her mom being cut out of Kerouac's *On the Road*. Is that true?"

"Could be, though probably not. Fumiko's mom died last year, but when I met her, she seemed to be full of it. Lots of conspiracy theories. Still, I don't doubt that's what she told her daughter, and I'm sure Fumiko believes it."

"She stands by her people, your lady wife."

"She sure does."

Andy lay down for what he thought would be a fifteen-minute nap, but when he awoke it was nearly six and Fumiko was in the kitchen cooking a pot of beef and udon noodles. The smell of chili sauce and green onions and ginger filled the room. Andy walked to his wife, put his arms around her, and breathed the aroma in deeply and appreciatively.

"You think your brother will make it to his hotel *and* to the show to-night?" she asked, leaning around Andy to stir the pot.

"He's a grown man," Andy said.

Fumiko smiled. "Like you."

"What do you mean, exactly?"

"You know what I mean," she said, turning down the heat under the pot and kissing him hard.

Chris's taxi pulled up in front of Live House Kyoto Nocturne just as Andy and Fumiko were getting out of their cab. There was a line of about fifty people waiting for the club to open, and when they saw the Fairley Brothers, they cheered and began singing a mix of "Whenever I Hit the Road" and "Take Me Till Tuesday," with one lone tenor voice wailing the chorus of "Never Believed You Anyway."

The brothers waved to their fans, and someone who must have been watching for their arrival via the camera above the door opened it up just wide enough for the three of them to slip inside.

Once in the building, two young men took their guitars and pointed up a flight of stairs. With Fumiko in the lead, they ascended to a club painted all in black with a low ceiling but a good lighting system and a mirror ball over the audience. The stage was two feet above the club floor, but the microphones were all set up, and the brothers only needed to perform "The Psychics Are Crying" to know that they were dealing with professionals. The sound was superb.

The two young men—could they be called "roadies"?—had placed the brothers' guitars in stands behind the microphones, so Andy and Chris went to the bar, where Fumiko was talking with the bartender.

"All sold out," she said to Andy when he leaned over her shoulder.

"So we were told," Chris said.

"Who told you that?" she asked.

"A fan we met this morning."

Fumiko raised her eyebrow and looked skeptically at her husband. "A female 'fan'?"

"We're big in Japan," Andy said, smiling at his wife.

Chris cleared his throat. "This is not a criticism in any way, okay? But I'm wondering if maybe we should have come straight to Kyoto? Instead of touring the hinterlands of Hokkaido?"

"Those 'hinterlands,'" Fumiko said. "That is why this tour is going so well now. If you hadn't played at Lake Akan, you probably would never have met Daisuke. His blog is responsible for much of this. He has tens of thousands of devoted followers, you know?"

"It wasn't the car commercial?" Chris asked.

"That was just the way in. Without Daisuke, this place would be half empty. If you were lucky."

The bartender looked at Chris and Andy.

"Beer," Andy said.

"Could you make me a margarita?" Chris asked. "Patrón Silver. Salt on the rim."

"Patrón Silver, salt. Yes."

"Very California," Fumiko said.

At eight, the owners opened the doors to Live House Kyoto Nocturne, and the crowd came streaming upstairs. A few people lingered at the bar, but most of them headed toward the front of the stage, jostling with one another for the best spots.

The Fairley Brothers and Fumiko were in the greenroom—a pleasant twenty-by-twenty space with a comfortable couch and two comfortable chairs—watching the club floor on a small black-and-white monitor. "It's filling up," Andy said.

"Too full," Fumiko said. "I'll talk to the manager and see about moving to another club tomorrow. It's your last night, and we're going to need a bigger space." She turned to Chris: "Unless you want to add some more dates?"

"I don't know. I've got my plane ticket already."

"You can change that," Andy said. "The tour will pay for it."

"Let me think about it."

Andy pointed to the monitor. "Hey! There's my crew from International Languages Japan. There's Jessica, Eduardo, and Cassie. And I think that's Doug Nakao." He turned to Fumiko. "He's from San Francisco."

"I know. You've mentioned that several times."

The stage manager knocked on the door and told them it was time, and when the Fairley Brothers took the stage, the masked audience erupted. Hands waved in the air. Cell phones were pointed at the stage. A scattering of audience members was soaked through—it must have been pouring outside—but they were, if anything, more enthusiastic than their neighbors.

The brothers began with "Don't Give It Away," a deep cut from *What the Folk?* that Chris regretted writing. It was the song that had led to the audience exodus at Telluride all those years ago, and he felt the chorus—"Don't give it away / Do what you can to make love stay"—was corny. However, Andy had argued via a text message earlier in the evening that the song had a lovely melody. "No one will know it," Chris had texted back, but Andy replied, "You'd be surprised."

And so Chris was singing, "The needle's primed, the ink is black / On your arm, a one-eyed Jack," and the audience was humming along with the verse, not exactly in sync, but not altogether out of tune. But they did know the chorus, and its mournful B minor strain filled Live House Kyoto Nocturne as though the club were a church, and the crowd its parishioners.

The blues rocker "Turpentine" went over well, as it always did, but when Andy insisted on a cover of Woody Guthrie's "Pastures of Plenty" both brothers expected a letdown. That didn't happen, and some of the audience even sang along: "My poor feet have traveled a hot dusty road."

Having established that anything they played would be well received, the brothers dove deep into their catalog, playing "Except the Dying" from *Never Believed You Anyway* and "Sunday Afternoons" from *Meet the Fairley Brothers* and "Portraits of the Insane" from *Dark as Dark Can Get*.

They resurrected The Byrds' "I'll Feel a Whole Lot Better (When You're Gone)," a crowd favorite from their very first days, and that met with thunderous applause, as did a cover of Joni Mitchell's "California."

Once they moved toward more familiar original material, an even bigger buzz filled the air, as though the Rolling Stones were shifting from *December's Children* outtakes to "You Can't Always Get What You Want." Howls of pleasure erupted as Chris strummed the chords to "On Your Own" and Andy sang the chorus: "All the maps of hidden treasures / They will never take your measure / You will have to find it on your own."

When the song ended, a chant came up from a group of young men toward the front of the stage: "Car in Kitchen! Car in Kitchen!" they repeated until the entire audience joined in.

Chris played an F chord, held it for a moment, then sang, "I parked the car in the kitchen / Kind of run into the kitchen sink." And the audience joined him, in a cacophony of voices: "But the refrigerator's still working / So I guess I'll get me another drink."

The mirror ball spun sparks of light in circles around the room. Nearly everyone was holding up their phones through nearly every song.

"We love you, Kyoto!" Andy said after the rapturous applause that greeted the conclusion of "Blue All Week Long."

"We love you, Andy!" several young women shouted.

Both brothers glanced over at Fumiko, who smiled grimly. Then she stood up and called out, "I love you, Andy!"

"I love you, too, Fumiko!" he yelled back, and the crowd went crazy.

The Fairley Brothers had recorded fifty-three songs across their four albums, and they played thirty of them that night, finally stopping in exhaustion at the end of their third encore, "The Psychics Are Crying," Chris holding the high C on his high E string—the highest note on his guitar—for a full twenty seconds before collapsing to the stage.

When they dragged themselves back to the greenroom, exhausted, sweating, ecstatic, Fumiko was there to meet them. Andy gave Fumiko a hug, then he dropped onto the comfortable couch, next to his brother.

There was a knock on the door. Fumiko opened it, and a man with gray hair and a face mask stepped inside and bowed at the brothers.

"I will talk to them, okay?" she said.

The man bowed again, and still without speaking, stepped out of the room and shut the door.

"What's the big mystery?" Chris asked.

"He is Mr. Minato Hara. He wants to make a film of your last concert of the tour."

"A film?" Chris repeated.

"He is an independent documentary filmmaker. I looked online. He has made two films. One is about the last Ainu people of Hokkaido, and the other looks like kind of a travelogue around Kyushu. But they are actual movies."

"Do we get any money out of this?" Chris asked. "I mean, we don't even have a manager. Who's going to look at the contract, assuming there even is one?"

"I could be your manager," Fumiko said.

"She practically already is," Andy agreed.

Fumiko pointed at a manila folder on the table. "He's already given me the contract. I can look at it tonight."

"And what kind of a cut do you get?"

"No agent fees. You and Andy split the full take fifty-fifty."

"Can't argue with that," Chris said.

"One issue. Mr. Hara can only do the filming on Friday, not tomorrow. However, I have already spoken with the owner of this club, and he has agreed to allow you to play at a larger venue on Friday night: the Rock Me Hall and Theatre Club, which he also owns."

"Doesn't that hold like five hundred people?" Andy asked.

"Five hundred and fifty."

"And you think we can fill it?" Chris asked.

Fumiko replied: "I know we can."

"I don't know," Chris said. "I mean, I love playing a great show, and all, but a big part of me wants to get back home where I can kind of process the last two weeks. Make sense of everything. I don't feel like I can do that in Japan."

"Mr. Hara will pay for changing your plane ticket," Fumiko said.

Andy looked at his brother. "It's *one* day. Come on, man." After a moment, Andy added: "What could it matter?"

Chris had been fiddling with a guitar pick. He stopped, put it in his pocket, and said, "Okay."

"All right!" Andy said, giving Chris a high five. "Now we can go party with the TEFL teachers! Believe me, they are *insane*."

They were, indeed, insane—Kayla, a twenty-something novice teacher from Kentucky; Eduardo, a suave graduate student from Santiago; Cassie, a plump middle-aged woman from Sheffield; and Doug, a divorced man in his forties from Daly City. Later, the group was joined by International Languages Japan's Kyoto branch manager Mr. Shimazaki, a man in his fifties with dyed green hair that was entirely at odds with his conservative business suit.

They were all full of an edgy electric energy, which seemed the natural state of the Club Brainsick, where Kayla had led them after the show. The club featured lasers; an LED-lit dance floor; dry ice; and a steady thumping of rap, techno, and J-pop and K-pop.

Andy's colleagues were genuinely excited that one of their own was something like a rock star—someone who, like them, powered through his days teaching children how to say their colors, showing teenagers how to enliven their language with idiomatic expressions, instructing businessmen how to negotiate accurately yet politely, and gently preparing older people for visits from children and grandchildren who no longer, or had never, spoken their mother tongue. It was hard work. Rocking out at Club Brainsick was so much more appealing in comparison.

"Listen," Kayla, drawled as she draped an arm over Andy's shoulder and spoke loudly and drunkenly into his ear. "You guys are better than Luke Bryan and Jason Aldean combined."

"Thank you," Andy shouted back, as Fumiko undraped the young woman's arm from her husband's shoulder. "Though I don't think we're really a country act. We've always thought of ourselves as folk rock."

"That song about the car in the kitchen sure is country."

"It's kind of a novelty song. But thank you, Kayla. We appreciate your coming to the show."

"Of course," she said, and gave him a big lipsticky kiss on his cheek, which Fumiko immediately wiped off with a tissue.

"She is not a nice person," Fumiko shouted in Andy's ear after Kayla had left.

"She's just young."

"That's what I'm saying."

The bass pumped and pumped, the dancers' limbs undulated along with the rhythm.

Meanwhile, Chris was backed against the bar, trying to drink a gin and tonic as he fielded questions from Eduardo, Doug, and Mr. Shimazaki.

Eduardo yelled, "Why did you guys stop playing together? You seem like you're pretty good."

"It's complicated," Chris replied.

Eduardo took a long swallow of his Moscow Mule and signaled to the bartender for another. "Okay, then in one sentence."

"People didn't want to listen to us anymore."

"Fair enough."

Doug slipped a JUUL from his coat pocket and inhaled deeply. He crossed his eyes, then blew the vapor out through his nostrils.

"THC?" Eduardo asked. Doug nodded and passed the JUUL to Eduardo, who took a monster hit. He looked over at their boss. "Mr. Shimazaki?"

"Fuck yeah," Mr. Shimazaki said.

"I wanna know something," Doug said, the tip of his tongue getting in the way of his words. "Why don't you have any songs about birds? I mean, birds...Jesus. That's a great subject for a song."

"Maybe it's because all the great songs about birds have already been written. There's 'Free Bird,' of course."

All three men raised a clenched fist in the air and exclaimed, "'Free Bird'!"

"That's right," Chris continued. "And then 'Rockin' Robin' and the Beatles' 'Blackbird' and 'When Doves Cry' and 'Fly Like an Eagle' and—"

"Don't forget 'Songbird,'" Doug shouted against the music, slurring 'Songbird' so that it sounded like "Slungturd." "Don't tell anybody, but I love Fleetwood Mac," Doug bellowed, "especially that Christine McVie. She's got a heart of gold. She didn't deserve all the shit she got from the bass player."

"Life on the road is hard," Chris muttered, philosophically, though he was pretty sure no one could hear him.

"Do you think Andy will leave ILJ to become a rock star again?" Mr. Shimazaki asked.

"He'll always be a rock star," Chris said. "I don't know about his career plans on a day-to-day basis."

The conversation paused, and Chris felt it was his turn to shout a question: "I've been meaning to ask my brother: Why do Japanese phones *always* make that loud digital *clicking* sound when someone takes a picture? Is that a cultural thing, or can you not turn it off?"

"Both," Doug said. "A lot of Japanese men were using selfie sticks to take pictures of women's underwear on the subway. So that taking-a-picture sound—those naughty boys made us all have it."

"Have any of you ever done that?" Chris asked.

Doug and Eduardo shook their heads no, but Mr. Shimazaki was noncommittal.

Chris was about to ask about the drinking exploits of salarymen when there was a sudden cry from the dance floor, with everyone pulling back, as though a dangerous animal had been set loose.

The four men moved toward the circle of dancers and found Cassie, the middle-aged Englishwoman, passed out in the center.

"She's got a drinking problem," Eduardo said.

"We all do," Doug agreed.

Eduardo and Mr. Shimazaki lifted Cassie to her feet, and she shook her head and seemed to be coming around, a little color entering her cheeks.

Doug gave her a light slap. "Cassie, Cassie, wake up."

"Whazzit?" she said.

"You fell down," Doug said, "you silly."

"Oh, I was," Cassie began, "so silly." Then she collapsed onto the dance floor once again, the LED lights making cheerful twinkling patterns beneath her recumbent body.

THE FAIRLEY BROTHERS'
CHRISTMAS ALBUM

Kyoto
Thursday, August 18

Chris was asleep when the sound of knocking entered his dream, first as the pounding on a kettle drum in an orchestra populated by Fairley Brothers fans, and then as the hammering on his head with a large but amorphous weapon wielded by a Japanese woman with shining green eyes.

He started up and made his way to the door of his hotel room. When he opened it, Andy was standing there, a heavy backpack slung over his right shoulder, his guitar case in his left hand.

Andy looked at Chris's rumpled hair and then down at his pajama pants. "Is that dynamite in your pocket, or are you just happy to see me?"

Chris moved his hand over his crotch. "What? Oh yeah. I have to pee."

"Don't let me stop you."

"I won't." Chris rubbed his eyes, opened the door wider for his brother, and went off to the bathroom. When he returned, Andy was still standing in the hall. "What are you doing here?" Chris asked. "Aren't you hung over from last night?"

"A little. How about you?"

Chris rubbed his temples. "More than a little."

"Drink some water," Andy said.

"I will. But what's up? I thought Fumiko said no gig tonight."

"That's right. Day off." Andy gestured with his guitar case. "Can I sit down?

"Sure, yeah, of course."

"I was thinking—" Andy began.

But Chris interrupted him: "First let me tell you about this dream I was having."

"Go ahead."

Chris sat down on the edge of his bed, and Andy took a seat in a chair.

"So," Chris said, "it was about our tour. Only there was one big difference."

Chris went on to describe a dream in which everything about their tour had been eerily similar to real life, except for the fact that a Japanese woman who was obsessed with him had been following them around the country, gradually becoming bolder and bolder in her attempts to win his affections. "She was, like, certain that I could solve all her problems, but I was like, 'I don't even know you.'"

Andy said, "Sounds kind of like a wish fulfillment deal. Like something you *wanted* to happen but didn't."

"On the surface, maybe, but in the dream, it was terrifying. I had no inkling this woman even existed, but she knew all about me through social media. When you started knocking, she was about to kill me for not living up to her ideals."

"It was just a dream, man."

"I know, but it was *so* real, like an alternate universe. Like I'd peeked inside this version of the truth that was hiding behind a thin membrane of...light, or whatever."

"How much acid did you do back in the '80s?"

"Ha ha."

"Actually, though, that's pretty weird because I had a really vivid dream last night, too. It was about Grandpa, Dad's dad, from Texas."

"Who died, what? Forty years ago?"

"Something like that. But in my dream, he pulled up in front of our apartment in Kyoto in that little old battered Toyota pickup he had. Do you remember it?"

"Totally. It was all rusted out, and he drove like forty-five miles an hour on the freeway, everybody honking at him while shit flew out of the bed of the truck."

"Right. Anyway, in he strolls, in short pants, which I'm sure he never wore in real life, and he sits down and starts whittling the wooden arm of our couch."

"Weird."

"Yeah. And I had that same feeling as I was waking up. Like time, or fate, or circumstances, or whatever, can go so many different ways that any single reality is just as likely, or unlikely, as any other."

Chris shook his head. "That's a little too much philosophy for me this early in the morning. Especially after last night's festivities. So, tell me: What's with the guitar and whatever's in your backpack?"

"I've got an idea."

"Oh, God."

"Just listen." Andy took his guitar from its case, tuned up, and strummed a combination of G, D7, and C chords. "Do you recognize it?"

Chris shook his head.

"'Silent Night.'"

"Oh, yeah, of course. A little out of season, wouldn't you say?"

"Maybe, maybe not. We have a day off before our last gig, right? I was thinking we could do some recording."

"And what would we record?"

"How about a Christmas album?"

"A *Christmas* album?"

"Sure.

"But *why*?" Chris asked, incredulous.

"First of all, a Christmas album, well, it's evergreen, if you will. For like six weeks of every year, it's an album that people are going to play, no matter how many times they've heard it. Think about all the ones we had at home. That was practically Mom's only interest in popular music, right? Remember Elvis? 'Santa Claus Is Coming to Town'? 'Blue Christmas'?"

"'Santa Bring My Baby Back to Me.'"

"That was a great one."

"The Beach Boys," Chris said, nodding.

"Right! 'Little Saint Nick,' with that great, obvious line about Christmas coming each time this year. And the Jackson 5 Christmas album."

"I forget what was on that one."

"You're kidding, right?" Andy said. "'I Saw Mommy Kissing Santa Claus'? 'Frosty the Snowman'? Michael was in fine form throughout. And then, like, Jim Nabors? Andy Williams? *Bobby Sherman*?"

Chris clenched his teeth. "I do remember that one."

"And the name of the album was always *Christmas Album*, so we have to do that too. *The Fairley Brothers' Christmas Album*."

"Are you serious? You want to spend our next to last day together in Japan recording a Christmas album?"

"Would you rather go out and see some more temples? More castles?"

Chris thought for a moment, then shook his head. "I suppose not."

"That's what I thought." Andy put his bulging backpack down on the low table in the center of the room, unzipped it, and took out a computer, a cord, a heavy Samson desk microphone, and two microphone windscreens. "It's got mics facing front and back, so we can do everything without over-dubbing."

"This is cool and all," Chris said, "but it's still pretty low-tech."

"All the better. It's indie. It's authentic."

"And what are you planning to do with the music we record? Who's going to listen to it?"

"I'll just upload it to SoundCloud, then have it sent out to all the streaming services—Spotify, Apple Music, Amazon."

Chris bit his thumbnail. "I don't know, man. This could go south pretty fast."

"Or not. There's absolutely nothing to lose. At your insistence, we're about to go on hiatus again for who knows how long. Come on, get your guitar."

Chris rubbed his temples again "I'll do *one* song."

"Do you want to get dressed, or anything?" Andy asked.

"My PJ pants are fine. It'll be like Christmas morning."

As though they had communicated telepathically, both brothers took out their iPads and attached them to their stands. Chris gave Andy the hotel's password and Andy AirDropped his file of Christmas songs into Chris's device.

Chris tuned up, and Andy said, "Let's start with something we used to sing when we were kids. With Mom? Something traditional."

"'O Come, All Ye Faithful'?"

"Sure thing."

Chris opened Andy's document. "Jesus, that's a lot of songs."

"Just some things to consider," Andy said, then he sang a long "Oooh."

After a moment, Chris joined him, and they both strummed G chords on "come," launching into the song.

As he sang, Andy thought of a Christmas when their father was still at home. Andy would have been no older than eight, and he remembered walking out from his bedroom on Christmas morning to find a cardboard submarine large enough for a child to climb inside; a spring mechanism allowed him to shoot plastic torpedoes at his brother. It was not a gift he had asked for or even known he wanted, but the moment he saw it, he felt it was the best present he would ever receive.

Chris was remembering that same day, though the movie playing in his mind was of his father handing his mother a gift. She unwrapped it. Clearly expecting something else, she made no effort to hide her disappointment. His father looked hurt for a moment, then angry, and he stalked out of the room.

Somehow, the song came to an end with both brothers striking the final G at the same time.

After a moment, Chris said, "That didn't sound half bad."

"What are you talking about? It sounded great. Let me set this up to record and we'll do it again."

"All right, but that second verse is kind of weird, all about 'Lo, he abhors not the Virgin's womb.' And 'begotten, not created.' It's this kind of perverted theological argument, or something."

"Let's skip it," Andy said.

"Okay. Verses one and three, then repeat one."

"Sounds good to me."

They recorded the song and played it back on a portable JBL speaker that Andy connected via Bluetooth to his computer.

Amazingly, there was a kind of magic to their rendition. Their voices were always in harmony, but there was a roughness to the timbre, perhaps from all the singing they'd been doing recently, or possibly just from growing older. The song felt sincere, as though the brothers truly were trying to exalt God to his highest glory.

"Wow," Andy said, after playing it back a second time.

Chris nodded. "What's next?"

"I was kind of looking into the permissions angle."

"Why does that not surprise me?"

"Anyway, a lot of Christmas carols are copyright free. Maybe we should stick to those?"

"Does that include the one we just sang?"

"Totally. And, really, all the other ones in that file I sent you."

"Play on then, Macduff. Play on."

For the next three hours, they scrolled through their iPads, playing and singing the opening verses of public-domain Christmas carols, agreeing on some, rejecting others, recording the ones that worked as duets.

It was like the old days, when the music really seemed to matter and one good idea led to the next, when the brothers' primary concern was to support one another, to make everything they did sound better.

They dismissed "O Little Town of Bethlehem" and "Hark! The Herald Angels Sing" and "We Wish You a Merry Christmas," but recorded "O Holy Night" and "God Rest Ye Merry Gentlemen" and "We Three Kings of Orient Are." Chris added a longish acoustic guitar solo to "Up on the House Top." They gave an acoustic-punk treatment to "The First Noel" and did a countrified version of "It Came Upon a Midnight Clear." Andy sang falsetto on "Deck the Halls" and a descant in Japanese over the third verse of "Away in a Manger." Together they sang "O Christmas Tree" as though it were the last song they would ever sing on this earth.

As they harmonized on that song's final verse—"That hope and love will ever be / The way to joy and peace for me"—the walls of the hotel room in Kyoto seemed to fade away, leaving them in some liminal space, halfway in the present, and halfway back in childhood. From beyond the faint smell of air freshener drifted the even fainter smell of pine needles from their childhood Christmas tree and wood smoke from the fireplace of the little house in Tarzana. For a moment Andy felt the comforting presence of his grandfather, while shivers ran up Chris's spine as, behind his closed eyes, he saw the woman of his nightmare coming at him with what looked like a long, curved sword.

They both broke off the song.

"Jesus fucking Christ," Chris said, blinking. "What the fuck was that?"

"Grandpa?" Andy asked.

"No, that crazy lady."

"Maybe too much Christmas music makes you hallucinate?" Andy said.

"Or puke," Chris said, putting down his guitar and rushing to the bathroom.

When Chris returned, wiping his mouth with a towel, Andy asked, "Feeling better?"

"I guess so."

"That's, what, eleven songs?" Andy asked, counting the files in the Logic Pro folder he'd created on his desktop. "I don't know about you, but I'm starving."

"A minute ago, I would have said, 'No way,' but come to mention it, I'm kind of peckish all of a sudden. Are we through here with our Christmas magic?"

"Let's definitely take a break. But I do have one more idea I'd like to run by you."

"Are you kidding me, Andy?"

"Come on, man. I just...I have this idea for a song."

"A *Christmas* song?"

"Right. An original. I've got the chorus, but I can't think of any verses, and I was thinking maybe you could help me."

"What's it called?"

"'Christmas in Japan.'"

"Brilliant."

"Whatever. Do you want to hear the chorus?"

"Why not?"

Andy strummed an E minor chord and began to sing:

Sitting with my baby
Looking at the lights
Holiday music
Everything feels right

I got her a present
Underneath the tree
It sure smells good
This bucket of KFC

"Wait," Chris said. "What?"

"Kentucky Fried Chicken. It's a Christmas tradition in Japan."

"And *why* is that?"

"I'm not totally sure. I think it was some kind of marketing gimmick back in the seventies."

"All right, I'll take another look at your song, but let's go eat lunch, and *no* KFC. It's disgusting."

They left the hotel and walked up Takakura Dori. The sky was overcast, and the humid air was sweltering. Andy guided them to a crowded noodle place that smelled of soy sauce and cleaning fluid. Using the iPad on the table, he ordered bowls of sesame soba and large Sapporos. A faded but angry-looking dragon snaked along the walls. "Not very Christmasy," Chris said.

"Well, we bring the spirit of the season with us, don't we?" Andy said, sighing.

As they sat eating and drinking, Andy told his brother about Christmas in Japan. Yes, there was a Santa Claus—Santa San—and lots of holiday lights, though mostly in shopping centers. However, Christmas was primarily a holiday for couples.

"Like Valentine's Day?" Chris asked.

"Kind of. But Christmas is wedged in between the Emperor's Birthday and New Year's, when the real gift-giving happens, so it doesn't feel super-special, the way Valentine's is supposed to."

"So, not very Christian?"

"Even less than America. And who can blame the Japanese? I mean, how much do Americans know about Shintoism? From our conversation yesterday, I'd say hardly anything at all."

Chris nodded and continued slurping his noodles.

"One of the funniest things," Andy said, "well, I guess it's funny, is when I first got here and was trying to explain Christianity to my students. I was projecting these Renaissance paintings, and my students were kind of shocked to see all these pictures of Jesus being whipped and hung up on the cross and everything. Finally, one student pointed at him all bloody and being carried away, and she said, 'Did he do something wrong?'"

"Good observation."

"I know. It depends on your point of view, right? But it just shows you how disconnected Christmas is from Christianity. In America, sure, but in Japan—I mean, they're not even in the same universe."

"Which raises the question: Why in the world do you think a Christmas album by the Fairley Brothers would be popular in Japan?"

"It's just a feeling I have. The Honda commercial, the fact that we're suddenly getting a lot of social media attention. The Japanese love quirky, nerdy stuff, and what's quirkier and nerdier than a Fairley Brothers Christmas album?"

"Right. So not exactly driven by market research, you're saying."

"We're pretty much done with the music part, except for the original. I'll do the rest. Then we'll just see."

Back in Chris's hotel room, the brothers spent two hours writing and recording "Christmas in Japan." Chris collaborated with Andy on lyrics for the verses. The brothers were particularly pleased with the couplets "I look into your eyes of gray / But today ain't no Valentine's Day" and "Your kiss is as sweet / As strawberry shortcake," which Andy had explained was another tradition of the holiday.

On the recording, Chris sang the verses and Andy sang the chorus, with Chris adding harmony vocals on "Everything feels right" and "This bucket of KFC." For the bridge, the brothers stole shamelessly from the melody of "Good King Wenceslas."

When they'd finished with a take they both found satisfactory, Andy disconnected the microphone. "It's after three. Do you want to do any rehearsing for tomorrow's gig?"

"Nah. We've been doing pretty good flying by the seat of our pants. Why jinx it now?"

Andy shrugged and began packing up. "You know," he said, "all this Christmas music is bringing up a lot of childhood memories."

"Not all of them good, I assume?"

"Definitely not. When I think about Christmas, I think about Dad not being there after the divorce. At Christmas dinner, no matter how hard Mom tried, it always felt like there was an empty chair at the table."

"She was a good woman," Chris said.

"I'm glad I was there when she passed."

"She was waiting for you to get home. From—"

"Côte d'Ivoire."

"Okay. All I remember was she was in that hospice bed in Reseda, fading and fading, and she kept saying, 'When is Andy coming home?'"

"I'm sorry, okay? I couldn't make it in America. You know what a fucked-up mess I was before I started teaching abroad."

"I get it. I was there in town. It makes sense that those duties would fall on me. Still," Chris said, placing his guitar in its case.

"'Still' what?"

"Still, it wasn't easy. You were teaching somewhere for Dad's last Christmas."

"Kazakhstan."

"Yeah. Well, that was pretty brutal. It was a different hospice, in Van Nuys—a crappier one. They didn't change his bedding frequently enough. It was kind of rancid."

"Sorry you had to go through that on your own."

"He wasn't asking for you, if you're curious. For me either. He was just moaning in bed about how unfair life was. I remember they had these grade school kids come in to sing carols to the dying people, and Dad was just like, 'Get the fuck out of my room, you little shits.' It was kind of shocking. A couple of the kids—they were probably in third grade—starting crying, and the teacher was all, 'Mister, I am sorry for your troubles, but you don't have to behave like an animal around innocent children.'"

"You never told me that story. What'd Dad say?"

"Nothing. He looked pretty sheepish. In fact, he said something like, 'Go ahead and sing,' but the kids wanted nothing to do with him and they left."

Neither brother spoke for a long moment.

Finally, Andy said, "We didn't really talk that much about our parents with Daisuke."

"Not surprising. It's not really his business, right? These are private memories."

Andy nodded. "What do you want to do tonight? Dinner? Go out and listen to somebody else's music?"

"If I'm honest, nothing really. Maybe just order room service and watch a movie in bed."

"You don't want to hit the town and take advantage of your burgeoning fame?"

Chris shook his head. "Go home to your wife."

"Could I take you on one more little trip, in the morning? One last bit of sightseeing?"

Chris shrugged and nodded. "I'll see you tomorrow."

ROCK ME HALL & THEATRE CLUB

Andy spooned rice from the cooker into two bowls, then ladled the miso soup simmering on the stovetop into two more bowls. He took two pieces of salted salmon from the refrigerator and placed them on two small plates. Then he took a sealed plastic container full of spinach salad with sesame dressing and forked it next to the salmon.

Fumiko, dressed for work, sat down at the table. "Very nice," she said. "What's the occasion?"

"Just celebrating our last show."

"Of course. By the way, is that chubby woman from your work all right? The one who collapsed at the nightclub?"

"Yeah. She texted me yesterday morning. Said she doesn't really remember anything after our first encore."

"Your teacher friends love to party. They seem sad."

"They are, I think. That's why they go so crazy whenever they have a chance. And this meal is also a celebration of the *Fairley Brothers' Christmas Album*. It's got a lot of potential."

"How so?" Fumiko asked, interested. "Commercial potential, you mean?"

"Absolutely. Maybe another tie-in with a corporation. If not Honda, then...who knows."

She nodded. "I will listen to the album tomorrow."

Andy sighed. "Tomorrow. Man, I have to teach again tomorrow. It's been a nice break. That job's exhausting."

"You could always do something else," Fumiko said, picking up a bite of salmon with her chopsticks.

"At my age? What?"

She smiled. "You could play in a band."

"That would be nice. To make a living playing music."

"The Fairley Brothers are very popular right now. If you could convince your brother to move to Japan, I think you could do it. You could always go back to ILJ if it didn't work out."

"And what about Chris? If it doesn't work out?"

"He goes home to his little life in Los Angeles. What is that expression you use sometimes? 'No harm, no foul'?"

"I'll talk to him today. I'm taking him to Nara. Everybody loves that place. Maybe it will make him want to stay."

"I can talk to him, too, if you think that would make a difference."

"I don't know. It might. Let's see what happens," Andy said, tweezing a bit of spinach with his chopsticks. "That was a great concert on Wednesday night. I know he felt the energy."

As was now his morning habit, Chris turned on the television and turned off the sound. A young couple walked slowly down a nighttime city street. It was raining and they shared a single umbrella. After what appeared to be an intense conversation, the woman squeezed the man's arm and rested her head on his shoulder.

Chris changed the channel. A woman stood in a bare white room, frowning. Then, through the magic of quick dissolve, she was smiling in a green blouse. She bowed, and the price of the garment flashed across the screen in huge hot pink numbers: ¥4,998.

The commercial was followed by a weatherman bowing deeply. The camera cut to video footage of people huddled under umbrellas, walking down rainy streets. The camera zoomed in on raindrops pounding the pavement, then zoomed back out and panned up to the gray and cloudy sky.

Chris turned off the TV, showered, and dressed. He was due to meet Andy at the train station at ten.

When Andy reached Kyoto Station, Chris was standing in front of the main entrance, surrounded by a semicircle of a half-dozen Japanese of varying ages. When he saw his brother, Chris waved frantically, and Andy hurried over.

"What's the problem?" Andy asked.

"I don't really know. I take it that these are fans of the Fairley Brothers, but no one really speaks English, and they seem to be asking me a lot of questions."

Andy spoke to the group in Japanese, responded to their queries, then bowed, and they bowed and dispersed.

"What was that all about?" Chris asked.

"They wanted tickets to our show tonight, but they're all sold out." Andy headed into the station. "Come on."

"Where are we going today?"

"It's your last day, so something special. Centuries ago, Nara was the capital of Japan. It's kind of an iconic place, definitely worth a visit."

At the turnstile, Andy scanned the two tickets on his phone. They boarded the train, found their seats, and soon were on their way.

Andy said, "It feels like the beginning of our tour."

"Yeah. But that wedding chapel in Sapporo seems like a million years ago."

"I know you're supposed to head home tomorrow, but do you think you might want to hang around and play a few more gigs? Or else head home but then come back in a few months? COVID's getting better, the visa situation is going to improve. Before long, tourists will be flooding in again. Our audiences can only get bigger."

"It's tempting, but I'm just not sure. Let's see how things go tonight. Sound fair?"

"Totally."

They exited the Nara Japan Rail station and began walking east on Sanjo-dori, up a gently ascending hill through a light misting of warm rain. For the first fifteen minutes, Nara seemed like any other Japanese city: banks and hair salons, little restaurants—some of them just opening up, others with their metal doors still down—apartment buildings, parking lots, construction sites, a 7-Eleven, a Lawson, a FamilyMart. As the only non-Japanese, Andy and Chris were noticed, obliquely, by everyone, but no one said anything until a middle-aged man, who looked as though he could be a banker, stepped politely in front of them and bowed. "The Fairley Brothers, I presume," he said.

"You presume correctly," Chris answered.

The man withdrew a fountain pen and a small, elegant notebook from his suitcoat breast pocket and said, "Your autographs, if you please." Above his surgical mask, his eyes were quizzical, but also a little excited, as the brothers each wrote their signatures on thick creamy paper.

"They don't make stationery like this where I'm from," Chris said.

The man grinned. "You allude to a song by Weezer, I believe."

"I do."

"Well played, Chris Fairley." He nodded, retrieved his notebook, and walked away.

They kept going and soon they were in Nara Park. "What's this?" Chris asked, when they stopped across the street from a five-story pagoda.

Andy looked down at his phone and read, "'Kofukuji Gojunoto. Iconic wood pagoda from the eighth century.'"

White-tailed deer ambled across the gravel paths, mostly taking no notice of the tourists who were taking pictures of them with their phones.

The brothers followed the signs toward Tōdaiji, past deer wandering the streets; deer asleep at the foot of temples; deer being petted by children, who were urged on by their picture-taking parents; and deer nudging their noses into the outstretched hands of visitors, gobbling up the pellets sold in vending machines. Scattered across all the lawns, like black and brown stones, was the scat of Nara's omnipresent totem animal.

"I'll bet there's a lot of deer pictures posted on Instagram," Chris said.

"Fear the deer."

Outside an enormous wooden temple, a plastic sign attached to the fence said, "NO DRONES." Inside was the Daibutsu, a fifty-foot-tall bronze Buddha, seated, his eyes barely open, right hand held up, palm forward, left hand on his lap, palm facing up. "I'm surprised he's not sweating," Chris said. "Everyone else is." Indeed, the late morning air was so humid that every person packed into the temple—saying prayers, padding around in their stocking feet to get the best angle for their photos—was dripping wet.

"It's part of the experience," Andy said, "though I don't know if I have the right mindset today. I just feel hot."

Chris nodded, wiping the sweat from his forehead.

They stopped at a small café with a counter and two tables and each ordered a salad and a glass of ice water. "The thought of eating anything hot right now is kind of overwhelming," Andy said.

"I know. Plus, this salad is pretty good. These cherry tomatoes are really fresh."

"Remember that one summer when Mom tried to grow cherry tomatoes? It was right after Dad left for good?"

"Yeah," Chris said. "She did okay at first. They were tasty."

"But we were supposed to water them every day," Andy said, "and we didn't, and she kind of forgot to check on them."

"And then she did check on them, and they were all dead."

"Remember how she cried?"

"Like somebody had died."

Andy nodded. "I guess that wasn't too far from the truth."

When they finished eating, they dutifully trudged around Nara, mostly not speaking in the heat, which grew more oppressive as the day plodded on. Periodically, Andy tried to sell Chris on the beauty of a particular view, but Andy felt as though he'd taken a sleeping pill, and he couldn't muster much enthusiasm.

In the temples were bronze octagonal lanterns with images of Buddha—playing the flute, standing on one leg, unshakably calm. Fierce wooden guardians raised their muscled arms, their thick eyebrows arched in anger. In the gardens stood rows of lichen-encrusted stone lanterns: the images carved into their sides were so weathered it was impossible to tell what any particular figure had once been. A giraffe? A dragon? A swan?

"Can we sit in the shade for a minute?" Chris asked. "And just be?"

"Of course," Andy said.

The brothers settled onto a stone bench by a shallow pond with red, gold, and white koi lazily swimming from end to end. "That was really weird yesterday," Chris said. "When we were playing that song, and then— *boom*. I felt like I was in another dimension."

"I know. Like getting swallowed up by a memory."

"Or a dream. I was thinking about it a lot last night, and just when I was about to fall asleep, I had this feeling, like, *It's okay. Relax. Weird things happen. It's just a part of life.* Then I shut my eyes, and I don't think I dreamt anything at all."

Andy took out his phone and took a slow-motion video of the koi. "I can't say it made that big an impression on me. But I'm glad you got something out of it."

A fawn poked its head into the clearing, looked at the two of them as though making a decision about something, then turned and vanished into the trees.

Chris stared at the passing clouds reflected in the pond's surface while Andy texted Fumiko. A warm breeze picked up, then died down again.

Finally, Andy said, "I know this was my idea, but I'm feeling a little 'templed' out. It's so hot, and there are so many people everywhere, I don't see how you're supposed to be relaxed and contemplative."

"Zen."

"What?"

"I was reading about it last night on my phone. You have to get this kind of Buddha-mind and let everything else go."

"So, you're like a *sensei* now?"

"I don't even know what that is. I'm just trying to find a little peace. I thought that's what you were all about."

"Yeah, well, I try. I'm just not feeling it right now. Maybe we can leave Nara to the tourists, and take the train back to Kyoto? I don't want to be exhausted for tonight."

"Let go, or be dragged," Chris said. "Act without expectation."

"Okay, you're freaking me out," Andy said, standing up. "Are you, like, possessed?"

Chris looked quietly at Andy, then burst out laughing. "I'm just bullshitting you, man. That's the sum total of everything I learned from the Internet."

"Okay, well, don't act so wise. It doesn't become you," Andy said, turning back to his phone and calling a cab to take them to the station.

It was after three by the time their local train pulled into Kyoto. They joined the crush of people hurrying up the stairs, at the top of which stood Daisuke Hayashi. He wore a small blue backpack and looked sheepish, like a child who knew he was in trouble.

"What the hell?" Chris said.

Daisuke put up his hands, in a gesture of surrender. "I come in peace, okay? Fumiko told me when your train was arriving. I asked her not to say anything because I wanted to talk with the two of you."

"No more interviews, Daisuke," Andy said. "We agreed."

"This isn't an interview. I just wanted to...explain. About why I've been so dogged in seeking the two of you out."

"You mean it's not our music?" Chris said, trying, unsuccessfully, to sound ironic.

"I like your music just fine. In fact, I like it a lot. But that's not why I've been doing these interviews."

"Why then?" Andy asked.

"It's kind of a long story. Are you hungry? I'll buy you lunch."

"I don't know," Chris said.

Daisuke put his hands together. "Please. This means a lot to me."

The brothers looked at each other, then followed Daisuke out of the station, across Shiokoji-dori, down an alley to a bar with chairs and tables set on the sidewalk beneath an awning. The air-conditioned interior was full, so they sat outside, the hint of a breeze barely stirring the damp afternoon air. Daisuke asked the brothers about Nara, and they gave short replies, waiting for his explanation, which he did not seem in a hurry to give.

It wasn't until after they had ordered, and their waiter had brought Daisuke a pizza margherita and each of them a large Asahi, that Daisuke said, "I know this is a personal question, but your parents, they are no longer with us?"

Andy nodded. "They're not."

"Wait," Chris said, "I thought this wasn't an interview."

"It's not, it's not. But may I ask how they passed away?"

"Where are you going with this, Daisuke?" Chris asked.

"Just cut me a little slack."

Andy said, "Our mother died of ovarian cancer. Our dad had a series of strokes, then a heart attack."

"I'm sorry to hear that," Daisuke said. "That must have been hard on both of you."

"It was, but it was a while ago," Andy said. "Again, though, why are you asking?"

"I want to tell you about the deaths of my own parents. I think I told you when we first met that my father worked for the United Nations and my mother was a translator?"

"Maybe," Andy said. "Sorry. I don't really remember."

"I do," Chris said. "I was asking about why you came back to Japan, and you didn't really answer, right?"

"I don't suppose I did."

Daisuke took a deep breath but said nothing. A sprinkle of rain dusted their table, then abruptly stopped. People rolled their luggage down the sidewalk, on their way to or from the station.

Finally, Daisuke said, "I came back to Japan when I was twenty. After my parents died, in 1996. They were on a road trip. They'd spent all their time in New York, and they wanted to see America. So they flew out to Saint Louis, I remember my father calling it 'the Gateway to the West,' and they rented a car—my father probably had not driven one since he lived in Japan.

"Anyway, they headed out, across Missouri and Kansas and into Colorado. Somewhere my father had read about the Black Canyon of the Gunnison, which was supposed to be one of the most beautiful places in the Rockies. They were driving along the rim road, probably to an outlook point, when some drunk redneck in a pickup ran them off the road. And not just off the road—off the *rim*, down into the canyon. Hundreds of feet, their car rolling and tumbling like in some bad movie."

"Jesus," Chris said.

"Their car didn't catch fire. I don't know why. Maybe they were almost out of gas. When the rescue crew finally got down there, they were dead of course, but the rescuers were able to get a CD out of the stereo, and they gave it to me, along with their clothes, and their luggage, and all this shit that I immediately, of course, just threw away. But I kept the CD."

Daisuke reached into his little blue backpack and took out a hard-plastic case that contained a single silver Fujifilm CD-RW. On the top, in black Sharpie, was written, "Fairley Bros. Mixtape."

"So, you see, I'm guessing your music was the last thing they heard when they died. I don't know which song, of course—there are eighteen of them on here, from all four of your albums—but they loved your music, so that's what I picture, just before the accident: They're driving down the road, the sun is shining, they're happy and listening to the Fairley Brothers. What happened afterwards doesn't matter."

A taxi pulled over in front of the restaurant, and a young couple got out of the back, laughing. They held hands as they walked down the street.

"I never went out there, to Colorado," Daisuke said. "I was a junior at NYU, and they left me well-off, so I dropped out of college and moved to Tokyo, where I didn't know anyone, and when I spoke, my awful foreign-born Japanese made everyone look at me strange. I didn't do much for about five years. Honestly, it's kind of a blur. But then one day I came across this CD here, and I started playing it, and then I listened to your albums, and then albums by Richard and Linda Thompson, and The Byrds, and Leonard Cohen, and the Indigo Girls. Some of the music I already knew, some of it I didn't, but I started writing about it online, and people read what I had to say. And because of Happy End, folk rock was already a thing in Japan, even though its popularity had diminished a lot since the seventies. At the time—this was in the early two thousands—the popular music was mostly heavy metal and pop, but I kept writing, and my audience kept growing, and that's why, twenty years later, when I post something on folkrockjapan, it's going to get read by a lot of people. And overall, I think I've done you a favor. I think I've paid you back for the pleasure I imagine you gave my parents."

"You did, yes," Andy said, "my God, of course."

"I'm sorry about your folks," Chris said. "I really am. But I'm not sure how what you just told us fits into the last interview we did with you. You were pretty hard on us. Poking around in our dirty laundry. Why'd you do that?"

"I don't know. Those questions weren't really planned. They just came out of my mouth."

The waiter returned and asked if they wanted more beer. They did.

They sat there for a while in the wet, humid late-summer afternoon, then Daisuke said to Andy, "Do you know *The Gateless Gate*?"

"I've heard of it. It's a Zen book, right?"

"That's right, from China, maybe eight hundred years ago. Forty-eight koans. The first one is probably the most famous. A monk asks this Zen master if a dog has a Buddha-nature, and the Zen master replies, 'Mu.'

"Literally, 'Mu' means 'Not Have,' 'Without,' 'Nothingness,' but in a larger sense, it means, 'Not no, not yes.' And, really, thinking you can answer the question at all is gate when there should be no gate at all."

"I'm confused," Chris said.

"Exactly," said Daisuke. "And if you were a Zen disciple, you'd keep puzzling over this koan until you passed through it. But that would be incredibly difficult, like 'drinking a hot iron ball that you can neither swallow nor spit out,' according to the teachings."

"And have you passed through this gateless gate?" Andy asked.

"I have not," said Daisuke Hayashi.

Just then, three middle-aged men who appeared to be on their way to their office walked by, paused, and turned back. "Hayashi Daisuke?" asked one. "The Fairley Brothers?" asked another.

"We are," said Andy.

"Picture?" the third man asked, and when Andy nodded, the businessmen crowded around them, smiling, mugging, flashing peace signs.

Andy's phone rang, and he held up his hands, gently dismissing the besotted salarymen, who bowed and went on their way.

"It's Fumiko," Andy said. He spoke to her in halting Japanese, with a few English phrases sprinkled in: "Yes, I get it." "Yes, I understand."

He turned to Chris, but before he could relay the contents of the phone call, Daisuke spoke: "We're not really Japanese, Fumiko and me. She's married to a *gaijin*, and I was born and raised in another country."

"Okay?" Andy said. "I'm sorry? Your point?"

"Only that life often feels like a dream, doesn't it? We look around and ask ourselves, Is this enlightenment or confusion?"

"Are you high?" Chris asked Daisuke.

"Just tired. I haven't slept in a couple of days."

"Anyway," Andy said, interrupting, "Fumiko says that this filmmaker wants us to come down there within the hour to do a proper sound check before the gig."

"Filmmaker?" Daisuke asked.

"They're going to do a documentary about us," Chris said, then added, "thanks to you."

Andy said to Chris, "She's going to meet us over there with my guitar. You just need to get yours."

"Like a real concert?" Chris asked. "Like the olden days, not just showing up a half hour beforehand?"

"Evidently." Andy pulled his wallet from his back pocket and took out three thousand-yen notes.

"As I said, my treat," Daisuke said, not reaching for his wallet.

"It's the least the Fairley Brothers can do," said Andy, putting the money on the table. "See you at the show?"

"Of course."

The three fans in business attire had only gone ten yards down the street, and all were furiously texting. When they saw the brothers leaving, the men moved to stop them. "Our friends here soon," said one of them. "More pictures."

"I'm afraid not," Andy said, sweeping past them in rock star fashion. "We've got a movie to make."

The 550-seat Rock Me Hall & Theatre Club was by far and away the largest venue of their tour. With its rows of stadium seating, it looked more like a small arena than a nightclub.

Minato Hara had already set up his equipment to record the concert. Remote video cameras, most of them no bigger than an old-fashioned handheld 35-millimeter camera, were placed on both sides of the stage, with two more downstage left and right. There were cameras in the rafters, and two men with handheld cameras were practicing moving unobtrusively across the stage.

"Already sold out," the manager said, as he led them down the center aisle up to the stage, where two Neumann condenser microphones were already set up and a battery of lights were pointed at them. "We could do another night tomorrow, easy."

"What do you say, Chris?" Andy asked, opening his guitar case and taking out his guitar.

"I'm not saying no, but let's see how tonight goes first."

Minato Hara, white-haired and wearing horn-rim glasses and an un-tucked silk shirt, walked up to the brothers and shook their hands. "It is a great honor for me to film tonight's show."

"Us, too, Mr. Hara," Andy said.

"Please call me Minato. For audio, I am using a splitter to copy the stage inputs before they are relayed to the front of house/monitor consoles. With the cameras, mostly we will try and stay out of the way, though the hand-helds will be crossing the stage periodically. Just do your best to pretend we're not there. And so now, we will get some footage, with the lights, if that's all right?"

"Of course," Andy said.

The brothers tuned up, the lights came down, then back up again, and they played "Whenever I Hit the Road."

"How does it sound out there?" Andy called to Fumiko, who was sit-ting in the fifth row.

"Pretty good," she said. "Maybe Chris's guitar is a little tinny."

"What does that mean?" Chris said into the semidarkness. "'Tinny?'"

"You know, maybe too much treble?"

Chris adjusted his tone control and played the first verse of "Sunday Afternoons."

"How's that?"

"Fine," she called back.

"Better," said the voice of Minato, directing from the sound booth. "Could you do another? Something quiet?"

They played "Don't Give It Away," and when the director asked for something loud, they played "Pickled and Juiced."

When they were done, the manager, Fumiko, and Minato convened on stage. "We were thinking," Fumiko began.

"Always dangerous," Chris said with a forced smile.

"That a little back-up instrumentation might not be amiss."

Chris turned to Andy: "Did you know about this?"

"Kind of," he said.

Minato said to Chris, "I am friends with a Japanese bass player, drum-mer, and keyboardist, all of whom are expert musicians and sworn fans of the Fairley Brothers. Would you be open to having them accompany you on select songs? I think it would add some visual and audio excitement to the film."

"Don't they need to rehearse with us?" Chris asked, skeptical.

"They don't, no. They can play every one of your songs, right now. And they won't be overwhelming the two of you. Just a...flavoring. Emphasizing what you already do."

"You're okay with this?" Chris asked his brother.

"I mean, we used to have backing musicians all the time. It sounds reasonable to me."

"Well then, why the fuck not."

The manager led the brothers to the regal greenroom—three plush couches and fresh fruit and bottles of Perrier and Veuve Clicquot chilling in buckets of ice. They agreed to leave their guitars and return at seven thirty, an hour and a half before the show.

"There's a good Kobe steak place around the corner," Fumiko said holding up her phone, then pointing to herself and Andy. "Our treat."

"Sold," Chris said.

"Good," Fumiko said. "I just made a reservation for the last three seats. But we need to be over there right now."

Ten minutes later, they were on the second floor of a sleek modern building seated in high-backed chairs around a rectangular counter. The back of the counter contained pots and pans and knives, while prosperous-looking diners filled the chairs on the other three sides. They were given black bibs, which looked slightly less ridiculous only because all the other customers were wearing them too.

The inner part of the counter was a flat-surface stainless steel grill on which several chefs sliced incredibly tender pieces of beef, searing them just long enough that they melted, like warm butter, in a diner's mouth.

Bites of steak were dipped in little bowls of ginger and wasabi, augmented with slices of eggplant and cabbage and Japanese squash, and followed with sips from cold glasses of Suntory beer.

They ate and ate and drank and ate.

When the meal was done, Fumiko said to Chris, "Do you want to take a walk with me? A quick one, while Andy pays the bill?"

"I guess so."

Outside, the lights had come on, though the sky was not yet dark. It had rained once more, and the air felt both cooler and more humid. Pedestrians, with their umbrellas still up against the chance of returning rain, stepped carefully around puddles and one another.

Fumiko walked slowly, her hands behind her back. "Andy told me he asked you to stay on for a while, to keep your momentum going."

"He did."

"And what are you thinking?"

"Not sure. If we're getting popular again, maybe we could try it in the States? You two could move to LA. Are you an American citizen now?"

"Japan does not allow dual nationality."

"Still, that doesn't mean we couldn't do an American tour. I'm just not sure I want to commit to Japan."

"You don't like it here?"

"I like it just fine. But it's not my home." He paused. "It's not Andy's home, either."

"He's made it his home."

"Yeah."

"But you're still thinking about it? At least in the short term?"

"Still thinking."

Fumiko turned around toward the entrance to the restaurant, where Andy was waiting, looking both hopeful and worried.

Fumiko shook her head slightly.

"Come on," Chris said. "Let's get to the gig."

The Fairley Brothers' last scheduled concert in Japan was, by all accounts, their best. Playing in the back of a gift shop in a flower farm or in a fish restaurant in Tokyo or beside a modern sculpture in a windstorm—these were all distant memories. Now, the Fairley Brothers were a band, the real thing, with a bass player, drummer, keyboardist, and a film crew ready to capture every solo and grimace and fabled harmony.

They began with acoustic versions of "Portraits of the Insane" and "Blue All Week Long," but when the other musicians kicked in at the start of "The Psychics Are Crying," both Chris and Andy looked at each other, happily surprised by how full their sound had suddenly become, glad for their accompanists to join them for the rest of the show.

As they had two nights earlier, the brothers played favorites like "Take Me Till Tuesday" and "Whenever I Hit the Road," deep cuts such as "Dead Man's Last Tale" and "Except the Dying," and amped-up covers of classic folk songs—this time "John Henry" and "Will the Circle Be Unbroken." Possibly it was just the energy of hundreds more fans in the audience, all of them screaming through their face masks, but the night took on a legendary feel—like Dylan at the Royal Albert Hall in 1966 or Springsteen in East Berlin before the Wall came down. Whether they were the musicians on stage, members of the audience, or the filmmakers looking through the lenses of Minato Hara's many video cameras, everyone would later claim to have had the feeling that this was a concert people would talk about for the rest of their lives.

When the third encore, "West Hollywood in the Rain," was over, the brothers and Ritsu, the bassist, Kenji, the drummer, and Tatsuki, the keyboard player, made several deep group bows, arms around each other, then exited the stage to one final roar.

Back in the greenroom, Ritsu, Kenji, and Tatsuki volunteered to play with the brothers any time, any place—then they bowed respectfully and left the room to Andy, Chris, and Fumiko, who was in the corner, speaking on her phone.

"Who was that?" Andy asked when she ended the call.

"An advertising executive from Honda. He was at the show tonight. They want to renew the song for another three months of commercials. They're even talking about the US market."

"See," Andy said. "The States, just like you wanted."

"That's nice," Chris said, noncommittally.

Andy said, "We could really do it now, Chris. What do you think? You're retired. No ties. Just move over here and we'll make it happen." There was a pleading note in Andy's voice that reminded Chris of when they were children and Andy really, really, really wanted Chris to play with him.

"I don't know. It's just...I mean, at some point, probably pretty soon, the commercial will stop being played. People will lose interest in the Fairley Brothers."

"Not if Daisuke keeps writing about us."

"I think he's done what he needed to do. I don't think we're going to be featured in his posts anymore."

"Sweetheart," Andy said to his wife, "could you give us the room?"

"Of course. But first I want to tell Chris that he has many female admirers on Instagram. Some are very romantic in their posts."

Chris felt himself blushing. "That's nice."

"*Very* nice. There is one woman who has commented on all your recent concerts, even though she has not attended them. Akemi from Shiranuka. She says to look her up the next time you're in Kushiro."

"I will probably do that."

Fumiko said, "She's been posting so frequently, I thought she might be here tonight. But I don't think so."

Chris shook his head. "You wouldn't want to break my losing streak, would you?"

Fumiko smiled. "I wouldn't want to do that."

She rose and headed for the door, and Chris crossed the room to give her a bear hug. "You're good people," he said, "and I want to thank you for all you've done for us."

"It sounds like you're saying goodbye."

"More like see you later."

Fumiko nodded, reached up and kissed Chris on the cheek, then left the room.

"So, it's a no," Andy said. "I had that feeling."

"I'm afraid so, little brother," Chris said, sitting down on the edge of a couch, poised to leave. "Stopping now just feels like the right thing to do. But I'm not saying it's over forever. I'll go home, work on those songs I've been writing for the past thirty-plus years. Who knows? Maybe we'll have enough material for another album. Maybe we can even tour sometime in the future. Playing music with you? I mean, these have probably been the most memorable two weeks of my life." Chris sighed. "But I'm not going to invest my life in a dream again."

"What else do we have but dreams?"

"Reality."

"Reality—yuck," Andy tried to joke, but he felt too heavy inside. Chris seemed ready to depart, and Andy held up a hand to stop him. "Before you go, I want to tell you a story. You know I taught ESL in Russia for six months, right?"

"Okay."

"After about a month, I stopped assigning essays."

"Why is that?"

"Because a couple of people would write everyone's essays. It was like this thing they had. Students were specialists in different subjects. If you were good at math, you did everyone's math homework. If you were good at physics, you did everyone's physics, and if it wasn't your specialty, then you didn't have to do the work in that class."

"I'm not sure I get the moral of that story, as it applies to us."

"The moral is that if we only think we can do one thing, then that's all we can do. But the reality is that we can do everything. Really—*everything*. Anything at all."

"I think there's a certain truth to that, but what I've learned over these past couple of weeks is that rushing around, trying to accomplish all these goals, it's a fool's errand. You hurry from place to place, and you miss everything in between. But when you're not hurrying, that's when you do see things. I felt that last night, sitting in my hotel room with the lights off. And today. As hot and sometimes boring as Nara was, when we stopped for a minute, I could really *see* it. The world, I mean."

Chris continued: "I won't say I haven't thought about making a comeback. I have, I definitely have. But why? What are we chasing? It's some illusion from our youth. I'd rather just live my life. Such as it is. Such as I make it."

"This all sounds pretty Zen."

"Yeah, I guess so."

"But why not keep trying? I get that you don't want to be disappointed again, and that life is an illusion and everything, but, man, couldn't you just do a couple more gigs while the band is hot?"

"I could, sure, but do you ever think any other gig could top this one?

Why not end on a high note rather than risk losing what we have tonight? Which is something close to perfection."

For a moment, Andy felt as though a forceful counterargument would leap into his brain—but it didn't happen. For one of the few times in his life, Chris was right. Andy walked over, knelt down, and put his arms around his brother. "I love you, man."

Chris gave him a long hug back. "That's a movie, I think."

"What?"

"That phrase. They made it into a comedy."

"I don't care. I still love you."

"I love you, too." He paused. "Man."

They hugged some more, then Chris rose, picked up his guitar case, and left the greenroom. He went down a dimly lit hall and exited through the stage door into an alley. He made his way toward the street, whistling a song he had not yet written. Perhaps he would jot down some notes back in his hotel room. But, no, better to let it go—if the song was worthwhile, he'd remember it.

He made his way from the alley out into the brightly lit avenue, more exhausted now than exhilarated. Tomorrow morning, he would be on a train for Tokyo. Tonight, for a while, he could rest.

The Fairley Brothers

The Fairley Brothers were a folk-rock duo consisting of Christopher Fairley and his younger brother Andrew. Chris and Andy are best known for their hits "Whenever I Hit the Road" and "Take Me Till Tuesday" from their 1985 album *Dark as Dark Can Get*. Their influences included the Everly Brothers, The Byrds, Richard & Linda Thompson, as well as the 1980s Los Angeles punk rock scene.

Meet the Fairley Brothers (1984) received airplay on alternative and college radio stations, and *Dark as Dark Can Get* achieved commercial success. However, their two follow-up albums *Never Believed You Anyway* (1986) and *What the Folk?* (1988) were increasingly ignored, and the duo disbanded after their fourth album.

In later life, the Fairley Brothers achieved a modest comeback. In 2022, "Whenever I Hit the Road" was adopted by Honda for use in a commercial promoting its CR-V compact crossover, and the brothers toured Japan that summer. Also that summer, they recorded *The Fairley Brothers' Christmas Album*, which was a surprise hit in Japan and the United Kingdom during the 2022 holiday season. A film of their final performance, *The Fairley Brothers Live in Kyoto*, was released independently.

Marcus Mumford of Mumford & Sons and Colin Meloy of the Decemberists have claimed the Fairley Brothers as influences. *Rolling Stone* ranked them no. 97 on its list of the 100 Greatest Duos of All Time.

Early life

Both Chris and Andy were born in Valley Presbyterian Hospital in Van Nuys, California (Chris in 1960 and Andy in 1964). They grew up in a small house in the nearby San Fernando Valley community of Tarzana.

Their mother, Nancy, worked as a nurse, while their father, Larry, was frequently unemployed. The couple divorced when the boys were young.

Music career

1984—1986: The Capitol years

In 1984, folk-rock impresario Bobby Tiryaki discovered the Fairley Brothers at Emil's Café in Encino and signed them to a three-record deal with Capitol Records.

Their first album, released that year, was *Meet the Fairley Brothers*, which peaked at no. 36 on the US charts. "Simple Soul" and "I'll Love You Longer Than a Bob Dylan Song" received some airplay on college radio, although neither song entered the Hot 100 Singles Chart. Another song, "The Crazies and Me," was criticized for its insensitive portrayal of the mentally ill.

Nevertheless, the Fairley Brothers' 1985 follow-up *Dark as Dark Can Get* reached no. 17 and spawned two Top 40 singles, "Whenever I Hit the Road" (no. 7) and "Take Me Till Tuesday" (no. 31). The album received widespread critical praise [citation needed] and resulted in an appearance by the brothers on *Austin City Limits*.

The Fairley Brothers' final album for Capitol, *Never Believed You Anyway*, was released in 1986 and peaked at no. 122 in the US. The album's single, "West Hollywood in the Rain," failed to chart. In addition to being commercially disappointing, the album was panned by critics, and there were widespread reports of tension between Chris and Andy [citation needed].

1988: Mother of the Groom Records and breakup

The Fairley Brothers' last album before their breakup was *What the Folk?* distributed by the independent label Mother of the Groom. The album was much looser and more experimental, both musically and lyrically, and sales figures were reportedly in the low thousands [citation needed]. Following a poorly received performance at the Telluride Bluegrass Festival in June 1988, the brothers stopped performing—other than several brief appearances in Ireland in 2017—for 34 years.

2022—2023: Japan tour, *The Fairley Brothers Live in Kyoto*, and *The Fairley Brothers' Christmas Album*

The popularity of their song "Whenever I Hit the Road," due to its use in a Japan-only Honda advertising campaign, inspired the Fairley Brothers to begin touring again. Initially ignored by fans and the media, the brothers' final concert was sold out and filmed by Japanese director Minato Hara. Released independently in January 2023 as *The Fairley Brothers Live in Kyoto*, the film received mixed reviews [citation needed].

During their tour, Chris and Andy recorded eleven traditional Christmas songs and one original, cowritten by the brothers, "Christmas in Japan." Andy uploaded the album to music streaming services on September 1, and in October, "Christmas in Japan" was picked up by the grocery store chain Aeon for a holiday television advertisement. The song became a hit in Japan, with over a million digital downloads, and in the United Kingdom, where it reached no. 19 on the UK Singles Chart. However, neither the song nor the album was popular in the United States.

Andy's death

On March 7, 2023, Andy Fairley died of a cerebral tumor in Kyoto. He was buried in Oakwood Memorial Park and Cemetery in Chatsworth, California.

EPILOGUE

OAKWOOD MEMORIAL PARK AND CEMETERY

Chatsworth, California
March 24, 2023

"Fairley Brother Dead."

The obituary in the print version of *Rolling Stone* had been a single paragraph, mentioning only *Dark as Dark Can Get*, their two radio hits, "Whenever I Hit the Road" and "Take Me Till Tuesday," and the former song's brief popularity in a Japanese commercial for Honda's CR-V.

A casual reader glancing at the headline who had a passing knowledge of the Fairley Brothers would probably have assumed the deceased brother was Chris, the older, less vivacious one. Had they also somehow heard of Chris's worries about prostate cancer, they would have been all the more certain the obituary was recording his demise.

But Chris Fairley was alive and reasonably well—his cancer scare having come to nothing—while his younger brother had succumbed to a cerebral tumor that grew, in his doctor's words, "faster than anything I've ever seen."

Andy had kept the secret from his brother until a week before his death, when he'd allowed Fumiko to call Chris, who had taken the next flight to Tokyo. He arrived on the second of March, 2023, having lost a day crossing the invisible boundary of the International Date Line.

On the Shinkansen down to Kyoto, Chris stared for the entire two hours and fifteen minutes at the back of the seat in front of him, studying the blue-green weave of its cover as though it were the surface of the ocean he had just traversed. He focused on his own breathing—in, out, in, out—and the occasional muted movement of the train as it sped along its preordained path.

Carrying only his hastily packed bag, Chris took a taxi from the station to Kyoto University Hospital Cancer Center, where he found his brother in a small bright room with an IV tube attached to his arm. Andy was watching TV, holding Fumiko's hand.

"You came," Andy said, weakly, and Chris bent down to engulf his brother in his arms.

"Careful!" Fumiko blurted out. Then, when Chris recoiled, she said: "Sorry. He's just in a lot of pain."

Chris tentatively touched Andy's arm, then pulled up a chair across the bed from Fumiko.

After some small talk about his journey, Chris said, "I don't get it. You were fine last summer. Better than fine."

"Yeah," Andy said. "I did have some headaches. But it seemed like the day after you left, things got worse. Nausea, blurry vision, I started having trouble remembering things. But I was so focused on getting our Christmas album out, and then there was that deal with Aeon for 'Christmas in Japan.' I don't know—it's all kind of a haze now."

"And there's nothing they can do?"

"Inoperable," Fumiko said. "Too advanced. I should have noticed sooner. It's my fault."

"I never should have left Japan," Chris said. "It's clearly my fault."

"It's nobody's fault," Andy said. "Except the cancer's."

That day—and the five that followed—either Chris or Fumiko sat by Andy's bedside. Often it was both of them, though they encouraged one another to take breaks—Fumiko returning to her apartment, Chris retreating to the business hotel across the street.

A palliative care team had been assigned to Andy, and a rotating group of doctors, nurses, aides, and social workers arrived periodically to check on the patient and his wife and brother. Most of them spoke only Japanese, and Fumiko would translate to Chris. However, one of the social workers was fluent in English and a fan of the Fairley Brothers. At her request, Chris and Andy signed a 1980s vintage CD jewel case containing

Dark as Dark Can Get, with Andy drawing a cartoon skull beneath his signature.

Generally, Andy was asleep, frequently with the assistance of the morphine that entered through his drip line, so Chris and Fumiko had plenty of time to talk quietly, telling stories about their childhoods and their struggles as adults. Mostly, though, they talked about Andy and his myriad kindnesses. "He's like Tarzana's answer to Gandhi," Chris said at one point.

Fumiko replied: "No, from what I've read, he's more tenderhearted than the Mahatma. And he has no agenda, other than making people feel better about themselves."

Before he could stop himself, Chris said, "He's not a saint." Chris rubbed his eyes. "Sorry, I must be exhausted. I don't know why I said that."

"He's not a saint, no, but do we really need saints?"

The penultimate day of Andy's life, he awoke only twice.

The first time, he opened his eyes to find Fumiko asleep, her head leaning awkwardly on her shoulder, her open mouth emitting a soft snore. He tried to reach his hand toward her, but he could not lift it past the railing on the hospital bed. He spoke her name, but it only came out in a whisper, and when she did not rouse, he closed his eyes and joined her in sleep.

The second time, Chris sat in one chair and Daisuke sat across from him.

Andy murmured something which neither of them could hear.

"Again, little brother?" Chris said, squeezing Andy's hand.

Slightly louder, though somewhat slurred, Andy said, "Another interview?" He coughed, then said, "The deathbed scene?"

Daisuke said, "I came to pay tribute to my favorite Fairley Brother."

"*What?*" Chris said, smiling. "Now that's a surprise."

Daisuke gently patted Andy's shoulder. "I just wanted to say that you and Chris have made some gorgeous music, music that changed people's lives. Not too many people can say that."

The left side of Andy's face was partially frozen, but a smile crept onto the right side of his mouth. He tried to speak, couldn't, grimaced and nodded his head instead. His eyes lost their focus as his gaze tilted toward the fluorescent lights in the ceiling, then he was asleep again.

On the final day of his life, Andy never regained consciousness. The frequency of the morphine dose had increased from every six hours to every three, as Andy's breathing halted for five, ten, fifteen, sometimes twenty seconds before he would take his next weak gulp of air.

The nurses assured Fumiko and Chris that Andy could still hear them, so they uttered whatever platitudes found their way into their addled brains. "Everything is fine." "You've done your best." "It's okay to let go."

When the silence felt overwhelming, Chris sang a cappella: "Sunday Morning" and "Don't Give It Away" and "Whenever I Hit the Road."

It was during their greatest hit that Andy's breathing began to slow tremendously. Chris stopped singing, and he and Fumiko each held one of Andy's hands. The lights had been dimmed, and they scooted their chairs closer as his chest ceased its gentle rise and fall. Then the only movement in his body was a slight pulse in a vein in his neck, which grew fainter and fainter and finally stopped altogether.

Thus, it was that at ten o'clock on the morning of Thursday, March 24, a little more than seven months after their final concert in Kyoto, more than a hundred people were squeezed together in a space meant for eighty at Gustafsson & Son funeral home in the San Fernando Valley. They were there to say goodbye to Andrew Michael Fairley, 1964–2023.

Chris had made no public announcement about the funeral—only mentioned it to a few mutual friends—but somehow, through Facebook and Instagram and text messages and phone calls, people had found out where and when it was.

Fumiko was there, of course. Daisuke and Jamie Ed Gainey had flown into LAX the day before. The other mourners were Andy's friends from kindergarten through high school. They were musician friends from his early twenties and studio musicians from the band's heyday. They were students and colleagues from around the world who happened to find themselves in Los Angeles on that day, or who had traveled from as far as Kazakhstan and Malaysia and Uruguay to pay their respects to their favorite teacher.

A week before the funeral, messages began pouring in, asking to speak at the service. Everyone, it seemed, had a story they wanted to tell about Andy's generosity and good cheer. Finally, the day before, Chris had written down the names of all those planning to attend on several sheets of paper, then cut them into separate slips, mixed them in a hat, and drawn three. The winners of the eulogy lottery were Lindy Bogan, their bass player on *Dark as Dark Can Get* and *Never Believed You Anyway*; Martín Suarez, a student of Andy's from Montevideo; and Nick Cooper, a friend from high school.

The three of them sat in the front row with Chris, Fumiko, Daisuke, and Jamie Ed. Andy's last appearance was standing room only, with men and women leaning against the walls or rocking slowly back and forth on the balls of their feet in the aisles, while the pews were crammed with people sniffling and weeping and generally looking miserable.

The service began with Erik Gustafsson, the titular son of the establishment, uttering a few bromides at the podium. Behind him, the closed coffin rested on a stand covered with blue velvet. When Gustafsson was finished, he gestured to Chris, who looked over at Lindy Bogan.

Lindy, a big man with a big stomach, ambled up to the microphone. "I would not say Andy and I were close friends," he sniffed, wiping away a tear, "but he made a very positive impression on me when we were recording, and then touring. He was always upbeat and interested in hearing about you and your life, even though, at the time, at least, he was the star.

"I was going through a divorce, and I really couldn't have had a better counselor than Andy. He always told me to stay positive, to keep looking to the future, that things would get better, and I guess those sound like clichés, but the way he said them, they felt real. And in the end, I guess he was mostly right."

Then Lindy told a long story about going out for beers one night with Andy while the Fairley Brothers were on tour. The bars they visited were near the club the band had just played, so patrons kept recognizing Andy and wanting to buy him a drink, but Andy insisted he was the lucky one because they had come to the show, so he kept buying drinks for the fans. For a rock musician, Lindy had a remarkable memory, and he recalled not only the names of the bars but also the types of drinks Andy had purchased. When he had finished, Lindy looked up at the vaulted ceiling, looked down at the beige carpet, then said, "That's all."

Martín took Lindy's place at the podium and told a story about how had been struggling in Andy's ESL class. It was very important to Martín's father that he excel in the subject, and Martín offered to pay for extra lessons. However, Andy said he would tutor Martín for free if he would show him the coffee shops of Montevideo. "At first, I was, you know, hesitant. Is this some kind of crazy weirdo, or something? But Andy wasn't like that. He just liked to meet new people and see new places. I took him to every neighborhood in the city: Tres Cruces, Pocitas, La Blanqueda, Jacinto Vera, La Mondiola—everywhere. By the time he left Uruguay, after about a year, my English was really good, and Andy could tell you where to find the best cup of coffee in any part of the city."

When Martín was finished, he gave a thumbs-up to Chris, then retook his seat.

Next was Nick Cooper, whom Chris had remembered as a morose hanger-on during Andy's punk rock days. "Andy Fairley was the best friend I ever had," Nick began, before spending ten minutes mostly talking about the loneliness of his own life, his disappointment in finding meaningful employment—he was currently working as an inventory clerk at a tire store—and his fraught romantic relationships—he was still looking for "Mrs. Right." Nick, who was tall and gaunt and had a floral neck tattoo, occasionally mentioned Andy, but mostly in passing, and primarily to emphasize how much richer and fuller his friend's life had been than his own.

From the corner of his eye, Chris saw Erik Gustafsson checking his watch, then sighing with relief when Nick finally concluded his tale of woe.

There was a brief lull, and Chris feared that the podium would be rushed by those wanting to eulogize his brother, so he softly squeezed Fumiko's arm.

"I can't say anything," she whispered. "I'm sorry. I'm too sad."

Hearing this, Daisuke rose from his seat and crossed to the podium. He carried a sheaf of notes, but after standing there for a moment, he rather dramatically ripped them in half. He cleared his throat. "I only met Andy Fairley, in Japan, this last summer, but I, like many of you, have known the music of the Fairley Brothers for the better part of my life. I say 'better part' deliberately, for there's something both gentle and sharp in their songs that reflects the personalities of both brothers and their views of life. Andy was famously the more...benevolent of the two, but he needed his brother's rough edge, just as Chris needed Andy's compassion. That's their music—that push and pull between high and low, optimism and depression, sunshine and darkness.

"And let's not forget that Andy was a man who knew his own mind. It would have been easier for him to have been buried in Japan, but he insisted that he wanted to lie under what, his wife tells me, he called his 'native soil.'

"And so, here he is. In his homeplace. In Japan, we have a number of complex rituals for the dead that I think Andy would have appreciated, but here in America you dispense with them, obviously. Therefore, I would close with this haiku by the poet Issa, written after the death of his daughter: 'The world of dew / Is the world of dew.'" The crowd leaned forward, ever so slightly, expecting more. Daisuke shrugged. "That's it."

He sat down, and big, burly Jamie Ed stood up and turned toward the assembled mourners. "I'd like to say something about Andy. I know a lot of us would, but I also know that it's painful for Fumiko to go through this, and so I think we should make the service as short as possible. I just want to tell you all that Andy would really appreciate your being here. He would. He was a guy whose heart was so full of joy and love, and that sounds corny, I know, but it's true. He felt love. For his wife, yes, most certainly, but I think above all for his brother. I think we should hear from Chris, and then go bury our friend."

There was a general murmur of assent as Jamie Ed sat and Chris walked up to the microphone. He took a few deep breaths, staring down the crowded aisle at the green EXIT sign above the door, then he said: "This is hard. Burying my brother. It's very, very hard.

"I do want to thank you all for being here. Andy, as you know, had hundreds of friends, probably thousands, and I was afraid his funeral would be flooded with people if I made a big announcement. Still, he's managed to fill up this little chapel pretty well."

A few people clapped, and Chris smiled.

"I could spend hours up here reading emails I've received and messages posted on social media. So please know that he was cherished and loved by far more people than could ever fit into this chapel.

"While we were physically separated for many years, I spent the very best days of my life playing music with my brother. Most recently, we had the opportunity, thanks to the tireless work of his widow, Fumiko, to tour Japan.

"I can't say every show we played was as wonderful as those last few nights in Osaka and Kyoto. There were times, especially early on, when I think we both felt more like street buskers than professional musicians. Not Fumiko's fault, I would emphasize. In fact, those crazy gigs—like playing one song over and over at a wedding reception, or playing in a mostly empty jazz bar, or practically having a riot with a rival band we'd never even heard of—those are the shows that really stick in my memory.

"Through it all, Andy was his steady, loving, patient self. I know he got frustrated with me. He had every right to. But he plugged along, always looking at the bright side, as Lindy said, always making everyone feel like his best friend." Here, Chris nodded at Nick. "I know this is something you hear at every funeral, but it's true about Andy: He was one of a kind."

It was a ten-minute drive along Canoga Avenue to the cemetery. Fumiko asked if she could ride alone in the hearse. Nick Cooper insisted on riding with Chris, Daisuke, and Jamie Ed in Chris's Camry, and a veritable convoy of vehicles followed behind them. Chris wondered what Fumiko was thinking as they passed the auto repair shops and gas stations, carpet outlets and nail salons, warehouses and liquor stores. It was an unlovely final drive for anyone. He hoped her eyes were shut.

However, when the hearse and the rest of the funeral train pulled into the gates above Oakwood Memorial Park and Cemetery, Chris remembered why he had chosen this place. It had been the rainiest winter in years, and the landscape was a rich green. Lawns that Chris guessed had been allowed to go brown during the seven-year drought looked as though they had sprung fresh from some 1950s version of Los Angeles, when the supply of water was seemingly inexhaustible. The boulder-strewn hills rising west above the cemetery looked like a Western movie backdrop, so vivid were the colors.

The hearse drove slowly down a winding path and pulled over beneath the shade of a cedar tree.

The director of the cemetery had informed Chris that due to recent insurance restrictions, there could be no pallbearers. Instead, two brawny men pushing a rolling gurney met the hearse when it parked. They opened the back doors, slid the coffin onto its metal surface, and pushed it across the lawn toward the open grave.

Rather than upright stones, the markers at Oakwood Memorial Park were flat in the ground, most of them rectangles of bronze in a concrete frame. Some had elaborate inscriptions, even pictures of the dead, but Chris had asked for a simple legend that gave Andy's name and dates, along with the inscription, "Husband, Brother, Musician."

As they walked toward the grave, one of the men pushing the coffin said to Chris, "No decorations, no pets."

"All right."

"And the hours are posted out front. Don't complain if you come when we're closed."

"I wasn't planning to."

"Okay then. We're sorry for your loss."

At the graveside, the broad-shouldered men slid the coffin from the gurney to another contraption, which straddled the grave itself. They lowered the coffin into the ground, then unlocked the gears to the straps, pulled them back up, and wheeled the device away from the grave.

The workers stood and waited while the group of mourners, which looked even larger outside the confines of the chapel, sniffed and shifted, uncomfortable and sad. Chris gazed out over the crowd. Among the friends and musicians and former students, he thought he recognized Andy's first wife. He wasn't sure of her name—Layla, Linda—something like that. She wore a black scarf and big sunglasses, and he was happy to let her go unseen by Fumiko.

"Andy wasn't real religious," Chris said in a loud, outdoor voice, "so I didn't ask for a minister or anything. I just thought, before they lay him to rest, we could all bow our heads and say a quiet prayer for him."

A cool breeze that smelled of sage and creosote blew down from the hills. The silence lasted a while, then someone began to sing:

There are loved ones in the glory
Whose dear forms you often miss,
When you close your earthly story
Will you join them in their bliss?

Then everyone began singing, a ragged chorus that included several distinctly off-key voices, but that was all the more moving for its imperfections:

Will the circle be unbroken
By and by, Lord, by and by?
There's a better home awaiting
In the sky, Lord, in the sky

There was a pause. No one seemed to know the next verse, so they sang the refrain again, repeating the last line, a conceit that had always seemed so preposterous to both brothers that Chris could not help but bend over and weep with the knowledge that he would never see Andy again.

The mourners stood respectfully until Chris was through, then Gustafsson appeared from the back of the crowd with a handful of dirt, which he placed in Chris's palm, nodding toward the coffin. Chris tossed it in, the clods making a hollow ringing as they hit the casket. Fumiko was next, and Daisuke, and Jamie Ed, and then everyone seemed to be stepping forward to help fill the grave.

Fumiko, standing next to Chris, reached over and briefly held his hand, then let it go. She led the group away from the grave, and soon came the noise of the workers, their shovels flinging wet earth against the coffin's lid.

Yet by the time the mourners reached the cemetery road, the somber sound of the burial had been replaced with the sweet and varied singing of a choir of birds. Those assembled looked around for the source of the trills and airs, but though the music seemed to come from near and far, its origin remained hidden from every living thing but the singers themselves.

ABOUT THE AUTHOR

DAVID STARKEY is the author of the widely acclaimed novel *Poor Ghost*, published by Keylight in 2024. In addition to writing fiction, he has published twelve books of poetry, most recently *The Moon Shall Not Give Her Light* (Vine Leaves Press, 2025) and *You, Caravaggio* (Pine Row Press, 2024). The Founding Director of the Creative Writing Program at Santa Barbara City College and the Publisher and Co-editor of Gunpowder Press, he is also the author of *Creative Writing: Four Genres in Brief* (4th edition, Bedford/St. Martin's, 2021), which for many years has been one of the most popular introductory textbooks for college creative writing courses. With drummer Eric Prothero, he records and performs as Falstaff Riley. You can learn more about David and his work at davidstarkey.net.